I'm in love with five bad boy rockstars. But

is our love strong enough

to overcome our tragedy?

Books By
C.M. STUNICH

Romance Novels

Hard Rock Roots Series
Real Ugly
Get Bent
Tough Luck
Bad Day
Born Wrong
Hard Rock Roots Box Set (1-5)
Dead Serious
Doll Face
Heart Broke
Get Hitched
Screw Up

Tasting Never Series
Tasting Never
Finding Never
Keeping Never
Tasting, Finding, Keeping: The Story of Never Box Set (1-3)
Never Can Tell
Never Let Go
Never Did Say
Never Have I

Rock-Hard Beautiful Trilogy
Groupie
Roadie
Moxie

The Bad Nanny Trilogy
Bad Nanny
Good Boyfriend
Great Husband

Triple M Series
Losing Me, Finding You
Loving Me, Trusting You
Needing Me, Wanting You
Craving Me, Desiring You

A Duet
Paint Me Beautiful
Color Me Pretty

Five Forgotten Souls Trilogy
Beautiful Survivors

Stand-Alone Novels
Fuck Valentine's Day (A Short Story)
Broken Pasts
Crushing Summer
Taboo Unchained
Taming Her Boss
Kicked

Books By
C.M. STUNICH

Violet Blaze Novels

(MY PEN NAME)

Bad Boys MC Trilogy
Raw and Dirty
Risky and Wild
Savage and Racy

Hers to Keep Trilogy
Biker Rockstar Billionaire CEO Alpha
Biker Rockstar Billionaire CEO Dom
Biker Rockstar Billionaire CEO Boss

Stand-Alone Novels
Football Dick
Stepbrother Thief
Stepbrother Inked
Glacier

Fantasy Novels

The Seven Mates of Zara Wolf Series
Pack Ebon Red
Pack Violet Shadow

Sirens of a Sinful Sea Trilogy
Under the Wild Waves

The Seven Wicked Series
Seven Wicked Creatures
Six Wicked Beasts
Five Wicked Monsters
Four Wicked Fiends

Howling Holidays Short Stories
A Werewolf Christmas
A Werewolf New Year's
A Werewolf Valentine's
A Werewolf St. Patrick's Day
A Werewolf Spring Break
A Werewolf Mother's Day

Academy of Spirits and Shadows
Spirited

Other Fantasy Novels
The House of Gray and Graves
Indigo & Iris
She Lies Twisted
Hell Inc.
DeadBorn
Chryer's Crest

Roadie

C. M. STUNICH
INTERNATIONAL BESTSELLING AUTHOR

Roadie

For information address Sarian Royal, 1863 Pioneer Pkwy. E Ste. 203, Springfield, OR 97477-3907.
www.cmstunich.com

ISBN-10: 1547015810 (pbk.)
ISBN-13: 978-1547015818(pbk.)
"Timeless" Font © Manfred Klein
"Autumn in November" Font © Misti's Fonts

This book is dedicated to the princesses who find their prince(s)

but also know how to wield swords.

There's no energy left inside of me for tears tonight.

My heart beats furiously as I sit up, tangled in black silk sheets, my body thrumming with the remembered touch of lips and hands and cocks. Putting both palms on my face, I drag my fingers over my sweaty skin and turn to glance down at the face of the boy closest to me.

It's Ransom Riggs, the dark eyed, dark haired bassist for Beauty in Lies.

Surprisingly, he's awake. Even more surprisingly, he's still naked, the faint scar on the left side of his face almost invisible when compared to the ones on his chest, partially hidden by black and grey tattoos. His eyes are locked on my face, and his mouth crooks into a sensual half-smile when he sees me looking at him.

"You alright, sweetheart?" he asks, and the honorific turns my own lips up into their own half-smile. A slight flush colors my cheeks, but mostly because of the carnal memories sliding up from my subconscious and not because Ransom's reached up to run his finger over my lips.

Tonight's been … interesting, to say the least.

"I'm okay," I say because I'm warring between two sides of the same coin. One face is ecstatic, brimming with affection and joy and anticipation of being with my boys. The other face is remembering Kevin's ugliness, Octavia's triumphant hate, and the cold feel of the cement beneath my bare legs. "It's just been a long night," I say as Ransom sits up, propping himself on an elbow and laying on his side to face me. Without the hood and the eyeliner and his usual hunched posture, he looks a lot less intimidating this way. For a second, I see the bright wink of a happy boy, a content and joyous young man unspoiled by grief. "I think I'm still …"

"Processing?" he asks in that thick, heavy bedroom voice of his. "Totally understandable. Lilith," he says and my eyes widen slightly in surprise at the sound of my full name on his lips, "we really thought we'd lost you tonight."

The graveness in his voice gives me pause, darkening that carefree glimmer I just saw.

"I … started imagining all sorts of shit," he says, sitting up and running his palm down his face. He won't look at me now. "You lying in a pool of blood like my mom …"

"Ran," I whisper softly as he glances back at me and closes his eyes for a moment.

I think of him shouting, jogging toward me, my name falling off his lips with a downpour of relief. I'm only just now realizing how traumatizing tonight might've been for him—for any of them. A girl with no family, no weapons, no self-defense training of any kind wanders alone into a big city she's never been to … and disappears.

The implications of that make me shiver.

I was drowning so deeply in thoughts of my family, my own misery, that I didn't even *think* about any of the other awful things that might've happened to me. In hindsight, Kevin and Octavia seem like small potatoes.

"I'm so sorry, Ransom," I say, but he makes this gentle sound in his throat and pulls my naked body to his for another hug. The scars on his chest are rough against the softness of my breasts, but I don't mind. I curl against him, fully aware of his bare skin kissing mine in every possible place but one …

"You're awake?"

I glance over my shoulder and find Michael standing in the doorway, watching me with Ran. His expression is hooded in shadow, but I can see that he's shirtless, bringing up this sharp sudden case of déjà vu when I think back to my first night on the bus. He looked at me with heat—a heat that pales in comparison to the brilliant fire of his expression now—and then he rejected me.

He's definitely not rejecting me now.

I pull away from Ran—not an easy feat to do—and crawl over to Michael, sitting up on my knees and feeling his muscular arms encircle my body. His touch is foreign and familiar all at once; I want more, more, more of it.

I got him; he's mine.

The thought repeats in my head and makes me smile.

Wow.

Five rockstars … all mine.

I try not to think of how unusual our situation is, how 'unfair' it might be to the boys, how fucking excited and shocked I am by the sudden turn of events. My life crashed to literal rock bottom last week; last night, I was afraid I was finally going to have to start living in the darkest part of that never-ending well.

But instead, here I am, hugging Michael Luxe, the lead guitarist for Beauty in Lies, burying my face against the side of his muscular neck.

"Would you like to come on our world tour with us?"

Derek Muser's words ring in my head as Michael's arms loosen and I glance over my shoulder to look for him, remembering that shattered, broken look on his face. Muse's story, when I finally get it, is going to break my heart in half; I'm already trying to prepare myself for the inevitable.

But Muse isn't in the bed; it's just me and Ransom.

"Everyone's in the living room," Michael explains as I unbend my naked legs and swing them over the edge of the bed, fishing around in the discarded pile of clothing for something to wear. I end up with Paxton's sweats and Copeland's t-shirt, standing up on the heated wood floors and glancing over my shoulder at Ransom.

He's already got his hoodie on, hood thrown up, and is crawling down the bed toward me. The sight is enough to fire my brain on all its synapses, reminding me that just a few short hours ago, I was naked and tangled up with all five men. For me, it was as close to heaven as I could get in this lifetime.

A miracle that, since I just so recently crawled up out of hell.

"It makes me want to go bloody fucking *mad* knowing that twat's sitting right there on the other side of this glass," Pax is saying when Michael slides the hall door open and we step into the kitchen. He pauses his rant to glance over at us, those sharp, cruel lips curling in a smile. "Miss Lilith Tempest Goode," he says as I smile back at him, at the two boys on the couch.

Muse is on his feet in an instant.

"Tea?" he asks, pointing at me, his expression back to normal but somehow oddly fragile, like whatever surge of emotions he experienced tonight cracked the careful, neutral shell around his heart. He pushes his glasses up his nose and pauses next to me, Cope rising to his feet behind him.

"Tea would be great, thank you," I say, feeling awkward and silly all of a sudden. But good, too. Really good. I mean, here are these five young guys fawning over me like I'm something special. At the time, if you'd asked me, I never would've dared to think that I really was. Later, I'd get my confidence back, my strength. For now, I felt loved. And it always feels nice to be loved.

I wave at them all dismissively and try to smile.

"You don't have to fuss over me—" I begin and startle when Michael makes a derisive snort beside me.

"Please," he says, drawing my attention back to him, to his violet eyes and pursed lips. "It gives these assholes purpose. Let 'em do it." But he's staring right at me when he says it and I get the impression that *these assholes* also includes him. We continue to look at each other, and I realize that for the last nine days, I've been staring at him with a filter over my vision.

Michael isn't just handsome … he's fucking *gorgeous.*

"Wasn't it just you that was nagging me to let it all out?" Pax asks, crossing his arms over his chest. He's wearing an unbuttoned button-up—as usual—with sweats and some ridiculous slippers that look like they should be paired with a gentleman's smoking jacket.

I sigh.

The asshole's right.

"Do you want another hug?" Cope asks, holding out his arms. This time, when he asks, I don't have to think about it. I *definitely* want a hug from him.

I slip into the circle of his warm arms as Muse fills the teapot with water and turns on the stove.

"Make a big pot," Pax calls when Ransom starts prepping some coffee. "I'mma be up all damn night. I'm not sleeping until I get a chance to fire Octavia—in person. Face to bloody face." He smacks his palms together and then slams one against the curtains covering the wall that separates our part of the bus from the driver's side.

"Tell us again what happened with Octavia," Muse says as he turns and leans against the counter, his gold-grey hazel eyes sparkling with anger behind the thick black rims of his glasses.

I sigh again and burrow against Copeland, the scent of laundry soap and new denim surrounding me in a cloud. And the way he holds me … it's a little bit different than it was before.

I guess I really did give these guys a scare. Well, hell, they gave me one, too.

I imagine myself curled up on a cot in a women's shelter, no money, no phone, my mother's ashes rumbling away inside their bus. If they really had left me in Atlanta … Ugh. No. I don't want to think about that. I should've known; I should've trusted them. But how can I? When I can't even trust myself.

"She told the security guards that I was banned from your shows for stalking … or something." I turn in Copeland's arms and let him hold me around the waist from behind, his chin resting on my shoulder. It's such a comfortable, familiar pose that it almost makes me cry again. I'm just a huge bundle of emotions tonight, I guess. But that's the way with grief; it strikes when you expect it, when you don't expect it, when you think you've finally beaten it down forever.

No, the only true immortals in this world are grief … and love.

I'll have to use the latter to defeat the former.

"She had me escorted off the property, across the street." I pause again because I've already told the guys that part of the story. I don't think that's really what Muse is asking. I close my eyes and take a deep breath. I had lots of ugly words thrown at me tonight, but the thing is … words are just words. Dad is dead; that's real pain, real grief. I can't let petty insults get to me.

"I always knew you were a whore ... I know it; you know it; your dead fucking dad knew it."

Fucking Kevin. I should've punched him when I had the chance.

"And she said a bunch of stuff that I just … I don't care to repeat," I say, Octavia's words layering themselves on top of Kevin's.

"You are nothing *to them. I've seen them do this a hundred times with a hundred different girls. You think you're different because they all fuck you? You're nothing but a shareable sex doll."*

"You don't have to tell us if you don't want to," Muse assures me and Michael snorts again.

"I just … what a day today," he breathes and I remember then that he went through some awful shit, too. His girlfriend, Vanessa, and his older brother, Timothy … having an affair. I watch him run some fingers through his dark hair, as shiny and black as a raven's feathers. Do I ask him about it?

I touch my fingers to the necklaces around my throat, and he notices the motion, going completely still.

Our eyes lock and my heart thunders in my chest.

"These are pretty," Cope says, reaching up to finger the jewelry. "This matches your bracelet, doesn't it?" he asks, and I feel my cheeks color slightly. I can deal with the sex stuff—*group* sex stuff, even—but the emotional stuff still gets me.

"Michael gave them to me," I say softly, drawing this terrible mocking laugh from Paxton's throat.

"Of *course* he did. Of bloody course. So how did you break up with that bitch anyhow?" he asks, moving away from the windows and coming to stand in our little circle in the kitchen. "I want to know what Vanessa's face was like when you gave her the boot." Pax pauses and points a finger at his friend. "You've been planning on it for days, haven't you? I could tell."

"I wasn't going to do it," Michael says with a small growl, looking away from me like he's ashamed. "I wanted to, but I wasn't … fuck. I've hated her for a long time now, but I felt like that was my punishment for the things I did before: the drugs, the cheating, the way I treated all those groupies."

"That's fucking ridiculous," Pax says, but Michael snaps his gaze over to his friend and shuts him up quick.

"Yeah, well, ridiculous or not, that's what I felt."

"Then what changed your mind?" Muse asks, looking at me and not at Michael. He smiles slightly and I smile back.

"I …" Michael starts and then he's looking at me, too, and then away again. "I caught Timothy balls deep in Vanessa."

"No bloody way!" Pax chortles, like that's the greatest thing he's ever heard in his life. "Those hypocrites! Oh, that's great. That's just … that's brilliant."

"The baby might not have been mine; she's been fucking Tim for years."

"Even better!" Pax says, slapping his tattooed hands

together. "We are free of fucking Vanessa! It's about time, Mikey."

"Please don't call me Mikey," Michael says, ruffling up his hair again and looking over at me. Our connection is so fresh, so new. I mean, it is with all the boys, but Michael and I … I have no idea what he's thinking when he looks at me, but his words from yesterday are still vibrant and fresh in my mind.

"I want to kiss you without restraint."

My cheeks flush with color again.

"I don't give a crap about Vanessa and Tim," Michael says as he moves over to stand in front of Cope and me. "I want to know what happened with *your* ex."

Copeland releases me to face Michael, my entire body thrumming with the desire to be touched by him. But he doesn't really seem like the cuddly, hugging type.

I decide to go for it anyway, stepping forward and sliding my arms around his bare waist.

His skin is warm and dry and he smells like his shampoo, the shampoo I've been using since the first night I climbed on the bus. For whatever reason, I was drawn to it. Maybe because subconsciously I related that scent to him?

Michael stiffens up for a moment, going completely still, his heart beating like the hooves of a thundering horse, this terrifying gallop that makes me wonder if I've just made a mistake. But then he puts his arms around me and pulls me against him; I can feel his arousal hard and insistent against me.

"It's been a long time since I've just been … touched," he says, as if he feels I need an explanation. A year. A year without sex … and hugs.

I lay my cheek against the hard muscles in his midsection

and close my eyes.

"Kevin was in line; he saw me walking by, asked if I wanted to have some coffee." Michael stiffens again, but he doesn't relax the strong band of his arms around me. "I thought … if I talked to him, maybe I could forgive him for all the shit he put me through and move on. But then we got into a fight and he tore the lanyard from my neck, set it on fire with his lighter and chucked it into a locked mailbox."

"Son of a *bitch,*" Michael curses, taking me by the shoulders and moving me back a step. He looks tall and fierce, his razored hair falling almost to his shoulders, his indigo eyes narrowed. And his tattoos … are just a sea of rich color, emphasizing the paleness of his skin. "Did he hurt you?" he asks, and he's dead serious about that question. I imagine that if I told him *yes,* he'd fly to Phoenix and beat the shit out of Kevin Peregrine.

"Not physically," I say, which is the truth.

Michael releases my shoulders and then pinches the bridge of his nose, closing his eyes for a moment.

"Last night could've been really bad," he says as Muse brings me my cup of tea, and I sit on the couch next to Cope. "I mean, you were *right* there and we couldn't find you. What if something *really* bad had happened?"

"Agreed," Muse says, handing a cup of tea to Michael. Somehow he always seems to know when someone could use a kind gesture. Michael narrows his eyes, but sits down on my other side, sending an excited thrill through me.

I feel strangely complete and excited right now.

The world tour.

They invited me on their fucking world tour.

I don't have to leave in a week.

I don't have to *leave*.

I get to *stay.*

I sip my tea to hide a smile and realize that Muse is staring at me over his shoulder as he stands at the counter to prepare his own cup of tea.

"You should try to memorize our numbers," he says, ever the practical one. He's already plugged them all into my phone, but like last night proved, that's not enough. "And our personal emails, just in case. We should put together a plan in case anything like that happens again. With the security on the tour, we're not the easiest people to get access to."

"No kidding," I say as I try to figure out what type of tea it is that I'm holding in my hands. It's got this warm, grassy taste and the color is slightly green. Must be green tea then, right? But it tastes different and it has this bright herbal scent that I don't recognize.

"What the fuck *is* this?" Michael asks, making a face. "It tastes like *grass.*"

Muse just laughs and grabs his mug from the counter, coming over to sit in the swivel chair across from Cope.

"What time is it ...?" I start, leaning forward to glance at the clock on the wall.

It's five in the morning.

"We're almost to Jacksonville," Muse says, closing his eyes and breathing in the white steam from his mug. "We should be pulling into the venue soon."

"Can I make you breakfast, honey?" Ransom asks, his voice as dark and sensual as it ever is. Even that simple question warms me up from the inside. Honey. That's a good term for him to use—because that's what his voice is like. Thick, warm honey.

"I'd love some," I say, realizing then that I'm *starving.* I haven't eaten since lunch yesterday. That, and doesn't it feel like emotional breakdowns just suck the life out of you? And then, of course, there's the *sex.* Fucking five men takes a lot of energy—especially when I can outlast *all* of them.

"I'll make my mom's pancakes," Ransom whispers and everyone goes quiet for a moment.

"So," Pax drawls, taking his cup of coffee over to the other swivel chair and sitting down, his storm grey eyes focused on my face. "Michael's in the club now, is he?"

"As if you need to ask," I say back, my voice barely above a whisper, "you were both inside of me at the same time last night."

"And so we were," Paxton says and that's that; everyone goes quiet again. This time though, it's a companionable silence, easy and comfortable. If the guys are at all weirded out by our unconventional little arrangement, they don't act like it.

I stare at Pax's face for a moment. He's the leader, too much of an alpha male to realize how much he's hurting. Covered in tattoos, hidden behind his well-pressed suits. There's a breakdown waiting to happen there, and I want to see it. There's so much sadness inside of him that he pushes down with anger, it must feel stifling …

Sitting there, enjoying the easiness of that one perfect moment, I don't wonder if the six of us will work as some kind of group, if one day the boys will make me choose, if eventually I'll want to choose. No. None of that matters. I've been taught many harsh lessons in my life; everything is temporary. Even things that are supposed to be forever …

With the band surrounding me, I realize then that I've never wished for anything to last so much as I wish for this.

I pick up one of Copeland's books and read for a while, but I can't get into the story because there's too much tension around me, too much waiting around for the bus to stop, for Pax to get off, for Octavia to face the band.

Also, as I sit there, I start to realize that no matter how glad I am to be back on this bus, how happy I am to have these wonderful men around me … none of that changes the fact that Dad is still dead. Cancer ate him and he's gone, and by the end of the week, I'll have to really face his mortality. All of this missing him and wanting him and needing him will finally hit its peak and then what? Time only helps in that it blows dirt over that dark, dirty hole in the ground, the one that's swallowed up the people you love. Grass grows, and sometimes, maybe even flowers. But if you pick them, if you dig, there's still this yawning pit waiting to swallow you up. The hole is never gone, just buried.

And that, that is the face of my own grief.

Putting the novel in the precarious stack on the back of the couch, I force myself to be brave, to get my phone and turn it on. It's been charging for hours, but I've been too scared to look at it. What if there's a message from my stepmother? From Kevin? Worse—what if there *aren't* any messages at all?

"Do you need something, sweet love?" Ransom asks and I get this warm spread of *feeling* all over my body when I look at him, standing next to me in an oversized black hoodie, those eyes of his like warm coffee on a cold morning. I want to drink him up, let him fill up every frigid part of me.

I manage a small smile as I pause next to the counter where my phone is sitting.

"Sweet love, that's a new one," I say and Ransom smiles. The movement pulls at the scar on his face, a scar left by a monster. Of course, physical wounds are *nothing* when compared to emotional ones, but this? This is the worst kind of both. These scars, every time he looks at them, they're a reminder of what happened to his mother, what happened to *him.*

I want to kiss them all, run my tongue along them, repurpose all of that hate with my love.

Love.

My heart constricts and I glance away.

Fuck.

I can't be falling in *love* with *five* different guys that I just fucking met. That's insane. That's beyond insane.

I run my fingers through the lightly tangled strands of my red hair and suck in a deep breath.

"I'm going to turn my phone on," I say and although the statement's innocuous as hell, there's an ominous ring to my voice. Ransom watches me as I grab the phone and power it up, closing my eyes briefly against the brilliant flash of light from the screen.

"We probably blew your phone up," Ransom whispers in that bedroom-dark voice of his.

It takes me a moment to realize what he's talking about and then … text messages, missed calls, voicemail. From my boys. My five rocker boys.

I flick through the messages, catch things like *Where are you, hon?* and *I'm sorry you missed the show—I played for you tonight.*

I glance up at Ransom and fight back another wave of emotion. I'm not weak. No, I *won't* be weak. I choose strength. Because sometimes, it *is* a choice. Bad things happen, people die, hearts are broken, but it's how we walk in the rain of grief that defines us. Do we cower in the downpour and let the frigid chill soak us through? Do we grab an umbrella and fight the storm? Or do we stand tall and let our heads fall back, open our mouths and taste every fucking drop as its coolness sizzles against the heat of our tongue?

That's the woman I want to be.

I drop the phone by my side and I smile in place of the tears that want to come.

Dad is still dead, but Ransom … Ransom is here.

"You were really that worried?" I ask, but it's a stupid validation question that I shouldn't have even bothered to ask. But still, Ransom smiles again and takes a step closer to me, setting aside the mug in his hands and wrapping his arms around me instead.

"We really were," he whispers, his breath hot against my ear, the smell of violets surrounding us in a fragrant cloud. I close my eyes and drink in all the sensations: the softness of his sweatshirt, the heat of his body, the frantic beating of his heart against my own. When he lets me go, I almost groan. I want him to keep holding me forever.

"Lilith," Michael says from behind me, drawing my

attention back around to his sleepy face. Shortly after he finished what he dubbed *that nasty as fuck grassy tasting hippie tea* he fell asleep on the couch, dreaming away the nightmare of the day as I ran my fingers through his shiny black hair. The style is razored, very rockstar, edgy as fuck, but god is it soft. I could spend all day with my fingers tangled in that man's locks.

Michael sits up and stretches his arms above his head, the muscles in his shoulders, chest, and tummy lengthening with the motion, drawing my attention with a sharp surge of desire, heating me up in all the places I need to be warmed.

"Did you think we left you?" he asks, but not like he's going to judge me for my answer, just like he's curious.

"I did," I say and he nods, like that's basically what he expected. He rises to his feet, the tattoos on his arms and chest this colorful art gallery of jewel toned pieces. The phoenix, rising from the ashes, dead center in all of it.

That's who I want to be, that phoenix.

Ashes. Mom, and now Dad.

Me.

Rising from them.

A bird of fire and flame.

"Let's just … get this out there," Michael says, drawing Pax's attention away from his phone. He's back at it again, frustratingly texting someone, ignoring their repeated calls. His parents again? Or something else? I still have a hell of a lot to learn about these boys, don't I? "This … thing," he says and then pauses for a moment, closing his violet eyes to catch his breath on the end of a yawn. I might've had a hard day yesterday, but so did he.

"This relationship," Muse corrects, glancing up at the ceiling in thought, his dark glasses perched on his face. "I don't like the word *thing.* It's too ambiguous. This is a relationship."

"Fucking Christ," Pax swears under his breath, but he just tosses his phone on the coffee table and tucks his fist under his chin, staring at me like he's just as confused by my attitude, my actions, and my presence as he was that first night when he cursed and ran out on me, leaving me tied up with his belt. What a dick. But a dick with a heart who's hurt, who misses his baby sister, who sings about her in the voice of a weeping angel.

"This relationship," Michael corrects, opening his eyes and glancing back at the other boys. Ransom stands at my side, looking at Cope of all people, the one who distinctly looks the *most* uncomfortable with this conversation. Huh. The boy next door type, the one who offered me a hug at our first meeting, who held and kissed me like I was his girlfriend the first night we had sex, is looking away toward the door with a gentle frown on his face and a sparkle of … something in his eyes that I can't read.

Is he regretting Muse's invitation? Does he wish this whole thing was as temporary as it seemed a few days ago? I stare at him, dressed in a white Misfits t-shirt and linen pj pants. No. I don't think so. The way he wrapped his arms around me earlier … There's no way. But something else is bothering him then. I want to know what it is.

"This relationship," I repeat when I draw my attention back to Michael and see his brow scrunched as he struggles for the right words.

"Well, I hope you're tickled bloody pink that he's involved now," Pax drawls, draping himself in his chair as he studies his friend, me, Ransom. Those steel grey eyes flick back to mine. "Because Michael is nothing if not intense."

"Shut your mouth, Pax," Michael says, but not unkindly. He tucks his hands in the pockets of his sweats and stares right at me. "This relationship thing we're doing then, it's not going to be willy-nilly or casual, not if I'm going to be a part of it."

"Okay," I say, blinking at him, watching him watch me and feeling this … heat swirl in my belly that takes over all my limbs and makes me wish I was naked and underneath him. Them. All of them. *Mine.* As soon as I fucked Michael, I felt it, this overwhelming sense of *primal,* of *beast.* I feel like a queen with a clutch of kings, like I have a harem.

Or … no, more than that. A female with her males. A wildcat with her mates.

A blush rises to my cheeks and I cross my arms over Cope's t-shirt that I snagged off the floor.

"To tell you the truth," Muse says from behind Michael, still situated in the leather swivel chair with a book on his lap. It's titled *Beautiful Survivors* and the cover features a woman … surrounded by men. It must be one of Cope's—and it might be something I'll need to read. All of this—the boys, the sex, the feelings, the dynamics—is completely new to me. I've been your average typical middle class American with the one boyfriend and the dreams of a house, kids, a decent, normal, average happy life.

This … has the potential for so much more. And yet, it also has the potential to go up in flames that would consume the heartache I felt at Kevin's betrayal and make it look like a match in an inferno.

This is a big risk … with a big reward.

Am I brave enough to take it?

"This wasn't really casual *before* you joined in—no

offense." Muse sets the book aside and rises to his feet, crossing his arms over the red wife beater he's wearing, his silver mohawk falling onto his forehead, wet and dripping from the shower he took while I tried to read. "But you're right—we should define the rules more clearly."

"Bloody rules," Pax says, rolling his eyes and rising to his feet like he doesn't give a shit. But when he passes by me, our arms brush and I get this scalding thrill through my body that doesn't lie. He really *does* give a shit. A lot of them, maybe. "Typical, yeah? Muse and Michael, taking the fun and turning it all bureaucratic. Don't you two ever get tired of being so fucking dreary?"

"No other guys," Michael says, crossing his arms over his bare chest, cutting into me with his violet gaze. "Just the five of us."

"No other girls," I say, almost breathless, my heart thundering in my throat. "Just me—and not just because of the no condoms thing. I mean no other girls *period.* Not with condoms, not to kiss, nothing." My throat gets so tight when I say this, lay it out there like that. It seems so unfair, doesn't it? That I'd get to fuck, date … fall in love with all of them, and they'd be limited to me?

I pause and glance at the heated hardwood floors under my feet for a moment.

"No other girls," I start and then look up at Michael, over at Ransom. Cope won't look back at me, still lost in whatever nightmare he's currently revisiting. "But I …" I think of Pax and Ransom kissing, and I don't know that they even liked it at all, if it was just for me, but … "I don't care what you do with each other."

I meet Michael's stern gaze dead-on.

He raises a dark eyebrow at me.

"Each other?" he asks, like the thought never even occurred to him.

"Yeah," I say, tucking some red hair behind my ear and nodding. "Each other. If we're in this, we're all in it together." When those words come out of my mouth, they feel *right.* "I know it seems silly right now, but that's how I feel. It's not just me, and you and you and you and you and you. This is an *us* thing."

"Okay …" Michael says, but like he doesn't see *that* particular avenue going anywhere. "No sleeping around with anyone but the people in this room. That's simple enough. Lilith," he says, and this is where he gets really fucking serious, "we will *not* end this thing like it was a fucking one-night stand or a fling. If we end this, we do it properly. We don't fuck around with other people and then apologize later: we end it first. We break up the right goddamn way—like a real relationship."

"So … if you get lost again," Muse says, coming across the living room and going straight into the kitchen to put on more water for tea—I'm assuming for Copeland this time, "then don't for a second think we've left you. Unless you hear it straight from our mouths, or we hear it from yours, this is happening, okay?"

I really do smile then, nice and big.

Boundaries and rules, like any other relationship. Some people feel stifled by them; I feel bolstered. To set rules, to care enough about someone breaking them, you have to actually *feel* something real.

"We won't leave you without talking about it first—*any* of us," Michael gives Paxton a look as his friend turns around with a fresh cup of coffee clutched in his tattooed hands and raises a blonde brow. But he doesn't say a damn word. "And you'll give us the same courtesy?"

I nod and breathe out a breath I wasn't even aware I was holding in.

"I promise," I say and then feel Ransom's warm hand curl around my own.

Fuck.

Did I just … agree to date five guys at the same time?

Yeah, I think I just did.

"So … if I happen to call you my girlfriend in the back room of a seedy BDSM club …" Ransom starts and my smile turns into a grin.

"What about the press?" Cope asks, speaking up for the first time, his voice slightly shaky and surreal. The other guys exchange glances, like they have some idea of what might be going through his head. I have no fucking clue, no idea about this guy who holds me like I'm precious, who takes me out to dance the Charleston. I *need* to; I want to. "Do we tell them?"

"Fuck the press," Pax says with a harsh laugh. "If they find out, then so be it." He lights up a cigarette and shakes his head dismissively. "We don't have to advertise our shit to them, but we also don't have to be ashamed of it."

He pauses and then his mouth turns cruel and cold.

"Do you feel that?" he asks and we all pause.

The bus is rolling to a slow stop beneath us, breathing out a mechanical sigh as the brakes are put in place. I grab the curtain on the window nearest me and pull it back, watching the marmalade wash of sunrise peak up above the Florida coast. The water sparkles and beckons, begging me to take a dip.

I realize then that it's been years since I've seen the ocean, and my breath catches in my chest.

I turn back to see Pax going for the door to the bus and my elation fades like a deflated balloon.

We're in Jacksonville, Florida, and it's time to see Octavia Warris.

"Wait," I say as Paxton reaches for the handle and pauses, glancing back at me with his cigarette hanging from his lips. Both blonde brows go up in surprise. "Let me throw something on; I want to talk to her, too."

"There's no need for that, love," Pax says, waving his tattooed hand dismissively. "I'm going to rapidly and succinctly fire her arse and kick her off this tour. You don't have to see her if you don't want to."

"I want to," I say, not entirely sure what it is that I'm doing. "Give me a minute. Just one minute."

I pad down the hallway and dig into the bags of clothing that Muse and Michael bought me, selecting a pair of white jeans and a tank top with an American flag on the front. I toss the outfit on, slip my feet into those stupid red heels I wore the first night I met the boys, and then rake my hair up into a ponytail.

When I step back into the living room, I get more than one appreciative look from the crowd.

"You look fucking hot, sweetheart," Ran whispers, giving me a kiss on the cheek as I smile and rub my suddenly sweaty palms on the white denim. Facing Octavia is either a really smart move … or a really stupid one.

"Thanks," I say as I head toward the door where Muse is now waiting with Pax.

"You ready?" he asks me, looking at me through the thick lenses of his glasses, his expression carefully neutral, like there are so many things he wants to tell me but isn't quite ready to yet.

"Is it okay if I do most of the talking?" I ask and Pax sighs, leaning his back against the metal wall of the short stairwell.

"You don't owe that bloody scrag a thing," he says and I smile tightly.

"I know."

Pax holds his hand out and lets me down the steps first—groping my ass as I go by, of course. I give him a look over my shoulder as I open the door and step into an already warm morning. It's in the late sixties and it's not even eight o'clock yet. For a second, I just stand there and close my eyes against the heated caress of an ocean breeze.

"Miss Goode," Octavia says as I open my eyes and find her standing nearby, her ever present clipboard and tablet clutched to her chest.

I stare at her brown eyes and let myself remember how awful and cruel they looked last night, narrowed and pinched with hate in my direction. She looks apathetically neutral now, face frozen in polite professionalism. I notice she doesn't look at Pax or Muse as they come down the steps to stand behind me.

"What did I do to you to make you hate me so much?" I ask, emotions warring in my chest as I try to figure out why it was that I wanted to come down here in the first place. I should've let Pax fire her and been glad that I never had to see her again. Instead, here I am, watching the warm morning wind tease brown hair around her face.

"I don't hate you," she says with a tight swallow and a slight lift of her chin, like she already knows what's coming.

"What you did to me last night …" I tuck some errant strands of red-purple hair behind my ear and look up at her. "That was fucked up on so many levels. You seemed really angry, Octavia."

"Let's just get this over with, shall we? I've already called the label and started making arrangements for a replacement to meet us in Montréal."

"Montréal?!" Pax asks from behind me. "Hell no. You aren't staying here until Montréal."

"Her name is Tamasin Perez, and she'll be coming in all the way from California. While she finishes up a project, I'll be getting her up to speed via email and video chat."

"No fucking way," Pax snaps, but I lift my hand back and curl my fingers through his, silencing him. Octavia watches the interaction with a pinched mouth and dark eyes.

"If you have until Montréal," I start as her gaze lifts to mine, "then you have plenty of time to face this."

"I'm afraid I don't know what you're talking about," she says with a slight sniff. But I can see the tremble in her hands, the tightness in her neck and shoulders. Being the manager for Beauty in Lies was a dream come true for her, and she doesn't want to let it go. Last night, I was ready to see her get her just deserts, lose her job, walk away with her head dropped in shame. This morning, in the easy glimmer of a coastal morning, vengeance doesn't seem quite as important.

"You made a huge mistake because you were jealous about Paxton and I becoming a couple."

"You're a couple?" she asks, and I feel like something awful's about to come out of her mouth as she flicks her attention to Muse.

"You have a week left to own up to your mistakes," I tell her with a slight shrug, dropping Pax's hand. I miss his warmth immediately and smile slightly. It feels good to miss something that I can still have. If I just reach back, he'll be there waiting. "And I don't have any friends." I pause. "Well, except for the boys."

"Are you saying you want to be *friends* with me?" Octavia scoffs, turning her head, her ponytail rustling around in the salty ocean air currents. "That's ridiculous."

"Only as ridiculous as you make it out to be. I was all ready last night to see you burn for your mistakes. This morning … I just don't feel like anymore suffering would negate the pain you caused me last night. I forgive you. I hope you can find it in your heart to apologize to me."

I turn away and head back up the stairs before I lose my nerve.

"Whoa," Muse says from behind me as I pause next to the swivel chairs and run my hands over my hair, adjusting my ponytail as I glance back at him. He looks impressed as he smiles at me, and I catch a snippet of angry conversation from outside. I can't stop whatever Paxton wants to say to Octavia, but I tried to take the high road out there. Hopefully that wasn't a mistake? "That, I did not expect."

"What happened?" Michael asks, appearing in the hallway with his shoulder length hair damp and feathery. He pulls a black t-shirt on as I watch, stretching the fabric over his lean muscular frame.

"Octavia's staying until Montréal," I say as I take a deep breath and put my hands on my hips, my heart thundering suddenly in my chest. I feel shaky and wired, like I'm standing at a precipice. This is the moment my new life begins, and I'm not going to start it by gleefully destroying a woman's career—not even a woman as mean-spirited and awful as Octavia Warris. "I told her that if she wanted, we could try to make friends."

"Have you completely lost the plot?" Pax asks, storming

up the steps in his expensive loafers, looking at me with a strange expression on his face, almost like he feels betrayed. "That bitch deserves the boot, not a goddamn handshake."

"People make mistakes, Paxton," I tell him softly and his grey eyes widen almost imperceptibly. "In most cases, it's worth it to give them a second chance."

His gaze snaps straight over to Ransom, who's frozen up next to the coffeepot like he's bracing himself for another fight. Dark brown eyes meet ash grey ones for a long, tense moment before Pax looks away and shakes his head.

"If you think you and Octavia will be holding hands by the end of this thing, you really are mental," Pax says, getting out another cigarette and pausing next to me, his breath hot against my ear. The sensation makes me shiver. "But it's your fight to fight, yeah? Let's hope you struck the right sort of blow."

He scoots around me, ignoring Ransom's tense shoulders, and disappears into the back of the bus, sliding the hall door closed behind him. I watch Ran for a moment as he relaxes with a long sigh of relief and pours himself some coffee. I want to see him and Pax work through their differences; that's one of my goals. It's something I've wanted to do since I first laid eyes on their conflict, but I didn't think I'd have the time.

I do now.

"I need a swimsuit," I say and the four boys left in the room with me seem to perk up considerably. Considering the shit storm that was last night, I feel hopeful, cheerful. I know it won't last indefinitely, this feeling. Grief doesn't just *stop.* That, and I know where this trip will end up by the end of the week: New York.

No matter how my plans with the boys have changed, I

have to go home and see the place I grew up one last time. I need that closure.

“Is there a chance we could squeeze in a trip before the show tonight? I could really use an afternoon at the beach.”

“We've got twelve hours to burn,” Muse says, putting his arms around me from behind and resting his chin on my shoulder. Last night, something broke in him. His touch is laden with need, tinged with fear. I really scared the crap out of him. “Neptune Beach is supposed to be a nice date spot, fairly mellow. And there should be plenty of shopping nearby.”

I reach down and curl my fingers around the tattooed bats on Muse's hand.

A date.

With all five of my boyfriends.

Holy shit.

I'm either the luckiest girl alive … or the craziest.

I'm sure that I much care either way.

Last night was weird for me.

I mean, I was freaked all the hell out that Lilith was missing, but now that she's here, safe and sound and browsing bikinis in a small seaside boutique, I should be okay. Only … I'm not. Each minute that ticked past, I imagined something awful happening to her. Each scenario was worse than the last, dredging up my own past like bones from a muddy grave.

“Are you alright?” Cope asks me, a few pairs of swim trunks tossed over his arm. His red hair is tousled into an easy mussed style today, not shaped into the small ridge of a faux hawk. But his eyes … those are worried and distant.

I'm not the only one with skeletons in my closet.

“Are you?” I query back at him, studying his expression as he looks at Lilith laughing at whatever stupid thing Paxton's just said. He stares at her for a moment and then glances away sharply. I know he's thinking about Cara, the girlfriend he couldn't save. It wasn't his fault yet he holds that failure so close that it's poisoning him.

“I don't want another girlfriend,” he whispers and I feel my mouth tighten up as I slip my hands into the pockets of my red skinny jeans. “I like Lilith, but I … I just can't do it.”

"You're not in this alone, not this time," I tell him, but when I try to put a hand on his shoulder he pulls away and heads for the dressing rooms. I watch him go and then turn my head to see Lilith following him with her eyes. As soon as Cope disappears through the archway that connects the two small rooms of the boutique, she refocuses her attention back on me.

I make myself smile.

"Is he okay?" she asks as she makes her way over to me, and I try to distract her from the question by reaching out and fingering the sleek shiny material of the black swimsuit in her hand.

"One-pieces?" I retort with a wrinkled nose. "Gross. Come on, Cutie, you could totally pull off a bikini."

"What's wrong with Copeland?" she asks again, tilting her head to the side, her red ponytail swinging with the motion. Those emerald green eyes lock on my face and I find it hard to breathe for a second there, my heart thundering in my chest. God. I've got it bad.

I reach a hand up and cup the side of Lilith's face.

"It's not my story to tell," I whisper, wishing I could just spit it all out, tell her that Copeland had a girlfriend named Cara, that Cara was sick in the head, that Cope tried to take care of her the way he took care of his mom and grandma. But Cara committed suicide and there was nothing he could do to stop her, no favor he could perform, no amount of love he could shower her with.

"It's Cara, isn't it?" Lilith asks, surprising me.

"He told you about her?" I ask and she shakes her head.

"No, but he mentioned her name …" Lilith trails off, sighs, and then puts a smile on her face.

I make myself return it because I feel damn lucky to be

standing here with her right now, alive and whole and safe. I know better than most how dark humanity can get, the awful things people do to each other.

Without even realizing it, I curl my hands into fists by my sides.

Don't think about it; don't think about it; don't think about it.

"You really want me to try on a bikini?" she asks coyly, turning and flipping her hair in my face. The soft strands brush across my skin and send shivers down my spine, turning my shitty fake half-smile into a real one. I can smell Michael's shampoo on the long, silky strands of her hair, some sort of body spray or perfume clinging to her clothes. "Help me pick one out and I'll try it on."

Lilith plays with the pair of necklaces at her throat as I step up beside her and start to slide hangers across a wooden bar, tiny scraps of bikini hanging from metal teeth and swaying with the motion. My tattooed arm, the one covered in bats, presses up tight against the bare empty canvas of her white flesh. The feel of her soft skin brushing against me ignites the slow burning ember in my belly.

Then the *rest* of last night comes rushing to the surface, the good parts of it anyway.

Fuck.

I've never had a sixsome before.

It was definitely a unique experience. I certainly know my friends better than I ever really expected to.

"You see this?" Lilith asks, taking a bikini and showing the cups to me. There's an eyeball on either one, artistically rendered with rainbow irises and diamond pupils, long dark lashes sweeping up to the halter straps. The bottoms have a grinning mouth with pink lips and vampire teeth. "I wonder what it takes to get your art on something like this? This is part of a famous painting by an up-and-coming artist from New York City. I used to have a print of it on my wall in Phoenix." She pauses for a moment and purses her lips. "Until Kevin burned it, that is."

Lilith rubs her fingers over the fabric fondly. I don't know anything about art outside of music, so I can't really comment on the piece or the artist, but I can hear the longing in Lil's voice, the desperate need to be seen, to be heard.

All artists feel that pull eventually. Some of us get lucky. Some of us don't. It's really only part talent, part drive … a whole lot of chancy dice rolling.

"We can find out," I say as Lilith pushes the bikini aside and keeps browsing. I trace my fingertips over hers and her breath catches. "We'll figure out some way for you to make a living with your art, if that's what you want. Just … promise me you'll keep trying while you're with us. I have to admit: you were right."

"About what?" Lilith asks, grabbing a white bikini with red hearts scattered across the fabric, little gold handled knives digging into the throbbing flesh. She adds that to her stack and keeps searching.

"You really are a good girlfriend," I tell her and she smiles, looking up at me with those full lips curved and shiny with red gloss. I lean over and brush my mouth gently against hers. "I don't want you to start taking care of me and the rest of these assholes and forget about yourself. Just promise me that, okay?"

Lilith pushes a few more swimsuits aside and I stop her, grabbing an emerald green and black striped one and pulling it off the rack.

"This one," I say and she raises her red eyebrows. "Just

trust me. And you haven't promised me yet."

I turn to face her fully and she does the same, pulling in a long, deep breath.

"I promise," she says and I smile, cupping her face again and pressing our mouths together for a long, languorous kiss, my tongue slipping between the cherry flavored softness of her lips. She kisses me back with a burning fervor that gets my blood pumping, turns my cock to diamond inside my red skinny jeans.

I wonder if she'll still kiss me like that once I tell her about my past?

"Your first official day without Vanessa metaphorically breathing down your neck," Pax says as he lounges on a rented chair under a blue umbrella and lifts his shades up to look at me. "Must feel bloody *fantastic.*"

"She blew up my fucking phone last night—everything from death threats to sobbing apologies. I'm thinking of blocking her."

"Thinking of it? Jesus, give me your phone and I'll do it for you."

I tap my cell against my palm and try to enjoy the warm sunshine on my pale as fuck skin. I look like a goddamn vampire. I could use some color.

"Tim's been texting me, too. I have no idea what to do about him. I mean, the way things went down it really seemed like he was trying to spare my feelings."

"By getting balls-deep in your girlfriend? Nah, sorry mate, but I'm gonna have to disagree with that. I say you block him, too."

"He's the only living family member I have left; I'm not blocking him."

"At least unfriend him on Facebook then? No? God, you're such a pussy."

"Pussies are a lot stronger than balls," Lilith says, startling both me and Pax. "Why would anyone say *he's got balls* to reference strength when a swift kick to the nether regions drops a man to his knees? As far as calling a weak person a *pussy,* well, pussies birth babies. Plus, they can take a pounding and *enjoy it.*"

"Keep saying *pussy* and I'll change my lingo however you want," Pax drawls, dropping his shades back into place. His mouth makes a dangerous curve as he studies Lil's hourglass figure, skin as white as cream, her black and green striped bikini sexy as hell, curving low on her hips, the top just big enough to hold her full breasts in place. "Michael, stop being such a pair of hairy bollocks and block that cheating bitch *and* that arsehole brother of yours. How's that sound?"

"Better," Lilith says as I cringe a little and watch her studying me with those big round eyes of hers. "Would you put this on for me?" she asks and my brows go up as she passes over some sunscreen. "I basically go from white to red; there's no in-between."

"If you think I'm going to say no to slathering lotion all over your back, you're dead fucking wrong. Give me that and take a seat."

Lilith hands the pink bottle to me as I lean back in the chair and put a leg on either side, my body responding to hers as she slides up close to me, her ass precariously close to my cock.

A year of celibacy. *Finally* fucking broken. And with the girl sitting in front of me?

It feels surreal, like Vanessa's noose is still around my neck.

"I haven't spoken to her since, in case you were

wondering," I tell Lilith as I squirt some of the lotion on my hands and rub it together to warm it up. My fingertips hover above her pale skin for a moment before she reaches up and unties the halter top, holding an arm over her breasts to keep the fabric from falling away.

My breath catches as I struggle to fight down a surge of wild hormones.

Holy shit.

This girl is beyond fucking hot. And she's my new girlfriend? It doesn't feel real.

I curl my fingers around her shoulders and Lilith shudders, goose bumps jumping up across her skin as I knead her warm flesh with my hands. My tongue runs across my lower lip as I struggle to keep my shit together. After a year of not touching anybody, I've got my hands all over a slippery lotion covered back.

Just beyond the circle of shade cast by our umbrellas, the sea sparkles and glimmers, the sand white-hot with the eighty degree heat. There are a few older people around, but there's no real crowd and we haven't seen any sniffing around from the media hounds—thank god.

"It's okay if you need to, for closure or something," Lil says, leaning back into my hands, murmuring with pleasure as I caress and knead her flesh, our little sunscreen session taking on an erotic edge. I can't help it. Since I came to Lilith in that kitchen, we've only had sex twice. Well, maybe three or four times if you break up last night's group session and count orgasms instead of actual sessions. "I'm sure there must be something you want to say to her?"

"I already said it yesterday: fuck you. That's all there is to it."

"What about your brother?" she asks me as I slide my

hands around her rib cage and dip my fingers under her arm to cup her breasts. Lilith gasps as I knead the tender flesh with my slick hands, feeling her nipples pebble against my palms. I scoot forward on the chair and press my erection against her back, leaning in to breathe against her neck.

My bare chest presses against her nearly naked back, making her gasp.

"I don't know," I whisper roughly. "I'm having a hard time thinking about my brother right now."

"You should—" Lil starts and then gasps when I squeeze her breasts harder, pressing my mouth to her neck. She smells like sun and sand, the faint whisper of my shampoo hiding beneath the scent of the lotion. "Oh God, Michael, not here," she whispers, but I can't help myself. Lilith is wiggling her hot, slick body against mine, the heavy weight of her breasts sitting in my hands.

"This is a public beach, you know," Pax murmurs from beside us, but he sounds like he's enjoying the show almost as much as I'm enjoying putting it on.

"People have been arrested for exactly this," Lilith whispers, pulling my hands away from her breasts and fastening her halter around her neck. "In *Florida,* too."

"That's fucking bullshit," I growl as I kiss her neck and slide my greasy palms down her arms instead, curling our fingers together. It occurs to me then that I don't even *know* this girl. I've spent the better part of a week treating her like shit. Honestly, I'm surprised she's even giving me the time of day let alone … *this.* "Puritanical crap. A hefty fine maybe, a slap on the wrist, a ban from the beach. But arresting someone for consensual sex?"

"Maybe so," she says, her breath coming in sharp, panting gasps. "But I don't want to spend two and a half years in prison." Lilith sighs and leans back against me as I add some lotion to my palms and rub them down her inner thighs. "The couple has to register as sex offenders, too."

"That's up there with the dumbest shit I've ever heard in my life," I say as I rub lotion across the smooth skin of her belly, up and over her collarbone, the front of her throat. I can feel Lil's pulse thrumming at my touch. "I bet they'd have gotten less time if they'd projected a video of a live murder on a screen for everyone to watch—just as long as they hadn't *actually* committed it."

"Violence is okay; sex and sensuality aren't," Lilith says, turning to glance at my face with a sad smile.

"But you don't agree with that?" I ask, curious as she takes the bottle from me and finishes up with her face, her hands, her feet. The movement of her palms sliding across her skin is fucking fascinating to me.

"I'm still coming to terms with my own sexuality," she says, her voice a near whisper that's hard to hear above the sound of the surf and the call of gulls in the distance. At the moment, there's nobody nearby. Ran, Muse, and Cope are in the water directly in front of us, but that's it. The six of us. I like it that way. "I think it'll take the public a lot longer to figure out that sex is just a part of life; it's not evil. I think the less we hide from it, the less it'll be flaunted, too. It's a double-edged sword. Demonizing sex turns it into a lewd form of theatrics."

"Well, this is getting too heavy for me. I prefer to swim in the shallows, thank you."

Pax rises to his feet and shoves his shades up and into his blonde hair.

"Enjoy your little pseudo intellectual chin-wag," he says, flicking his fingers dismissively at us. "While you're at it, make sure you cover politics and religion, too." Pax grins and tucks his fingers into the black swim trunks hanging off his thin hips, swaggering off to join the others at the edge of the water.

"This is probably the first real conversation that we've had," Lilith says and I smile.

"Maybe the first one where I haven't been a fucking asshole. I'm sorry about that, by the way. I completely misread you. I don't know how I ever thought you were just another random groupie."

"And now I'm the *only* groupie," she says, and I don't miss the smile in her voice. "Since we're at it already, are you religious?"

"I'm spiritual," I say and she laughs.

"Cop-out. Politics?" Lilith draws a D in the sand with her foot on one side of the chair and an R on the other.

"Democrats or republicans?" I ask and she nods. "Fucking *neither.*"

"Good answer." I watch her curvy body unfold as she stands up and holds out a hand to me, green eyes sparkling. The pair of necklaces I bought her—the rhodonite heart and the opal tear—swing as she leans over and smiles at me with those full lips of hers. "As fascinating as I find this conversation, there's no way I came all the way down to Florida just to talk. It's been years since I've been anywhere near the ocean, let alone an ocean I could swim in."

I take Lil's hand and stand up, deciding to be bold and yank her against me, swing her up in my arms. The press of her body against mine takes my breath away, especially when she reaches forward and pulls off my shades, fisting a hand in my hair and pulling my mouth to hers for a kiss.

I made so many mistakes with Vanessa that I can't even

remember if we had it good in the beginning or if I just imagined it. I won't make those same mistakes with Lilith.

Our kiss breaks off with reluctance on both sides as I carry her down to the edge of the beach and jump straight into the waves. Lilith squeals as I toss her into the water and she disappears under the easy rolling surf for a second, popping up with her red hair slipping out of her ponytail and sticking to the sides of her face.

"About time you two showed up," Muse says, ruffling up his mohawk with a smile, giving me a look that trails over to Ransom, shirtless and staring up at the sun with his eyes closed. The fact that he's *not* wallowing in shadow and drowning in one of his big baggy hoodies is a miracle. But then I look over and see Cope kneeling down to pick up a seashell, examining it with a strange sort of intensity and then standing up to chuck it into the water.

He looks almost miserable standing in the sea and sun and surf.

It's gotta be about Cara. Has to be. But I get a feeling that if one of us fucks this thing up, the whole ship sinks with him.

I just got fucking started here and I'm not letting the heavy weight of *anyone's* baggage drag us down.

Not even mine.

The speakers on either side of the stage ripple with the sound of a bass, guitars, and drums, the soft sexy sound so similar to Ransom's decadent voice that I get chills down my spine. I clap my hands and pump my fist, cheering along with the crowd as the animated short finishes playing on the curtain and it rises up to reveal the boys.

My boys.

A ripple of pleasure snakes through me at the idea, so thrilling in its newness, so fucking exciting. It doesn't seem possible to feel this … *good* after last night, but I do. Our day at the beach was as relaxing as it was fun, and I felt like I got to spend some quality time with Michael. I had such a good time that I don't even mind the slight burn I got on the back of my neck or the glare Octavia was throwing my way when we came back with sand in our hair and clothes, slightly tipsy from a small beachside bar that we stopped into after we finished swimming.

"*I'm broken and cold with no place of my own,*" Paxton sings in a soft low voice, kneeling near the front of the stage and panning his grey gaze across the audience. His suit today is white, his tie bloodred. "*You trashed and bloodied my only home.*" He rises slowly after the next verse, hooking his left hand around the mic stand and tilting it toward the hushed faces of the crowd. The lights are so low, they shadow his face as they spin around and away, across the rest of my boys and then back to Pax as he raises his voice. "*You stole the light, snuffed out the flame. You destroyed the entire world as a game.*"

His face splits into a wry grin as he lifts his chin and belts out the next lines with a force that turns my blood to ice. I can *feel* the emotion there; I just can't decide if it's *his* emotion. If I didn't know any better, I'd say this was *Ransom's* song.

"*I have nothing left except this song. Just this song ...*"

Pax drops his voice again on the last word and then Ran joins in for the hook as their words swell and amplify through the mics, crash into me and leave me breathless. God. The two of them together is like magic. I just don't think they know that yet.

"*I'm just a man; I'm not invincible. This is my goodbye, my farewell to the world!*"

Cope's drums take over for a moment as the lyrics trail off and the lights overhead flicker and flash, spotlighting him for a moment, the resigned expression on his face. He's been great to me, as nice as ever. But there's something deep down that's haunting him, something that was triggered either by last night … or this morning.

I swallow through a slightly dry throat and try not to think too hard about. I *just* claimed all five of these guys as my own … what would it feel like to lose one already? It feels like an inevitability that my happiness will end someday. I mean, surely a relationship with *five* men—five straight men? I'm not sure—and one woman can't last. One day, they'll want families and wives and houses like everybody else.

Right?

"*So fucking sick of wandering alone. The things you've done have cut to the bone. I have nothing left except this song. Just this song ...*"

Pax sighs and the lights cut off Cope to highlight him and Ran again, plucking at the strings of his dark purple bass. He's rocking it hard, teasing the strings with his bare fingers, his face dark, eyes closed for a moment as he digs into the rhythm. In his black leather boots, black holey jeans and hooded tank with the green skull and crossbones on it, he looks like a specter. I let him sweep his shadowy wings over me with the grinding depth of the bass and close my own eyes.

"*I'm just a man; I'm not invincible. This is my goodbye ...*" The two boys sing together, their voices booming and haunting both at the same time.

"*This is my goodbye ...*" The other three repeat softly, Muse sharing a mic with Ran while Michael shares one with Pax; Cope has his own positioned so he can reach it while he plays his drums.

"*My farewell to the world,*" Pax and Ran continue. "*I'm just a man; I'm not invincible. This is my goodbye ...*"

"*This is my goodbye ...*"

"*My farewell to the world!*" they finish as Pax leans his head back again and taps one of his expensive brown loafers against the shiny red floor of the stage. I'm not sure what it's made out of, but when the light hits it just right, it looks like the boys are standing in blood.

"*I think I hate you,*" Pax continues on his own as Ransom layers his voice atop his.

"*I won't leave this world alone.*"

"Come see me; I'm through."

They both stop singing as the lights swing over and spotlight Muse and Michael as they step up close to the stage and lean back to back, their picks moving across their guitars at a speed that's hard to follow, breaking up the distant melancholy of the song with some electrified notes. They're both so into it, biting their sexy lips and thrashing their heads. Muse likes to let the tip of his tongue stick out when he's really into it.

I cheer and bounce with the crowd as they both slide to the ground, continuing to play their instruments and then pausing suddenly, leaving a small sharp moment for the crowd to snatch a gasping breath.

When Pax and Ran break through their mics to sing the hook again, I get more chills and find my arms crossed tight over the short pink dress I'm wearing, this one a gift from Ransom. He saw me looking at it in the shop today and bought it without my knowing. When he gave it to me, he said he liked the way we looked together, light and dark like that.

They repeat the hook twice more, the sounds of their voices melding and twisting until it sounds like only one person is singing. As they trail off, Pax shoves his mic back in the stand and steps back with his arms raised, head down.

Muse and Michael rise to their feet and take over the ending as Cope stops drumming and the three string instruments carry the song to its natural conclusion.

"We're Beauty in Lies," Michael shouts into the mic, short on breath as Pax smiles and claps his hands along with everyone else, pausing to adjust his tie. Surprisingly, it's still around his neck tonight. Usually he takes it off and chucks it at the crowd. "A big fucking thank you for having us,

Jacksonville."

Cope pummels his kick drum a few times and then stands up, throwing his sticks into the crowd as the confetti cannon explodes and I reach up to catch some on my palm. Instead of just confetti, I end up with one of Cope's sweaty sticks, pulling it down to stare at it with wide eyes, my palm stinging from the impact.

I feel like I've just caught a wedding bouquet or something.

Tiny white hearts fall all around me and cling to my hair as Michael hands his guitar off to a roadie and heads for the front of the stage, sitting down and sliding off to land hard on his brown boots.

Sweating and shaking with adrenaline, he reaches out a hand and I take it, letting him lead me down the narrow walkway between the security fence and the raised platform of the stage as the audience screams and demands another song. I don't think I've seen a concert yet where they don't at least try.

"That was really intense," I say as Michael drags me into the frenetic chaos that makes up the backstage area, slipping his arm around my waist. My pink dress has a drop waist, the short skirt fluttering around my thighs as sweat drips down my legs. It is hot as *hell* in here. But with Michael's hard, muscular arm pressing into me, each drop of sweat is a tease, a reminder that if his fingers were to trace that same path, my body would be on fire.

"It always is when we play that song," Michael agrees, still trying to catch his breath as we both catch sight of Octavia, gathering the VIP badge holders into a group. She doesn't meet my eyes when her gaze pans across the room, glazing over me like I'm not even there. For a second, I wonder if I've made a mistake in trying to give her a second chance. But no. No. If she wants to shit on the opportunity I've given her, that's her choice to make. It'll dictate the true content of her character, and it won't sully mine.

"Did Ransom write it?" I ask as Michael's violet eyes drop down to mine and my heart starts to race. He's wearing a tight purple tee that brings out the color in his eyes, and a pair of dark jeans. Simple, casual, but with his tattoos, his hair, his eyeliner, he's got the rockstar look all the way.

"Pretty obvious, huh?" he says as the rest of the band makes their way toward Octavia and Michael puts a hand on my shoulder. "Hang out here until we're done?" he asks and I smile. After last night, I guess we're all a little paranoid.

"Sure," I say as he leans down to give me a quick kiss, thrilling me all the way down to my toes. My heart patters in excitement as I watch the band gather together … and notice that Copeland is missing. I look around the glimmering dark beauty backstage and catch sight of a guy in a white tee slipping out the back door toward the buses.

It's most definitely Cope.

I start after him, squeezing between roadies and past the crazy lead singer of the opening band, Tipped by Tyrants, and her neon pink mohawk.

Outside, it's a little cooler but still balmy, the breeze from the ocean making the whole world seem vibrant and tropical and alive. I move across the pavement in my pale pink Docs and flash my badge at the security guard standing at the bottom of the bus steps. She must either recognize me or remember talking to Muse about the redheaded girl on tour because she barely glances my way.

"Cope?" I ask as I open the door and move inside.

He's not in the living room, but I can hear the shower

running.

I pause then, playing with the charm bracelet on my arm and running my tongue across my lower lip in thought. I mean, technically Copeland Park and I are dating now … right? But then, I've only really known him for a week. That, and he never really agreed to all of this explicitly, did he? Michael did; Ransom did. Paxton and Derek did.

Cope's been … a little off today.

I wonder then if I've made a terrible mistake, just assuming that this arrangement is something he wanted to participate in. Maybe I completely misread him?

Taking a deep breath, I move over to the sliding door that leads into the hall and push it aside, stepping into the darkness beyond and closing it behind me before I raise my fist to knock.

"Cope, it's Lily," I say, listening to the sound of running water and glancing down to see steam sneaking out from underneath the door. "Are you okay in there?"

I wait a few moments, knocking a little louder the second time, but there's still no response.

The door to the kitchen slides open and I find Ransom standing there with one hand tucked into the front pocket of an enormous hoodie.

"Is Cope in there?" he asks and I shrug.

"Copeland." Ran lifts his fist and hits the door with a surprising amount of strength, rattling it in its frame. "Hey, man, you have to show up to all the VIP shit. If I have to suffer through that crap, so do you."

He waits for a moment and we exchange looks, my heart thundering in my chest.

"I've got a key," Ransom whispers, his voice warm milk and honey even in a moment like this. He moves around me, his body brushing against mine as he heads over to one of the small drawers on the left side of the kitchen, yanking out a ring with a bunch of tiny gold keys on it. "That stupid motherfucker better have earplugs in or some shit …" he mumbles, and I notice his hands are shaking as he tries to fit one of the tiny keys in the lock.

"Here, let me," I say, wrapping my fingers around Ransom's, stilling his quivering with my touch. I would smile if I wasn't so worried about Cope. The lock turns and then Ran's grabbing the door and shoving it open.

Copeland's standing in the shower, the hot water dragging his auburn hair over his forehead and into those turquoise eyes of his. He's completely naked, and I feel a slight warmth suffuse my cheeks as I study his muscular form, palms outstretched and pressed against the wall, head hanging slightly.

The steam rushes into the hallway and swirls around my legs, giving me chills as Cope glances over and sees us standing there, his mouth turning up at the corner in a slight smile.

"You caught one of my sticks," he says, like he didn't hear us calling his name or knocking.

"Dude, are you fucking deaf?" Ran whispers, voice barely audible above the rush of the water.

"Sorry," Cope says, standing up and running his fingers through his hair, so much darker now that it's wet. It looks more brown than red at the moment. "You guys were knocking?"

He turns toward us, his entire body exposed, water sluicing over his muscles, across the pair of heart tattoos on his chest, dripping down his half-hard cock. I feel my breath catch when he sees me looking and crooks a slightly naughtier smile.

"Sorry," he repeats, shaking his head. "I guess I was a little out of it."

"Well get back into it," Ransom says, voice heavy and dripping with shadows. "We have a meet and greet. There's some famous local reporter there and she says you're her favorite; she wants to write a piece on us."

Copeland leans against the wall and focuses his attention on me, still clutching the stupid drumstick. I wasn't even aware that I was still holding it.

"Is it me?" I ask, refusing to keep secrets or hide from the truth. Neither of those things have served me very well in life. And this, this is my new start. Today. Right here. "Am I the reason you're so upset?"

"Of course not," Ran answers for him, but then he looks from Cope to me, back to Cope again. "Are you fucking serious?"

"It's not you," Copeland says, leaning back against the silver and black tiles, the tattoos at his wrists vibrant under the rush of water, almost like they're being magnified. "Not exactly. I just … can you stall Octavia for a few minutes? I'll be right there."

"I'm not leaving until you explain what the hell is wrong with you—" Ransom starts, but I grab hold of one of the baggy sleeves of his sweatshirt and clutch the material tight, bringing his attention down to me.

"Will you buy us a minute so we can talk?" I ask, my heart hammering, my stomach twisting in knots. Shit. I knew this was all too good to be true. I start to wonder if by the end of the week, more than one of the boys will be asking me to leave.

"Fuck. Fine. But I want to know what the hell's going

on after."

Ran leans down and presses a kiss to the top of my head that I appreciate more than I can even say. I watch him go, carefully sliding the hall door shut behind him.

Without even thinking about it, I go into my strength pose—ankles crossed, hands laced behind my head, chest pulling in damp lungfuls of warm air. I can't let every little thing topple me. And today, I felt like I was on top of the world. That's as good a place as any to start a hard conversation like this, right?

"Do you want me to give you a second to get dressed?" I ask, but Cope just stands up and moves across the tile floor, reaching out a hand and curling his fingers around my wrist. He pulls me into the bathroom and shuts the door, penning me in against it with a hand on either side of my head.

"Lilith," he says, and he sounds so boy next door, so apologetic, that I can hardly even believe he's breaking up with me. Well, maybe he's just ending something that never really got started in the first place? "I don't know if I can do this."

Fuck. Fuck, fuck, fuck.

"Okay," I say, trying to take calm, slow breaths. It's hard because the bathroom is so steamy and Copeland is naked, and his cock isn't just *half*-hard anymore. *He* might not be able to do this, but his body seems more than willing to try. "Can't do what? Share me?"

"Date," he says firmly, reaching down and uncurling my fingers from around the drumstick. "I can't be somebody's boyfriend. I told you one of the reasons why …"

"Not looking to have kids right now," I say, trying to smile through the pain. But shit. This *is* fucking painful, more so than I even thought. The agony is right up there, gnawing at me along with the grief from my father's passing. It shouldn't hurt this goddamn much, not after a week.

I feel like Cinderella again, but this time, she's sitting back and watching her prince take the glass slipper … and shatter it into pieces.

"Right, but …" Cope says, finally freeing the stick from my fingers and letting it drop to the floor. His eyes are so bright, like the ocean today when the sun hit it just right. Beautiful. I can't handle the intensity of that stare, so I refocus on the single ring pierced through the center of his bottom lip. "That's what one-night stands are for, fucking and hanging out for a little while and knowing it doesn't have to go anywhere. Dating is … seeing if there's the possibility of a future somewhere."

"And there's no future with me?" I ask, just to confirm, beads of moisture clinging to my skin, joining the sweat from the show. My skin feels tight, hot, and not just from the steam or the nearness of Cope's body, but from my own fear of losing him when I just finally, *finally* got all five of them to be mine.

"Oh, Lily," he says, his voice low and sad, almost resigned. But that's the part I just don't understand: resigned to *what?* "It's not you," Cope says softly, trailing his wet knuckles down the side of my face, my neck, fingering the thin pink straps of my dress.

My body lights up like a switchboard, electricity crackling in all the places he touches me. How can he do that, make me feel this way at the same time he's saying he doesn't want to take this risk, this leap off a high cliff into a tumultuous ocean? But the thing is, there are four other people down there besides us, waiting with life rafts, ready to rescue us if the waves get too rough.

It's got to be worth the risk. It is to me anyway. I need Cope to feel that, too; I won't force him.

"It's not you, it's me?" I ask, lifting my eyes back up to his face and finding his expression tired and withdrawn. "That's a little cliché, don't you think?"

Copeland sighs, leaning down to nuzzle the side of my neck for a moment. The gesture, the action, it's too tender for somebody that truly wants to cut and run. Maybe he doesn't really know *what* he wants? I've been there, done that before.

"I know you've heard me say her name before," he whispers, his voice cracking for a split second, showing me this thread of vulnerability that makes my heart hurt. "Cara."

The way he says her name makes me think of my father. *Roy.* I haven't said his name once since he died. Roy. Even thinking it hurts.

My breath catches and Cope pauses, leaning back to look into my eyes, letting his long fingers trace down the length of my arm.

"Once or twice," I say, chest tight, throat tight, wondering what the hell we're doing standing here with him naked and hard, the hot shower still running behind the smooth muscular planes of his back. All I want to do is place my fingers against all of that naked flesh, run my hands across Cope's wet body, put my mouth against the throbbing pulse in his neck, feel the hard curved length of his cock slide into me.

Based on the signs his body is giving me—hard nipples, harder cock, dilated pupils—I get the feeling that that's all he wants, too. For a split second, I wish neither of us had a past, wish neither of us had experienced the kind of pain that rips through you and leaves you a bleeding mess on the floor. But then, it's our pain that drew us together in the first place. I don't know who I'd be without it, who Cope would be.

And if it takes pain for us to be together then I don't know that I'd shed the cocoon of hurt around my shoulders if I could, snap my fingers and stop missing my family.

"She was …" he starts, pauses, flicks his eyes away from me for a moment. "She was everything to me, Lil. *Everything.*" I watch his breathing, the rise and fall of his chest, the pair of heart tattoos on his pec, and I wonder if that image is for her.

He glances back, catches me looking, and smiles tightly.

"This," he says, pointing at it, "this is for my mom and grandma. Cara … she was my best friend and my lover all the way from junior year of high school to my sophomore year of college. In fact, we never actually broke up. But our relationship … it was too messy to tattoo. She hurt me in ways my fucked-up family never did."

I stare into Cope's eyes, blinking against the white steam swirling around his handsome face, around that penetrative gaze of his that makes me want to spill all my hurts and hopes and worries. I told you—I *told* you—that guys like Copeland Park were the most dangerous. The nice ones, the sweet ones, the ones who promise that everything will be okay with a single look.

They're the ones that fuck you over the hardest.

"What happened?"

"Well," Cope says, glancing away from me and stepping back.

My breathing starts again in a rush, making my heart pump faster, my pulse thunder in my throat. Now that he's moved away, I can see all of him again. All of him.

"She killed herself," he tells me finally, licking hot moisture from his lips and shaking his head. "I thought I could take care of her the way I always took care of my mom and grandma." Cope closes his eyes and moves back into the water, letting it sluice between his full lips. "I spent every single fucking day worrying about that awful moment, knowing it was coming, fighting as hard as I could to stop it. Prescription drugs, therapists, love. None of it was enough —not even me."

He opens his eyes again and the sight is *breathtaking.*

I remember his words from just a few days ago: *I've had to hug a lot of people through a lot of things.*

This must be one of those things.

"I couldn't take care of her Lilith, no matter how hard I tried. I wasn't enough. And I'm sad, and I'm tired, and I just … I can't go through that again. At least not yet. I'm not ready."

"Cope," I say, taking a small step forward, feeling my skirt swish around my thighs. "You don't have to take care of me like that."

"All I want to do is take care of you," he says, eyes half-lidded as he studies me with undisguised desire, want, a surprising amount of affection. "All I want to do is hug you and hold you and make the pain go away. And I'm good at it. But not that good. I can't be the man any woman needs me to be, not in the long term." He pauses, takes a deep breath and looks at me with an unbelievable amount of sadness etched into the beautiful lines of that handsome face. "For a night or two, for a few weeks maybe. Not forever, as a boyfriend or a husband. I just can't. I should've said something this morning, but … god, I was so happy to see that you were okay."

"Cope …" I start, and I have to really breathe slow and deep to stop myself from shedding any tears. For him, for me, for … whatever else. But honestly, I don't really care how compelling his story is. I don't want to let him go.

He steps toward me again, closing the distance between us, and pulls me into the water with him.

"Can you forgive me?" he asks, brushing wet red curls back from my face as warm water streams over us. I blink past it, licking hot droplets from my lips. "You can stay, you know, with the other guys. You can still have the Bat Cave, still come on the tour with us. I'm not asking to put a stop to any of that."

I close my eyes as he cups the side of my face and kisses me with that gentle easiness of his, that comforting slant of lips that says his words are a lie, that I *am* his girlfriend, that he would never think to put the brakes on a start as beautiful and interesting as this. We have a connection, Cope and me. The idea of killing it before it even really gets started is … it's sad is what it is.

I let him kiss me anyway, press my palms to his wet chest as his tongue teases mine, slow and sensual and languid, like we have all the time in the world. In reality, we have no time at all. It's over. It's over already and I just got started. I just claimed my boys, just pulled Michael into the group.

I feel like Cope is chiseling a chunk of my heart off, chipping it away and making me bleed.

When his wet hands slide up under my now sopping skirt and grip my ass, I don't protest. I don't want to. I want *him* is what I want.

Cope curls his fingers under the waistband of my panties, some stupid frilly lace boyshorts I put on to impress the guys after the show. We're supposed to go back to that little bar by the beach, but … the thought of going without Copeland makes the whole thing seem pointless.

He pulls his mouth away from mine for just a second, pulling my panties down and helping me step out of them. He tosses them aside, next to the discarded drumstick and then stands back up. For a moment we just look at each other.

And then he lifts me up, turns us so that my back is to the tiled wall. Cope presses me into the wet tile with his body, my legs around him, the spray from above soaking us both as we kiss and I wrap my arms around his neck. I can feel his cock pressing against my opening, blocked by the wet pleats of my skirt. It's maddening, to have him so close and yet … not at all. The physical complication of our bodies is just mimicking the emotional complication, isn't it?

Behind Cope, the door slides open again, much harder this time.

It's Michael.

"What the fuck is going on in here?" he asks, his ire dissipating slightly at the sight of us tangled hot and wet together. "You need to be at the meet and greet," he says, voice trailing off as his violet eyes take in my face. Something about my expression must give the moment away. "And what's this about you having some kind of problem with Lilith?"

Copeland sets me down so reluctantly, I swear he believes this is the last time we'll ever touch.

"I'll …" Cope looks back at me and our gazes lock tight, emotions traveling through the connection like lightning. "Shit."

"Shit, what?" Michael asks, angry and panting, his arousal obvious by the bulge in his dark jeans. But his rage, that's also obvious, written all over his face. I almost smile, seeing Michael turn that ire of his on its head, using it on my behalf instead of against me. "Shit, *what,* Cope?"

"I can't be a boyfriend right now, Michael," Copeland says, sounding about as destroyed as I feel inside, studying me like he's trying to memorize my face. "I'm just not ready to try that again."

"Cope," I start, but Michael's scoff causes me to pause.

"Are you fucking *kidding* me?" he growls, stalking forward and grabbing his friend by the arm. "Do you realize that I just broke up with Vanessa *yesterday?* That I just ended a five year relationship and found out that the baby I've been mourning all this time was probably my niece or nephew instead of my kid?" He's panting with the force of his frustration, flicking those blue-purple eyes my way and then back towards Cope. "You don't screw up an opportunity like this because you're not *ready,* you stupid shit. None of us were ready for this, but it bit us in the ass and so here we are. Life doesn't wait for you to get ready, Copeland."

"I ..." He leans back against the wall for a moment, breathing almost as hard as his friend.

"Fuck," Michael says, raking his fingers through his dark hair. "Take a second and get your shit together. Stop being such a fucking ball sack and grow some ovaries," he continues with a slight smile for me, referencing our conversation at the beach. While I appreciate his reversal of traditional gender bullshit, I don't seem to have it in me to smile back. "Come on, Lil."

Michael takes my hand when I step out of the water, realizing that it's actually gone ice-cold while I was standing there. I hadn't even noticed.

We step out of the room and Michael pushes the door closed behind us.

"Let's get you a towel," he says as I pause there for a moment and stare at the black lacquer surface of the wood. Michael digs into a cabinet in the other bathroom, but I don't wait for the towel. Instead, I rip the door open again to glare at Copeland.

But he's already right there, stumbling into me and knocking us both into the wall.

"Fuck," he whispers, putting a palm up next to my head to steady himself.

"Do you like me?" I ask him as his turquoise eyes catch on my lips and lift back up to find my gaze hard and steely.

"More than any girl I've met since Cara or …" He doesn't finish that sentence, but it feels like a loaded gun, so I decide to leave it for later.

"I'm not sick like Cara, Copeland."

"It shouldn't matter, even if you were," he says with a long sigh, putting his forehead against mine. I'm hyperaware of the fact that Michael is standing just inches away, tucked into the second bathroom, listening. But it doesn't feel like an invasion. No, he's got just as much right to be here as I do. "Lilith, I'm just … I think I'm fucking scared to try again—especially with someone like you."

"Someone like me?" I ask as he adjusts his mouth, puts it precariously close to mine. I can feel his warm breath feathering against my lips, smell the clean sharp scent of bar soap, the slight mineral tang of the water.

"Someone I like as much as you," he corrects, and then he's kissing me again and I don't have the resolve to resist, not when he kisses me like that, uses his whole mouth, his lips, his teeth, his tongue. Cope cups the side of my face and holds me there, romancing me with his kiss, scrambling up the thoughts in my brain.

His hand slides around my back and drags my zipper down before he reaches up to my shoulders and pushes the wet soppy fabric of my dress to the floor. It falls easily off of my curvy body, the liquid heavy cotton hitting the floor with a splatter of warm water.

I'm standing there panting, wearing nothing but my pink Docs and my bra when Cope glances at Michael for a moment and then back to me, his expression impossible to read. *What is happening right now? Is he changing his mind? Am I? Are we still together?*

Copeland picks up me with his hands under my ass, the same way he just did in the bathroom, picking up right where we left off. But this time, instead of my back hitting the wall, I feel myself press against Michael's hard, warm body. He's so strong, so immovable, he may as well be a fucking wall.

Cope's warm wet hands slide along my thighs, gripping me under the knees, while Michael takes hold of my hips. I wrap my arms around the drummer's neck and lean into Beauty in Lies' lead guitarist, his warm lips on my neck, kissing and sucking at my wet skin, drawing gasps from my throat.

Pressed between the two men, I can feel two distinct heartbeats, one against my chest and one against my back. Cope's is frantic, like the flurried beating of his kit, and Michael's is low, strong, steady.

With one hand, Copeland reaches between us and guides his shaft to my opening, penetrating the slick, swollen heat of my sex. I'm so ready for him that he slides right in, no resistance, filling me up and capturing my lips at the same moment.

I'm too busy kissing him, tasting him, praying that what he was saying to me means he's changed his mind, that he really will give this a try, to notice Michael grabbing some lube from the bathroom cabinet—these boys have it stashed *everywhere*—and slicking up his shaft. He finds my ass as easily as Cope found the liquid heat of my cunt, pushing in slowly, carefully. I'm so warmed up from my make out session in the bathroom that all I feel is pleasure, this tight heavy fullness, like my body's stretched to its limit and enjoying every second of it.

My fingers dig into Cope's wet auburn hair, fisting tight, pulling his face to mine as I rock my hips, pleasuring the three of us with the rhythm of my body. I feel like one of the guys when they're onstage, confident, sure of myself. Michael and Copeland are *mine* to play, the notes escaping their throats a song of my own design.

I've never been confident when it comes to sex before. No, when Cope first asked me that awful question—*is there something in particular that you like?*—I had no idea how to answer him. Kevin didn't ask me questions like that. Hell, he didn't care enough about me to even *think* about questions like that. Sex with him was rough, clumsy, oftentimes boring.

A week with these guys though … it's been the perfect environment to explore my sexuality.

"Lilith," Copeland whispers against my mouth, his eyes opening halfway, the lids heavy and drooping with desire. I feel weightless suspended between these two men, their strong arms sharing the weight of my burden like it's nothing at all. Together, they've got no problem keeping me afloat.

But I do like the strain of their arm muscles, feeling my

way up Cope's wet biceps, to the definition in his deltoids, all those perfectly masculine muscles shaped from making *art,* and not from working out. It's unbelievably attractive to me, knowing that there are two talented artists inside of me.

"Is this good for you, Lil?" Michael asks, his lips against my ear, the sound of his voice so foreign and strange, so new. It's exciting, hearing him speak to me like that, talk to me while he's buried so intimately inside my body. I want him to keep talking to me, keep fucking me, until his voice and his body are as familiar to me as my own.

"This is wonderful," I whisper, my gaze focused on Copeland as Michael's hands tighten on my hips and he pushes us all back into the wall. Cope leans into the grey painted surface as Michael's hips surge like pistons, taking over the song like he does during a guitar solo. Lead guitarist, huh. Used to being in charge.

My attention stays with Copeland, my pelvis pushing against his, grinding my clit to Michael's new rhythm. The lace of my pink bra scrapes against Cope's chest as my breathing picks up speed, the kisses on the back of my neck helping to send me over the edge and into a violent orgasm. I arch my neck back and gather Cope's head against me, my hair sliding against Michael's face as he groans into my ear, the sounds almost as wild and ragged now as they were yesterday, when he broke his yearlong celibacy against the kitchen counter.

The boys take a little longer to find their own conclusions to our shared pleasure, but the slip and slide of their bodies doesn't stop feeling good when the shock of my orgasm passes. No, it just keeps getting more intense, the slickness of my sex tender and aching, the two cocks working in unison to massage that fine veil of tissue between them.

There are so many nerve endings there that my brain feels scrambled from the rush of sensations—Michael's hard hot body behind me, Cope's wet warm muscles in front of me, the bestial churn of their cocks moving in and out of me.

I swear, when I close my eyes, I see rainbows of vibrant color.

That's what an orgasm looks like to me: a fucking *rainbow* over grey clouds, wild and rebellious against a stormy sky.

Michael's the next person to find his archway of color, pressing harder against me and Cope, grinding us into the wall as he gasps sharply, biting down on my earlobe and making me whimper.

"Shit," he murmurs, still holding me up but sliding out of me, giving my body over to Cope.

His mouth presses against my ear as I wedge the soles of my Docs up against the wall, using the immovable strength of Michael behind me as leverage as I curl my fingers around Cope's shoulders and start to ride him.

Those turquoise eyes watch me with a little shock, a little wonder, as I grind my pelvis against his, his muscular body trapped between my thighs, my ass held up by Michael's hands. He takes the majority of my weight as I fuck Copeland into the wall and make him come with a hard, violent shudder. It takes over his entire body, drops those heavy lids over his Caribbean blue eyes, and spills his seed inside of me.

I'm still panting, my legs shaky and weak as the boys set me down between them, my boots loud against the wood floors beneath my feet.

"The meet and greet," Michael says and then lets out a string of almost unintelligible curse words as he sweeps some red hair over my shoulder, and I glance back, finally able to look at him, at dilated pupils over purple irises, parted lips, and a sweat streaked face. If he goes back to the VIP get-together looking like that, there won't be a person there who questions what he was up to back at the bus.

"You two should go," I say, bending down to gather my wet dress up off the floor.

I look right at Cope as I rise to my feet, clutching the fabric against my chest.

I have no idea where we're at with this conversation, but … it can wait an hour or two.

"Lilith," he says, but then he just stops and takes a deep breath, playing with the single ring in the center of his full bottom lip with his tongue. "You're right—we should go. Did you want to come with us?"

"I think I'm going to grab a cold shower," I say with a crooked half-smile, the warm trickle of semen between my thighs making me bite my lip. "I'll see you when you get back."

I push past him and into the bathroom, shutting the door and locking it behind me.

"So what are you planning on doing?" Michael asks, his hands in the pockets of his dark blue jeans as we move across the parking lot and toward the back door of the venue. My hair's still wet, but the warm hands of the breeze tease it as we walk, drying it into what I hope is a tousled rockstar sort of a look. I guess freshly fucked is a good style to wear?

But shit.

I am such a goddamn idiot.

"I don't know," I say as I run my hand over my face and feel just god-awful sick inside. My whole life, I've taken care of women, not pulled them into hot steamy bathrooms and tried to fuck them after I just told them there was no future with me. Maybe my mom and grandma's shitty genes are finally driving me crazy? Or maybe it's those asshole genes I inherited from my grandpa and my dad?

"Jesus," Michael curses, giving me a long, angry once-over. He takes in the new outfit I slipped on—my other was trapped in the locked bathroom with Lilith—and scowls at the dark bootcut jeans and flip-flops. "I mean, come on, Cope. You're better than this."

"Am I?" I ask as we pause outside the door, roadies coming and going, moving around us like we're rocks in the middle of a raging river. Groups split around us carrying equipment, disappearing into the night with the scent of pot and beer clinging to their clothes. "Michael, for nine years —check it, *nine* years—I've avoided any real relationships."

"Exactly my point," he says, violet eyes accusatory as he pulls out a cigarette and lights up, his leather jacket slung over his shoulders, looking the part of the classic bad boy with his tattoos, long razored hair, and eyeliner. I know who I'm supposed to be—the nice one, the boy next door, the good guy—but all I feel like right now is the dick. "Nine years. That's a long time to punish yourself, Park."

I breathe out, long and low, and run my fingers through my hair.

Man, I'm almost thirty years old. Thirty. I feel a million years older than any of the other guys, than Lilith. She's eight years younger than me. God, that's a lot, isn't it? Especially at this age.

"She doesn't need my baggage," I say and Michael just throws his hands up like I'm crazy.

"Jesus, I can't believe I just fucked you," he says, and then he's yanking the door to the venue open and heading inside, leaving me standing in the warm evening air by myself. Well, really, there's a whole crowd around me—our staff, venue staff, a few members of the other bands—but I feel completely alone.

The thing is, I don't have to be, do I?

I follow Michael inside, through the backstage area and over to a long hallway that leads to a small sit-down restaurant. It's been emptied for the event tonight, just the guys and a handful of VIP badge holders sitting around a table with Octavia hovering off to the side.

She doesn't even look at me when I walk in, even though

in the past she would've ripped me a new one for being so late.

"Well, well, well," Pax drawls, his hand curled over the top of a glass tumbler, swirling the amber liquid around inside it, "look who the cat dragged in. Where the fuck have you two been?"

Michael's just pulling out a chair, shrugging out of his leather jacket, as I take the spot next to him. He doesn't look at me, but Ran does, raising a dark eyebrow inside the shadow of his hoodie.

"Oh, Copeland," a woman with strawberry blonde hair says, smiling at me from across the table. "I've been waiting to meet you. I have so many questions."

I smile back at her, but that's just about all I've got at the moment. My mind is too preoccupied with Lilith to think about anything else, much less care what a reporter wants.

I wait for either Pax to fill in the silence (he usually does) or for the woman to introduce herself, too far away to reach out and shake her hand properly. I focus instead on some t-shirts and records that make their way over to me along with a silver and a black Sharpie. My hands are shaking slightly as I take hold of the pens and attempt to add my messy signature to my bandmates' swirls.

He knew she was the right girl for him. Knew it in his head, his gut, his soul. Knew it in the blood that his heart pumped, in the veins and arteries that decorated his wrists and his cock, in his pulse that thundered when he saw her, in his eyes that fell lidded and heavy at the sight of her naked body in his bed. He knew all of those things and yet ... for whatever reason, he wouldn't let himself go to her.

I scrawl *Copeland Park* on the front of a pink, white, and black record with our newest album art on it. It's in the same style as the animated video that plays before our sets, with the convertible and the stick figures and the bloody knives raining from the sky.

You're thinking in book lingo again, I tell myself. But that's only because books speak the truth our mouths are too afraid to voice, our minds too cluttered to parse out.

"Can you make that one out to Gillie?" a girl two seats over says excitedly, her voice quivering with joy at just being in the same room as us. I wonder if she'd still feel that way if she knew how messed up we all are inside? Really, Lilith is the perfect girlfriend for each one of us. Hurting, but still holding onto that burning desire to *live,* to fight through, to grieve properly but move on. Why can't I take my goddamn cues from her and let nine years of pain just *go?* I've had more than enough chances to grieve Cara. I don't have to stop missing her, but why am I letting her loss mess up the first really good thing to happen to me since then? "G-I-L-L-I-E."

"And you can make mine out to Bridget," the blonde adds as I pass over the first record to Michael and glance up, meeting the penetrating intensity of his gaze. Fuck. That man knows how to throw a look that cuts deep. I sign the next record, pass it on, and turn my attention to an oversized white t-shirt with a yellow sticky note that says *Gillie* on it.

Duly noted.

"Bridget's a reporter from the *Florida Times-Union*," Muse says from my right, sandwiched between me and the hyper-excited girl with pink glasses and a retainer. Her smile, when I glance in her direction, is … profuse. I make myself smile back and then look over at the blonde again.

"The *Florida Times-Union,* huh?" I ask as I write out the young girl's name and then pause, realizing I've actually just written *Lilith* instead.

Fuck.

"You know what?" Muse says, reaching over to grab the t-shirt and tugging it from my fingers. "This is one of our old designs. You want a few new shirts and a hoodie—my treat, of course."

"Could I?" the girl asks, eyes glittering as she rises to her feet.

"Sure thing," he says, giving my shoulder a squeeze as he turns away and gestures for her to come with him. He drapes the ruined tee over the back of my chair as he goes. "Follow me and you can pick out whatever swag you want."

He guides her away, down the hall, as I move onto the other items in my stack.

"I was hoping I might be able to do a brief interview with you? I've already cleared it with my fellow VIP guests and your manager, so—"

"Oh, but she won't be our manager for long, will you, Octavia?" Pax smiles cruelly in Octavia's direction. Her face tightens, but she doesn't look directly at him. I want to feel sorry for her, but I just … don't. Not after what she did to Lilith.

Lilith.

What about what *I* just tried to do to Lilith?

"Interesting," Bridget says, placing her smartphone down on the table, screen up, and looking around at us as she pushes a button. "By the way, is it okay if I record our conversation for the article?"

We all mumble some form of consent as the woman smiles with shiny nude painted lips.

"Okay, so the world is just dying to know about your romantic lives. You're all so close-lipped in your other interviews? Is there a reason for that?"

Pax smirks and downs the rest of his bourbon, but he doesn't respond. Usually, he's the one that talks us through these things. Ransom glances away and smokes his cigarette, his hand disappearing inside the shadows of his hood as he puts the cigarette to his lips. Michael yanks the last t-shirt from my hand, leaving a long black line trailing from the tip of my pen.

"Mr. Park?" Bridget asks, focusing her attention on me, smiling from ear to ear. Normally, I don't like reporters. For whatever reason, I like this one. She reminds me of my mom—when she's on one of her good days, obviously. On her bad days … there's nobody more cruel, more angry, more righteously pissed off at the world. She throws things at me, screams at me, threatens suicide. "Recently, a photo was published online of you in a bookstore with a redheaded young woman. May I ask if she's someone special to you?"

"You're asking if I have a girlfriend?" I say as I cap the pen in my hand and lean back, knocking the messed up t-shirt to the floor. I lean down to pick it up, dragging it into my lap and rubbing my thumb over the name in black ink. My body's still wired up and hot from our threesome in the hallway, my cock half-hard again, my nipples pebbled beneath the pale pink t-shirt I've got on.

"We're all dying to know," Bridget says, grinning excitedly when Michael finishes with her shirt and record, passing them to Pax to hand over to her. Three other girls sit next to the blonde reporter, but none of them speak. They're all young, pretty, probably looking to be groupies. I recognize the licking of lips, the tucking of shiny hair behind ears, the coquettish smiles.

But we already have a groupie.

A girlfriend.

"The woman asked you a fucking question," Michael says, drawing both Ran's and Pax's gazes over to me. "Answer her for Christ's sake."

He'd made so many mistakes in his past, mistakes that haunted him to this day. Why should he chance making her another one when walking away would solve the problem of having him in her life? But damn it, he didn't want to. With every part of himself he wanted to stay.

"I have a girlfriend," I say, heart thundering as I stare at the t-shirt in my hand, my throat closing up, sweat slipping down my spine.

Fuck.

I look up at the reporter and see the surprise written all over her face. If she's such a big fan of the band, she must know all the trouble we've had with girlfriends in the past. The shit with Chloe, Kortney; she'll probably even know about Cara. Vanessa. I think the only person in the group who *hasn't* had a fucked-up relationship is Derek.

"You do?" she asks with another smile. "Can you tell me her name?"

"No," I say, looking back at the six letters on the white fabric. "I won't tell you her name."

"Won't? Interesting choice of words. Is there anything you will share about her?"

I look back at Michael, but his face is closed off and he still looks pissed.

"Would you like to take some pictures with us?" I ask instead, suddenly desperate to get back to Lilith. I can't leave this shit hanging, not even for a second. I'm supposed to take *care* of girls, not treat them like shit. It goes against everything that I am. And this girl, this time, she needs me for more than a single night. Even if it scares the crap out of me, I have to step up.

And Muse is right—I don't have to do it alone this time.

"Because I really need to go. Whatever other questions you have, the guys can answer."

I rise to my feet and so does the reporter.

Luckily, Muse comes back with the glasses girl, Gillie, and finds me standing there with a wild thundering heart and a pulse that sounds like one of Ran's bass lines running through my head.

"Pictures," I tell him and he nods. Octavia steps back in for a second, acting like the manager she was before last night, but Paxton doesn't let her forget for even an instant that she's done something wrong. The way he's treating her, it's not entirely unwarranted, but it does make me think of the way he treats Ransom.

That … there's nothing warranted about that.

We take a few group shots, a few with my arm slung around the reporter, the girl with the retainer. And then I take off, leaving the others to drink and chat with the badge holders, give them their money's worth.

"Lilith?" I call out when I get back on the bus.

The living room is empty, the bathroom door open and empty.

I find her sitting on the bed in the Bat Cave, the curtains and windows open, letting the warm Florida breeze sweep around the room. She's sitting cross-legged in a black tank and tiny pink shorts, her phone in her hand. There's the slightest kiss of tears on her cheeks and I wonder immediately if any of those salty drops have something to do with me.

She looks up at me with big green eyes and then tries to

breathe past the crying, smiling at me.

"Hey Cope."

"You don't have to pretend for me," I tell her as I feel my heart lift into my throat, trying to choke me with emotion. "Do you want another hug?"

"I don't need you to take care of me," she says firmly, leaning back on the bed and looking up at me. "So if that's the real reason you don't think this can work, scrap it. You'll have to come up with something else."

"I do need to take care of you," I say and her mouth flattens into a line as I crawl onto the bed next to her, sitting on my knees. I take the big white t-shirt in my hand and slip it over her head. Lilith pulls it the rest of the way down, putting her arms through the sleeves and then glancing down at our signatures. As soon as she sees the word *Lilith,* she reaches up to touch it. "We should all take care of each other, I think. It's something we should've been doing all along. But … it got messed up somewhere along the way. Ran and Pax are a mess; Michael's withdrawn. Muse has always been a little distant."

"And you?" she asks me, holding her phone in her lap, balancing it in the hammock the giant shirt makes when she pulls it over her knees.

"I've …" I start and then notice several incoming texts hit her phone. "Can I ask who that is?"

"You mean *what* this is," she says with a long sigh. "This is the shit hitting the fan."

Lilith pushes the home button on her phone and shuts the screen off, looking up at me.

"But I want to hear what you have to say first. Ran is hurting; Pax is mean; Michael is self-absorbed; Muse is closed-off. What's your sin, Copeland?"

"Fear," I say, my breathing still coming in rapid-fire bursts as I look at this redheaded girl with all the right curves and the biggest green eyes I've ever seen in my life. "I've been living in fear. I've been living only in *books*. Which is fine, but … I don't want to *just* read about romance anymore, Lilith. I want to try living it."

She smiles at me, but it's only a half-smile.

"What does that mean exactly? You've changed your mind?"

"I could understand if you didn't think I had that right," I whisper, the crashing of the ocean waves like a lullaby the earth sings to the sky. It's beautiful. I lean back on the bed and put my arms behind my head. It's dark in here now. The only light was the light from Lilith's phone, but now that it's off, everything is black. "Considering I tried to break up with you, fucked you, and then tried to get back together with you in the span of a heartbeat."

Lilith lays back, too, her body lined up next to mine. She bends a knee and then puts one foot between my thighs, so that her leg's draped over my own.

"Do you miss Cara?" she asks, surprising me.

I close my eyes for a moment, enjoying the warmth of her body next to mine.

"Yes and no. I miss the good parts of her, like the way she always laughed at her own jokes or how she used to write me notes on the toilet paper."

Lilith chuckles, and I find myself smiling slightly.

"But she was … she was really sick, sicker than my mom. I think that's why I was drawn to her, as fucked as that sounds. I felt like I had to be the one to save her. I don't miss all of that worry and that fear, all the nights I waited up for her when she didn't come home. She cheated on me a lot."

"I'm sorry, Cope," Lilith says, but I just reach down and grab her hand. That's not her sin to apologize for, and I've long since forgiven Cara for the things she did.

I sigh, perfuming the darkness with the sound of my past.

"She didn't … really know what she was doing," I say on the end of another long sigh.

"At least you know the other four guys I'm sleeping with, right?" Lilith asks, trying to lighten the mood. I let myself smile again and turn toward her. I can barely see her profile in the darkness, but her skin is so pale that it practically glows.

"At least there's that," I say, lifting our entwined fingers. "I'm sorry. I've been moping all fucking day instead of just talking to you about it. I should've discussed it before I said all of that shit."

"No, I get it. Trust me, the last thing I thought I needed after breaking up with Kevin was another boyfriend … was *five* new boyfriends." Lilith laughs softly as I press her knuckles to my lips and close my eyes, imagining her trying to dance the Charleston and totally screwing it up. My smile gets a little more real. I wish it wasn't so dark so she could see it. "But here you guys are …"

"Here we are," I say, wondering if it was fate that put us together at that gas station in Arizona. I usually go on a run when we get to a new city, but we'd had bus trouble and showed up so late that I had one of the roadies drive me to a gas station so I could grab some snacks instead. He parked down the road a ways to smoke pot. I didn't give a shit since it gave me a second to myself as I walked up to the convenience store.

I never expected to meet a girl there.

"I panicked last night … this morning. But if you give me a chance, I'll do what I can to make it up to you. I want to see what it feels like to really belong to someone. Not just for sex, not just for a night, but … indefinitely." I pause and listen to the sound of Lil's breathing. I'm not sure if it's intentional or not, but it seems to mimic the heartbeat of the ocean. "What do you think? Can I have another chance?"

"I wasn't going to let you run away," she says, finally turning her head to look at me. I might not be able to see her eyes in the shadows of the Bat Cave, but at least I can feel her breath on my mouth. "I don't think Michael was either. Did you see how pissed he was?"

"Michael's always pissed," I say, but then I lean forward and close that small distance between our mouths, cupping the side of her face, letting myself kiss my *girlfriend.*

We belonged to each other. It was inextricable, our love. Undeniable. Inevitable.

More book lingo. I can't help it. My reading permeates my thoughts.

Our tongues dance together as the clouds shift and moonlight spills in the window, highlighting the signatures on the stolen white band tee, shifting over Lilith's face. I close my eyes and kiss her deeper, try to let myself go for a second, drop the act for once and see what happens when I'm not trying so hard. When I'm just being me.

Lilith's phone beeps again, breaking up the gentle quiet and the easy blackness of night.

"Shit," she says as she grabs it and sits up. I follow after her and wait as she glances at the screen. "Right after you left, I started getting messages from both my stepmom *and* Kevin."

"What the hell does he want?" I ask, feeling strangely

possessive. Or maybe it's not strange at all. Last night, when I heard what he'd done … I wanted to fucking kill the guy. What kind of loser treats a woman he used to be in love with like that?

"Look," she says, passing me the phone. I take it and scan through Kevin's barrage of hatred. Lilith hasn't responded to him, but that hasn't kept him from texting her almost nonstop for the last hour or so. I see all the typical insults: whore, bitch, cunt … *groupie.* But he can't have that last one. We're keeping that for ourselves. "I got upset with him when he started saying I must be fucking all the roadies. I told him I was sleeping with the band. And then *he* called my stepmom."

I see Lilith's mouth tighten up in a frown, highlighted by the glow of her phone.

"And now she's calling and texting me. Now. After I begged her for help and she turned me down, abandoned me when I needed her most."

She takes the phone from me and switches over to a text conversation from *Susan Goode.*

Lilith, Kevin is worried about you.

He says you're selling your body to a rock band.

I frown, too, and keep scrolling, watching as her stepmother gets angrier and angrier, even though Lilith doesn't respond. Or maybe *because* she doesn't.

I can't support this kind of disgusting behavior from you.

Call me now, Lilith, or I'll have to assume it's all true.

Fine then. Just remember your father is looking down on you from heaven. Is this the kind of thing you want him to see you doing?

And then lastly, *I'll leave your share of the ashes in the living room with your things. Hopefully you get the chance to get them before the first showing with the realtor.*

“Jesus Christ,” I say as Lilith sighs and leans forward to put her head on her knees. “Are you okay? And it's alright if you're not,” I add, trying to smile as I lift up a hand and rub her back in small circles. “Don't edit yourself just because I was a dick earlier. It's not you that I'm afraid of. It's me.”

She lifts her head up and glances over at me with another half-smile.

“I just think it's ironic that when I was at my lowest, the two of them didn't give a shit about me. Now that I'm …” She stops to smile a little wider. “Starting to feel like I might just be able to survive without my dad, they want to crush me into the dirt. It's pathetic is what it is. How can she even *think* of using my father's ashes against me like that, like a threat? He's only been dead for ten days. Ten.”

I scoot closer and wrap my arms around Lilith, pulling her tight against me.

She settles in, snuggling up to me and making my half-hard cock rock solid, speeding my heartbeat up again. I don't mean for the former part of that reaction to set in; it just happens. I'm really fucking attracted to this girl.

“What the *fuck* is this about you two breaking up?” Pax snarls, shoving the door to the Bat Cave open and startling us both. He points a sharp finger at me. “You better be taking the bloody piss, mate.”

“Relax,” I say, trying not to smile. “I didn't know you cared so damn much.”

“Yeah, well,” he says, looking slightly chagrined at the sight of us sitting cuddled on the bed together. “I didn't agree to this shite only to have it fucked-up in less than twenty-four hours.”

“It's not fucked-up,” Lilith promises, glancing back at

me, and then turning to Paxton again. "Cope and I worked it out."

Pax leans his back against one side of the doorframe and digs out a cigarette, lighting it up as he watches us for a long moment and then nods briskly.

"Good. Because I was about to kick your skinny arse halfway back to Seattle. Get up then and let's hit that bar on the beach, the one we had drinks at this afternoon. Maybe if you're not moping around this time, you'll actually enjoy yourself."

He stands up and moves back down the hall as Lilith and I look at each other.

"Are you still up to go out?" I ask as she takes a deep breath. "Because we can stay here if you want."

Lilith shakes her head at me, dark red hair falling over her shoulders with the motion.

"Nope. You promised me that we'd spend the rest of this tour exploring each city. I intend to hold you to that."

She stands up, slides to the floor, and then turns to offer me her hand.

I don't hesitate, just reach up … and take it.

For the second night in a row, all six of us sleep in the Bat Cave together.

I can't explain how good that feels, our little group curled up in black silk and satin, the duvet twisted around heavily sedated bodies, bodies that were too drunk last night to do much but sleep when they stumbled back to the bus.

Stretching my arms above my head, I yawn and try to resist going for my phone first thing. Looking at hateful texts from Kevin or Susan won't do me any good. In fact, I should probably block one or both of them.

I sit up and look down at Ransom, brushing some chocolate dark hair from his sweaty forehead before I stand up and scoot off the end of the bed, leaving four of the boys behind me and finding Michael in the living room by himself.

He's shirtless and fucking gorgeous, as usual, wearing jeans and nothing else. One of his legs is tucked up on the couch, an elbow resting on his denim cloaked knee, a glass of orange juice in one hand, his phone in the other.

"OJ? Does it help with the hangover?" I ask, drawing his violet eyes up to mine.

"This?" he asks, swirling the liquid around for a moment.

"This isn't just orange juice. This is the hair of the dog that bit you." He smiles with that ridiculously beautiful mouth of his. Looking at him now, it's easy to see that he was a heartbreaker. Everything about him says *warning: bad boy in residence.* And it's not just the tattoos or the leather jacket he always wears. No, it's in the way he holds himself, the shape of his mouth, the puncturing gaze that stabs right through me. "Vodka and orange juice."

"A screwdriver," I say as I pad across the heated hardwood floors and sit down next to him. I take the drink when he hands it to me and sip it slowly. It's fucking *strong.*

"I needed it to deal with this fallout shit."

"Fallout?" I ask as he drops his knee and squeezes his hand around his phone. It's got a padded black case with a skull on the back of it. It almost looks like he might crack it he's gripping it so hard. "From … Vanessa and Tim?"

"I walked in on them, her gold bikini pushed aside, his ass in the air …" Michael grits his teeth and glances away from me, toward the door of the bus. We're not moving anymore, so I figure we must already be in Charlotte. It's barely a six hour drive from Jacksonville, so we didn't leave until early this morning. According to the clock on the wall, it's just past noon. "Anyway, I finally blocked her number. We have nothing to say to each other. The texts and voicemails she's leaving me are all bullshit, just her flinging insults my way."

"Kevin started doing the same to me last night," I tell him, drawing his attention back to me. He's kind of scary when he's pissed like that, Michael is.

"Are you fucking serious?" he asks, looking shocked and incensed on my behalf. "Why?"

"He called my stepmom and told her I was whoring

myself out to Beauty in Lies."

There's a long pause and then, "give me the phone."

I blink up at him, at those long lashes over eyes the color of aubergine.

"Why?"

Michael holds out a hand covered in tattoos and gestures at me, the phoenix on his chest brilliant in the early afternoon light leaking through the curtains.

"Because I'll verbally fuck him up, that's why."

I smile and turn to face him, dressed in that baggy shirt Copeland gave me last night. Michael looks at me and then down at it.

"You're missing my signature," he says, reaching out and running a finger over Cope's handwriting. I still don't know why he wrote my name on it; I didn't think to ask.

"It's not missing," I tell him as I stand up and grab my purse, digging a pink Sharpie out of an inner pocket. I grab my phone, too. "It's the last one to be added, a little behind the curve."

He smiles at me, this razor-sharp version of the expression that leaves my heart in my throat and my body in a state of heated bliss, remembering the thickness of his cock inside of me last night, the strength of his arms as he held me up.

"But I wouldn't have wanted you if you'd cheated on Vanessa, so …"

"So give me the damn pen," he says, and I reach out and drop it into his palm. Michael grabs a handful of my t-shirt and tugs me toward him, pulling me into his lap. He pulls the cap off the pen with his teeth and yanks the fabric taut, scrawling his name in swirling pink letters diagonally across my belly. "You still smell like my fucking shampoo," he whispers, his voice a little ragged, a little hoarse. "Goddamn it."

Michael tosses the pen aside and pushes me back into the couch, covering my body with his. I swear, my legs spread of their own accord, welcoming him in as he presses the hardness of his crotch to my own.

"It's been so long, I might be a little crazy for a few days …" he explains, like he's trying to apologize for his own libido. But I guess he just hasn't realized that I've got one to match. His eyes are so goddamn intense when he stares down at me that I find myself struggling to catch a breath, getting caught up in them, in all the wild anger buried down there. I want to see him unpack it all, feel myself standing in the middle of the storm when it happens.

I must be crazy.

Michael slants his mouth over mine, curling his fingers around the side of my throat. The kiss is as possessive as it is arousing. He claims me with that kiss, puts a possessive stamp right over my mouth that tangles me up in him completely. Fuck, he practically *demands* that I surrender to this intensity of his. It's so much, almost too much, but I'm slick and hot and aroused when he shoves my shorts to the side and unbuttons his jeans.

With a quick thrust, Michael's inside of me, grinding his pelvis to mine, taking me so hard and fast that I barely have a moment to catch my own breath. He fucks with these deep, long movements, searching me out, seeking me in a way I've never felt another man do.

I don't know how Vanessa ever hid anything from Michael when she was sleeping with him; it feels impossible to keep secrets, like he's deeper inside of me than just the place where his cock is moving. But then, maybe he didn't fuck her like this? Maybe this is just for me?

I pretend that's the truth because it feels good, so damn good.

He never stops kissing me, not even for a second.

I don't expect to come, not with this quick, wild rutting, but I do. I lock my legs around him and arch my back, digging my nails into his strong shoulders. I gasp against the onslaught of his tongue, the relentless motion of his hips. They're merciless, driving right through my orgasm, into the hypersensitivity on the other side. I have to squeeze Michael tight, grip him hard, just to be able to *breathe* through the pleasure.

His orgasm hits him like a baseball bat, tightening up every muscle in his body, drawing this awful pained sound from his throat. I feel like I'm soothing a wild animal for a second there, taming it with my silken heat.

It's the wildcat metaphor again, I guess.

"Holy shit," he whispers, sitting up, looking down at me like he's never seen me before. "Who the hell are you that you can fuck like that?"

"Me?" I ask as he sits back and fixes his jeans in place. "I don't think I was the one doing the fucking."

I adjust my shorts and sit up, too, my legs lying across his lap.

"Guess not," Michael says, grinning at me as he leans over and slides a pack of cigarettes across the table, pulling one out and putting it between his lips. He settles into the cushions and looks over at me with this look of pure male satisfaction on his face.

It gives me the chills—in a good way.

"Want one?" he asks, offering me a cigarette.

"No thank you," I say as he swings the lid closed and

tosses the pack back on the table, lighting up with a silver lighter from his pocket. Michael looks me over carefully as he smokes, a white cloud drifting up toward the open window behind the couch. I can tell it's open because a slight breeze ruffles the curtain, dripping molten orange sunlight into the room. "My dad …" Fuck. This shouldn't be so hard to say, but it is. I can barely squeeze the words out. "And my mom," I add, taking a few shallow breaths to get my grief under control, "they both died from cancer, so I try to stay away from cigarettes."

Michael cringes slightly and then looks at the cigarette in his hand with a chagrined sort of expression.

"Well, shit," he says, putting it out in a glass ashtray that's sitting next to his bare foot on the black lacquer surface of the coffee table.

"You don't have to put it out on my account," I say, but he shakes his head, dark razored hair falling around his face as he leans forward and trades out his smoke for the discarded screwdriver. "I don't mind if you smoke; I just choose not to."

"Maybe later," he says, noticing my phone sitting on the edge of the couch cushion near his leg. I think I dropped it there when he grabbed me. I was so caught up in lust that I don't quite remember. "Can I make that call to Kevin now?"

I smile as he grabs one of my feet with his free hand and examines the painted surfaces of my toenails, covered in hot pink gloss.

"He's a fucking douche; you won't get anything productive done with that call."

"It'll make my morning," he tells me as I cross my arms over my chest and watch him watching me. His gaze is predatory, but protective, too. An interesting mix.

"Do I get to call Vanessa after?"

He shrugs loosely, offering the drink up to me. When I shake my head, he downs it and sets the glass on the table.

"If you want to. She's a crazy bitch though. I wouldn't if I were you."

"Okay then," I say, throwing up my hands in surrender. How can I say no when my lips are swollen and tender from his kisses, when my body feels languid and warm and satisfied? "Call Kevin Peregrine and ask him why he burned all my paintings, stole my laptop, and changed my cloud drive password."

"Alright, now you're fucking with me," Michael says, turning to face me with my phone in his tattooed hands. "He burned your art?"

"In retaliation when I called him out on his cheating, on the …" I can't even say the word *syphilis.* That word is just loaded with negativity, with betrayal, fear, disgust. "On the disease he gave me," I whisper and Michael's lips purse.

He looks away for a moment, and I wonder if he's thinking about the mistakes that he made with Vanessa. The fact that she was cheating on him doesn't wipe the record clean of his crimes. But then, I got to see firsthand how intensely he was committed to keeping his promise of changing his ways. Our attraction was fierce, heady, but he didn't give in. He held on tight all the way through to the end.

"Here. Unblock his number and I'll call."

I take the phone, my fingers brushing against Michael's. Despite the fact that he's still touching my foot, that we just had sex, I get a thrill up my arm that travels straight to my heart, making it beat fiercely and wildly with want.

"There." I unblock the number and hand my cell back to

Michael, waiting with nervous butterflies in my stomach as he hits the screen with his thumb and makes the call.

"No," is how he answers the phone, his voice this low, dangerous razor of sound, "this isn't the quote *crazy bitch* on the phone, it's her fucking man."

Her man.

I have to smile at that.

"Yeah, motherfucker, you heard me. It's Michael Luxe." *Michael Luxe.* I love his name, the way it rolls off my tongue. His first name's so ordinary, so plain, but paired with the unusual last name, it sounds … well, kind of like a rockstar's name. "I'll bet you do, you son of a bitch."

I glance back as Paxton steps out of the hallway in black sweats and nothing else, looking stupidly sexy with his hair tangled and wild on top of his head.

"Who the fuck is he talking to?" he asks on the edge of a yawn. "And where the hell's my coffee? That little bastard over there knows to make me a pot if he gets up first."

"Listen to me: you give me that goddamn password to Lilith's cloud drive and I won't get on the next plane out of here to come and kick your sorry ass to next Sunday."

Pax's brows go up and he walks over, staring at his friend with a vaguely amused expression on that devilishly handsome face of his.

Michael sits up, his jaw tightening, his purple eyes darkening with anger.

"You think I give a shit about lawyers? Will a restraining order keep my foot out of your ass? Give me the password or I'll make good on my threats. I can have people at your place within *minutes* with a single Facebook post. Or would you rather pictures of that tiny dick of yours made their way around social media?"

There's a pause as Michael bends down and grabs the pink Sharpie from the floor. He places the tip of it against his own bare midsection and writes the word *carrie89124* across his washboard abs.

"What about the laptop, you limp dick?" he asks as my own eyebrows go up. "Then you'd better *un*delete that shit and email it to Lilith. She has so much crap on you, man. I've seen the pictures on her phone. If I were you, I'd seriously consider fucking off."

Michael hangs up the phone and tosses it onto the coffee table.

"Bloody hell, Mikey, what the fuck are you doing?" Pax asks.

"Don't call me Mikey," he says, slipping out from under my legs with a slight smile. "I was just having a conversation with Lilith's ex."

"One day in and you're already calling to intimidate past boyfriends. I warned you it'd get heavy with this man around," Pax says, watching his friend disappear down the hallway and then reappear with a computer in his hand. He passes it over to me.

"Log onto your cloud drive with this," he says, ignoring Paxton and pointing at the password on his abs. I flip the lid and try it, not really expecting much—or anything at all—from Kevin. But when I click through and find myself face to face with pages and pages of digital art that I never thought I'd see again … I lose my breath completely.

"Fuck," I whisper as I quickly change the password to something Kevin will *never* guess.

"Is Carrie the name of one of the girls he cheated with?" Michael asks, sitting back down next to me, studying the expression on my face as I click through the colorful images and feel my heart racing wildly. There are even photos of the physical paintings that Kevin burned. It's all here, all of it.

"No … it's … *Carrie*'s his favorite movie," I whisper as I try not to cry again. I've been crying all week at sad, horrible things; the last thing I want to do is cry at the happy ones, too. "But not because he actually likes the film, just because he thinks young Sissy Spacek is hot."

"So did it work?" Michael asks, lounging on the couch with that bad boy swagger of his. It's different than Pax's, rougher, wilder, more … animal. If I had to compare them to supernatural creatures, I'd say that Paxton was the vampire … and Michael was the werewolf. Equally hot, just different.

"It worked," I say, tugging down the lid of the computer so I can look at Michael's face. "All my art is here."

"Do you actually have any pictures of your ex's cock?" Paxton asks, the song lyrics on his chest catching my attention for a moment before I slide my eyes back up to his face, that cold cruel perfect face of his. But God, it's hiding so much hurt. So, so much. Now that I'm here to stay, I'm going to try to pick him apart, I know I am. I can't help it.

"None," I admit with a sad smile, closing the computer completely. "I told you that I was repressed sexually. I didn't think to take any, not for my own purposes or for any future thoughts of revenge. I thought Kevin and I would be together forever."

"That's what I thought about Chloe," Pax says, but he doesn't elaborate, just heads over to the counter and starts making coffee. Michael watches him for a moment and then turns back to me, taking my phone and unbuttoning his jeans again.

"What are you doing?" I ask, a slight flush coloring my cheeks.

"Giving you the upper hand," he says, snapping a picture of his junk and passing the phone back to me. He looks so fucking confident when he does it, like there's not a thing in the world that could sway him from this path. From *me.* Our third official day together and he's so goddamn intense.

I love it.

"I don't think I could use this to blackmail you the way I could've used Kevin's," I say and he laughs, the sound so different than it was a few days ago. "But thank you anyway. I'll keep it close." I lift the picture up in salute and then set the phone back on the coffee table.

Michael's eyes never leave mine, locked with my gaze, breaking through all my walls without even trying. I feel so bare and naked in front of him, it's a little disconcerting.

"Okay, guys," Muse says as he steps out of the hallway and leaves the door open. I can hear the shower running, can see Copeland moving around in the dark, digging things out from under his bunk—more books by the look of it. "I just called one of the local art museums and guess what? They rent that shit out."

"An art museum?" Pax asks, turning and leaning back against the counter, his mouth in this sideways smirk that I find intriguing. "For our little artiste over there?"

"Exactly," Muse says, an unzipped sleeveless hoodie over his bare chest and a pair of long black cargo shorts over combat boots. Unlike the other two boys in the room, I don't think he's just lounging; I think he's already dressed for the day. "What do you say, Lilith? You want to visit an art museum after hours?"

"Do I?" I ask, feeling this lightness in my chest that I

know can't last. My dad hasn't been gone long enough for the hurt to fade into a shiny pink scar. No, this wound is just scabbed and like with any injury, there's a chance it'll be ripped off, torn clean, scraped away. I could still bleed. And I know, deep down, that the end of this portion of the tour puts me back at home, face to face with my own reality. But why shouldn't I ride the highs while I can? "Are you kidding me? That would be a dream come true."

Muse grins, pushing his hood back and revealing the perfect curve of his black and silver mohawk, his hazel eyes sparkling like the wings of a dragonfly.

"That's my specialty," he says, perfecting a small bow, "making dreams come true."

"If we're going to spend all of our post-show evening in a dreary old museum, then I want fucking sushi beforehand," Pax says, pouring two cups of coffee … and bringing one over to me, complete with cream and sugar.

My cheeks flush and I almost squeal as he sits down right in my fucking lap.

"You like fish, Lilith? Because I know I do."

"You're so fucking crude," Michael says with a slight roll of his eyes, getting up to make his own coffee.

"I happen to love fish," I tell him as he rolls that tempest-tossed gaze down to my face, studying me with a practiced eye, one that I'm sure is used to picking up on the weaknesses of others. I look right back at him, let him see as deep into me as he wants. It's almost a challenge. *Here are all my faults, Pax, all my fears and worries and dreams. Wield them against me however you want.*

He breaks our gaze when Ransom slips out of the bathroom, also shirtless—wow, seriously? five shirtless guys in one room?—but with a towel slung over his head like a hood. He carries that scarred but perfect body of his into the kitchen and leans against the wall near Michael while he waits for a turn at the coffee.

I swear, as soon as he enters the room, I smell violets, even from all the way over here. The scent is intoxicating.

"I can't take all the credit for the museum thing though," Muse continues as he starts water boiling for his usual cup of tea. "Cope and I came up with it together."

I share a secret smile with Copeland as he carries his shirtless butt into the room and takes one of the chairs across from me, putting his feet up and propping his head on his hand.

"He damn well better have," Ransom whispers, "after that shit he pulled last night."

"Eh, that was nothing compared to your sins though, now was it?" Pax asks and the room goes quiet. Fuck. I thought they were starting to work through their shit? But I guess ten days is nowhere near enough to clean up four years of bullshit.

Ransom ignores his friend as Paxton adjusts our position so that he's sitting less on top of me and more next to me.

"What's this about a museum?" Ran asks instead, eyes heavy-lidded and dark as he turns back to the room with his coffee.

"Big family date at the art museum," Muse says, slipping one hand into his pocket and observing his friend carefully, studying his mood. "You want to see some, uh, *American Art created from the Colonial Era through the Second World War?*"

"I have no fucking clue what that means," Ransom says with a husky bedroom laugh, "but I'll look and pretend like I have an opinion that matters. I'm sure Pax'll be good at this, what with his expensive education and all that."

Ransom's tone is friendly, conversational, but at the casual mention of his name, Pax goes completely cold and detached, turning away and focusing on the front door with an acuteness to his gaze that scares me a little.

"Do you have an art background?" I ask and Paxton snorts.

"I have an uptight boarding school background," he says, and that's that. I can tell he's done talking about it.

"Okay," I say softly, laying my hand atop his. But I'm not done trying to pull Paxton's layers apart.

I'm just getting started.

The show in Charlotte is an early one, the doors opening up before the sun has even set.

"Love what you've done with the shirt," Cope says, examining the mutilated white tee with the boys' signatures and my own name scrawled across the front. I've shortened it to mid-thigh, cinched the waist with a few careful stitches, and cut off the sleeves. I also added a deep V-neck, slanted just right so that it doesn't cut off any of the band's signatures. Paired with black high heels and some bracelets, I feel like a rockstar's girlfriend.

Mmm.

Like the rockstars' groupie?

Either one. I've decided it doesn't really matter. Labels aren't as important to me as they used to be.

"Thank you," I say, waiting as the boys gather up together in the living room, dressed in their finest. It looks like tonight they've all pulled clothes from the trailer that one of the roadies tows with a truck. Ransom took me over there to take a look earlier. It's practically a fantasyland in there, laden with alternative clothes and shoes, like the glittering hoard inside a dragon's cave. It seemed surreal, all of that beauty in one place like that.

Anyway, the guys are all wearing things I've never seen before, each one of them hot enough to make my thighs clench, my pussy heat and swell, my tongue run across my lower lip. It's almost too much, the sensory overload. My nipples pebble beneath the white shirt-dress and I find myself touching my hand to the pounding rhythm of my heart.

"You guys look … fucking amazing," I say as Ransom slides an arm around my waist, dressed in a red mesh hoodie over a black tank with a white cross on it. I think he wears it ironically since I doubt he's in any way religious.

"It's not just us that look good tonight, sweetheart," he says softly, stirring my hair with his breath, the wicked sexy press of his lips against my forehead almost enough to drop me to my knees. "You look goddamn *edible.*"

"Do I?" I ask, trying to be coy, totally failing because when I look up into those eyes, they look as deep and dark as wet earth on a forest floor, nourishing and anchoring the trees that tower above it. There's so much in Ransom's gaze that it'd take a lifetime to discover all his little nuances. I find myself wanting to at least try.

"Scrumptious," Muse agrees, plodding down the steps in big loud silver boots and kicking the bus door open. He hops to the ground and holds out an arm to prop it open for Ran and me as we head outside and into a brief dry spell. The weather here's been a little crazy today: windy, humid, alternating rain and sun. In the distance, I can hear the faintest growl of thunder.

"So basically you all want to eat me?" I ask, unable to hold back a smile as I meet Muse's eyes, see his dark brow raise up flirtatiously. The four black piercings above it catch the light streaming from the bus' open door and make it look like they're winking at me. He's got on another low slung pair of jeans, flashing his black and white striped boxer briefs and the waistband with the brand scrawled across it. But at least he's wearing a shirt tonight—some black and silver tank that's shredded and ripped, gaping holes torn in random places.

"Eat you out," Muse corrects as the rest of my boys join us on the wet pavement, all of them dark and glittering and unique. For a moment I'm reminded of the night we went to the Silver Skull, that BDSM club, when everyone was dressed up and sparkling.

They look even better now.

Or maybe I'm just imagining that they do because our relationship has changed? Because Michael's now a part of it? I'm not sure.

"Maybe if you're lucky, I'll let you after the show?" I tease as I meet Michael's violet eyes, Copeland's turquoise ones. Paxton is drinking from a small silver flask that he holds out to me. I hesitate for a split second and then take it, tipping it back and finding some kind of flavored whiskey. Cinnamon, I think it is.

"Maybe at the art museum itself?" Muse continues, walking backward so he can look at me as we move toward the back door of the venue, Ransom's arm still strong and comforting around my waist. Derek's eyes dance with amusement, but I can still see that flickering shadow in his gaze, the one that appeared the other night and has made its home in his multicolored irises.

Poor fucking Muse. Whatever it is that's eating away at him, I want to know about it.

I take another drink and hand the flask back to Paxton.

"Maybe," I say as we head around the corner and down

the narrow alley that leads to the back entrance. Red brick walls tower up on either side of us, giving us a brief moment of privacy.

"Let's wait out here for a few," Pax says, checking his phone and then leaning the expensive lines of his navy suit against the wall nearest the door. "We're early enough, and the last thing I want to do right now is look at Octavia's face." He shakes his head and gives me a look. "I can't even believe you gave that fucking twat some sort of invitation to redemption. That's the *last* thing she deserves." He pauses and flicks a quick glance Ransom's way, their eyes locking for the briefest of seconds before Paxton looks away.

"Yeah, well, at least if I give her a second chance and she blows it, I'll know I took the high road," I say, leaning against the wall opposite the boys. They look like they're posing for a poster or something, all lined up like that, one glittering dark beast next to another.

I smile.

"I've never been much of a hiker," Pax says with a cruel smirk, flicking cigarette ash into the wind as he gives my new shirt-dress a scalding once-over, tearing me apart with his grey gaze, making my knees feel weak enough that I have to lean my weight against the bricks behind me. "The high road is just too much damn work."

"So I've noticed," Ransom whispers, his voice like hot fudge over ice cream, melting me even as I'm worrying about how Pax is going to react. But all he does is grit his teeth and continue smoking his cigarette. I guess that's an improvement over the way he was treating Ransom last week?

A couple of roadies move down the alley between us, Michael nodding at them in greeting before they pass through the sticker plastered surface of the back door, the rowdy sounds of the venue leaking out into the relative quiet of the alley.

To my left, at the end of it, there's a chain-link fence with pieces of black painted plywood attached to it, blocking off our view of the street. To my right, I can just barely see the buses and trailers in the parking lot.

The wind howls down the narrow walkway, ruffling the short cotton dress around my pale thighs. I glance down, at the black gladiator heels that crisscross up to my knees, and then back up at the boys, noticing that there's more than one set of eyes on me.

"What do you guys normally do right before a show? Since I've been here, you've just sort of been hanging out with me."

"A huge improvement over the usual, I assure you," Muse says, pushing off the wall and coming over to stand in front of me in his torn tank and low-slung jeans, penning me in against the bricks. Even out here, with a storm brewing and the wind dragging strands of red hair across my face, I can smell Muse's smoky tea/incense scent.

"And the usual was …" I start, my eyes drawn to the fullness of Derek's mouth, the way it parts slightly as he looks down at me, still smiling.

"Getting fluffed by groupies," Pax says and ends up with an elbow in the ribs from Michael.

"Yeah, sure. Like when did that ever fucking happen?"

"Oh, please, I remember a good dozen times I caught you with a groupie before a show, your pants around your ankles —" Pax starts, interrupted by a growl from Michael.

"That was a long goddamn time ago. Why do you have to bring that shit up?"

"It was *two* years ago," Paxton corrects, giving me this scalding look over Michael's shoulder. "And I just think Miss Lily oughta know what she's getting into with you."

My gaze swings over to Michael, those purple-blue eyes of his boring into me as Muse drops his lips to my neck and my eyes get heavy and half-lidded.

"Yeah, I'll cop to it," he says as he steals the cigarette from Pax's fingers and takes a drag on it. "I was a horrible piece of shit. Maybe I did fuck groupies before our shows? Honestly, I wouldn't even remember if I did."

Michael pushes up the long sleeve of his black shirt, turning his arm over and rubbing at the crook of his elbow with a thumb. There are tattoos there, but when he steps over to my side of the alley and lifts my hand, I can feel the rough bumps of scars.

Track marks.

Muse rests his chin on my shoulder and looks at his friend, the tall crest of his mohawk briefly obscuring my view.

"Pax, you sure like to stir the pot, don't you?" I ask him as Muse steps back and leans against the wall next to me, pressing our arms together as Michael does the same on the other side, crossing his arms over his chest, sleeves still pushed up.

"Me? No, never," he says, but his voice is low and dangerous, edgy. He's been getting phone calls all day today, ones that he's been ignoring and then answering with angry flicks of his thumbs across his cell's screen as he texts back. I hope curiosity doesn't really kill the cat because I'm almost desperate to see who he's talking to and why.

"I was an awful human being," Michael continues as I stand there squashed between him and Muse, looking across the way at Ransom and Copeland. "But I got a second chance, and I'm trying to use it right."

He looks down at me, and I think of the wild, frantic sex we had that morning, my cheeks flushing slightly.

"I think you're doing great," Muse says, locking his fingers together behind his neck. "And trust me, I was no fan of Vanessa's, but I think you handled the situation as well as it could be handled."

"Yeah, well," Michael starts, still smoking, looking the part of the fucking badass in his long-sleeved *Beauty in Lies* tee, his tattoos sticking out the rolled up sleeves, his pants this tight leather that cups his body in a way that should be criminal. His boots are this dark green turquoise that mimics the color in his tattoos, the laces missing, the silver eyelets glimmering in the soft peach colored afternoon light. "That I'm not so sure about, but thanks."

There's a quiet moment where I just stand there and take in the scene. Ransom's dark hair is sticking out of the small holes on his red mesh hoodie, the hood pulled up as usual. And Cope is draped in necklaces and bracelets with little pewter charms, a white and black bandanna tied through one of the loops on his dark brown jeans. I can smell Muse's smoky scent mixing with Michael's spicy pomegranate shampoo, weaving together with the rosewater perfume I spritzed on before we left the bus.

Standing here like this, with all these rockstars waiting for the show, I feel like … I want to take care of them. I know, I know, I need to stop doing that. All I ever *did* was take care of Kevin, but I can't help it. And besides, my skin feels … hot, achy, needy. My fingers curl against the bricks as I take in my boys with a hungry gaze, one that I know they must feel as it sears across their skin.

They're mine, I think as I look at them, one by one, dirty thoughts ticking past inside my head.

"What the bloody fuck are you up to over there, Miss Lilith Tempest Goode?" Paxton asks as he kicks one of his expensive loafers up against the wall. "You look like you're ready to go on the hunt or something."

"So … you've never had a groupie take care of you before a show?" I ask, and I almost don't recognize my own voice. It's thready, husky, low and dripping. I sound a little like *Ransom* in that moment.

"Did I say that?" Pax asks with a challenge in his voice as a smile curves my lips and I glance down the alley. I don't see anyone out here, but that doesn't mean anything. It was like a highway earlier, all the comings and goings in opposite directions, people in edgy clothes carrying instruments and lights and confetti cannons.

At any second, we could have an audience …

I am definitely losing my mind here. But maybe in a good way?

I just … if these boys are mine, then I *want* them. I want to touch them and hold them and fuck them. It doesn't matter when or where or why. I just do.

I turn to Muse first, penning *him* in against the wall this time as he smiles a slow, easy smile at me. God, that's what I really like about him, how unpretentious he is, how straightforward, how practical. But there's also something magical about him, too, some … glimmer of fire deep inside that says that this man, he's a fucking fighter. Now, I might not know what he went through in his past, but anyone that can get emancipated at fifteen and fight their way into a multiplatinum selling band deserves some serious props.

And maybe a quickie outside the venue?

"Is there something you wanted?" he asks me coyly as I slide my fingers over his shoulders and lean forward to press a kiss to his mouth, one that he definitely *doesn't* take for granted. We kiss slow and easy for a moment, like we've got all the time in the world.

"You're on in about a half hour," Octavia says just after I hear the door swing open. There's a long pause, like maybe she's watching me and Muse, but then she disappears and the vibrating rhythm of the music from inside the building disappears, cut off and leaving us in the eerie quiet of the coming storm.

"Thirty minutes," I say as I pull away from Muse and bite my lower lip gently, looking up at him from under my lashes. "That's about … six minutes each."

"Holy shit," Muse breathes, and then I'm kissing him hard and fast, letting him spin me around and press my back into the wall.

The rough brick teases my thighs as Derek slides his warm hands up and under my shirt-dress, finding the lacy black panties he bought me at the mall, when he snuck away from me and Michael. They have a slit down the center of the crotch, making them quite convenient for … times like this.

"Oh, god," he groans, closing his eyes and leaning his forehead against mine for a second. "You didn't. I thought I was totally grasping at straws when I bought these."

"Well, you grasped the right straw then I guess," I say as I wrap my arms around his neck and he reaches down to undo his jeans, freeing his already hard shaft. I don't look at anything but the gold-grey of his eyes as he lifts me up with his hands under my ass and slams my back into the wall.

Those eyes … they remind me of the clouds above our

heads, the grey swirl of the storm mixing with the cheerful golden rays of the spring sunshine, the tiny drops of rain that are beginning to fall like the blue flecks in Muse's irises; the whisper of leaves on the trees at the edge of the lot are the green bits in his gaze.

That's what Muse is like, like the weather. In some ways, it's predictable, but only if you really know what you're looking for. And yet, sometimes, it can throw you completely off-balance.

I feel like I'm metaphorically stumbling as I guide Muse to my core and he thrusts into me, shattering the aching heat in my skin to pieces, making it feel like it's sliding off and away, leaving me bare and open to the world.

I wrap my black gladiator heels around his back as he rides me into the wall, not kissing me, just looking at me, studying me with that all knowing gaze of his.

"*We'll figure out some way for you to make a living with your art, if that's what you want. Just ... promise me you'll keep trying while you're with us.*"

He just met me and already, he knows me too well.

But what is all that empathy hiding? What was the cost of all that intuition?

"Lilith," he whispers, pressing his mouth to my ear, groaning as our hips grind together, my bare ass pressing into the bricks. I'm sure I'll have some cuts and scrapes after this, but I don't care. I don't want to stop. The rough feel of the wall mixes with the sweet agony of sharing my body with another, that hot slip and slide that tugs at all my heartstrings, makes me wonder if I'm even capable of *just sex.* If any of the moments I've spent with these guys were ever *just* anything. Even that first night, when I slept with one after the other, there was something else going on.

Just like there is now.

I breathe out deep and refuse to let myself tap into any of my own emotions. My soul feels like a butterfly trapped in a gilded cage of grief; I just want to open the door and set it free. I want to do the same for all these boys, release them from their own agony.

The sex … is just a stepping-stone on our way to healing, an easy and obvious way to connect with another human being. Right now, with Muse buried inside of me, I can feel his heartbeat against my chest, taste his breath on my lips, know that he's alive. No, more than just alive—*awake.*

He fucks me hard and fast, getting harder and faster as we go. One hand holds me up under the ass while he presses his palm against the bricks with the other. Something shifts in his expression, something dark, and Muse glances away, thrusting a few last times and finishing with this pained, quiet sort of sound.

"You're breaking me up, Lilith," he whispers in my ear, just before he puts me down and steps away. I open my mouth to ask what exactly he means by that, but then Michael's right there, taking me into his arms.

And oh, fuck. I want to make sure they all know before they take that stage where their hearts and minds should belong. Maybe I'm being selfish, but I can't help it. I've got that queenly feeling again, that sense of being worshipped and adored, and it feels too good to resist. Why should I?

I briefly catch sight of Paxton over Michael's shoulder and he looks … jealous?

It's a surprising emotion to see on his face, especially after all the things we've been through this past week, but I can't stop. No, the torrid whisper of Michael's hands moving over my body is too mesmerizing, drawing my attention back to the wild expression on his face.

Paxton is an alpha; Michael is an alpha.

I wonder if they're going to be able to deal with each other?

Michael has his pants undone and me lifted up before I can take a solid breath, crushing our mouths together in that same way he did outside the venue that one night, when I was wearing the green dress. If he made my lip bleed then, I don't know that I even want to see the mess we're making tonight.

I respond to the frenzied need of his kissing with the desperate urge to soothe it, to take some of the edge off his almost limitless desire, imagining myself as some kind of dark fairytale princess. But instead of the prince kissing me to wake me up, I'm kissing *him* to relax him, calm him, soothe the ruffled feathers of his jagged passion.

Because Michael *is* jagged and broken. Those two years he fought to stay faithful to Vanessa, he was only melting the tip of the iceberg of his problems, that small obvious piece that the whole world could see. But there's enough floating beneath the surface to sink a ship. Michael is angry, and he's been alone for a long time. There are so many different kinds of loneliness, but his breed, the monster that was born the day his parents died, it's been feeding off of him for a while.

Michael drives into me like an animal and I *love* it. Part of me still feels guilty, like I shouldn't, like sex should be saved for dark rooms and quiet evenings. Yet … out here, with the storm rolling in above our heads, shedding tiny droplets of rain, I feel so fucking alive, charged, even dominant.

That's not something I've really … ever felt.

Not that I was submissive to Kevin or anything, but I think I let him walk on me without even knowing it. And now, here, with five strong personalities, I feel more in *charge* than I ever did back then.

Michael's driving thrusts are so different than Muse's, and I can tell he's still working more from instinct and need than anything else. I want to change that, break through it, really *connect* with him. Because we have something here, something that needs to be explored.

I run my hands over Michael's shoulders, down his arms, loving the feel and touch and smell of him. For days, I had to watch him at a distance, feel this *thing* between us stretch and twist and trip us both up. And now we get to throw ourselves into it headfirst, see where it takes us.

I imagine places high.

"*Fuck,*" he groans as he pumps into me and comes hard, making my head tilt back, my lids droop. When Michael finishes, he doesn't let go right away, holding me for a moment, claiming me with another searing kiss, one that steals all the breath in my lungs and leaves me panting. "Fuck," he says again, reluctantly sliding out of me and letting me put my heels against the pavement.

We watch each other as I walk around him and find fingers curling around my wrist and tugging me close.

It's Paxton.

Of *course* it is.

"I'm supposed to be impressed by that?" he calls over my shoulder and I glance back just in time to see the angry expression flash across Michael's face.

"I was," I say, looking back at Pax as he stares down at me from that too perfect face of his. Eventually, it's going to crack and I'm going to see all the things inside of him that he doesn't want anyone else to see. It's fucking inevitable.

"Well, well, then let's see what I can do to change that?"

I start to back up against the wall on the opposite side of the alley when he spins me around and pushes my cheek to the bricks, my head turned toward Ransom. I can see him watching from those dark eyes of his, the scent of violets in the air, even with the few feet separating us. That smell surrounds me like a hug, competes with the sharp glaze of Pax's cologne.

"You alright, sweetheart?" he asks, ready to protect me, beat the shit out of Paxton if need be. I believe he could do it, too, if he really wanted to. That's one of the things I don't understand about their relationship, why Ransom *lets* Paxton treat him like crap.

"I'm perfect," I say as Paxton unzips his slacks and teases me with his cock, sliding it against the wet aching heat between my thighs, that explosion of nerves, that desperate thirst that I can't seem to quench. "I can't seem to get enough," I whisper, having a conversation with Ransom even as Pax grips my breasts through my bra and squeezes them tight enough to make me gasp.

"What a delightful problem to have," Pax says, slipping the head of his shaft against my opening, teasing me with an inch, two inches, making me squirm and press back into him. My palms splay out against the irregular surface of the red-brown stones, and I shove my hips back, impaling myself on Paxton's warm cock. "Bleeding hell," he whispers, slipping his hands back down my sweaty body to my hips.

He grabs hold of me and starts to move with these long, slow strokes that tickle all the right spots, make my chest and throat feel tight. When he moves one of his hands down around to my clit, I have to bite my lip to keep from screaming. My body ripples and tightens, my sex clamping down on Paxton and holding tight, pausing his movements for several agonizing seconds.

"Paxton," I say, but I can barely get his name past my lips before he teases the hardened nub of flesh in tight, rapid circles, using the juices of my own desire as lube, rubbing me until my self-control breaks and I come around him. My orgasm is like the distant lightning lighting up the sky in the west, cracking the grey-gold afternoon into pieces.

I'm so wrapped up in the shockwaves of pleasure that I barely notice his orgasm, the switch of cruel, cold hands for warm, calloused ones.

I notice then that I'm not looking at Ransom anymore, but at Cope.

Ransom is behind me.

"Are you sure you want more?" he asks before he does anything more but lay his hands on the tight sweaty expanse of my skin. I feel like I'm trapped in it again, inside a vortex of want and need.

"I need more," I say as Copeland's blue-green eyes connect with mine.

I have to close them as I feel Ransom's hands on my body, sliding up and freeing my breasts from the confines of my bra. I might be wearing panties still, but they're soaking wet and my dress is pushed up, my breasts hanging free.

I may as well be naked in this damn alley.

"I'll give you whatever you want, darling," he tells me, caressing the torturous rawness of my breasts, his thumbs grazing the sharp points of my nipples, connecting the aching desperation of my pussy with my chest, my heart, my head. I'm all wrapped up in this, desperate to finish my last two boys before the show.

If we're not done when Octavia comes to collect them … I might not let them go.

Ransom's hands draw away from my breasts, one palm slicking up my spine, the other taking hold of my hip as he finds the ardent proof of my desire, soaking my crotchless panties and wetting my inner thighs. I know I have the others' proof all over me, too, their come inside of me.

"You're such a beautiful girl, sweet thing," he tells me, filling me slowly, pushing inside of me with a single breath. "Such a beautiful fucking girl."

I move my hips back against Ransom's, meeting the low thrumming bass that seems to be his natural rhythm. That instrument, the way he wields it onstage, that's how he works my body, easy and low and slow. Ransom moves inside of me like he's already in love with me, like he's trying to make me sing along with the deep decadent notes of his own groans. The sounds he makes when he's having sex with me are like after dinner coffee and desserts, that part of the meal you spend all night waiting for, when the lights are dim and the candle on the table's melted away to almost nothing.

Intimate. Esoteric. Transcendent.

That's Ransom Riggs.

We slide together, our movements almost coordinated, finding each other in the suddenness of the storm as wind sweeps down the alley and chills my heated skin. Goose bumps break out all across my body as my breasts swing like pendulums and I drop my head in pleasure.

My cunt is liquid, molten, scorching across Ransom's shaft as I let his darkness twist through mine, find its melancholy partner. We process things so much the same way that I wonder how good it is for us to be together. Last week, when I thought this was temporary, I was worried.

Now … I just like him too much to care. I really, really do.

I use my body to drag the demons from his, make him come in me, just like the others. I claim him, mark him, take the proof of our connection inside of me.

"Oh, shit, baby girl," he says, and I swear there's a sob inside of his voice. But when I stand up and turn around, his dark eyes are dry and he's looking at me with a small smile.

"Five minutes," Muse warns as I lick my lips and lean back against the wall with my breasts exposed, my shirt-dress pushed up around my hips.

Cope approaches me slowly, takes Ransom's place as my scarred, twisted lover steps aside to fix his pants.

"You look like the cat that got the cream," Cope whispers in my ear, taking my face in his hand and kissing me like the girl next door instead of the one half-naked in an alley with a bunch of horny rockstars.

When he lifts me up and I wrap my legs around him, it feels like we're together in some distant place, just the two of us. When he enters me, I can't help it—I have another orgasm. This one is a slow, sneaking shadow that takes over me, makes me shudder in Cope's arms, melt against his chest as he makes love to me outside the venue door. On this side of the alley, I can actually feel the music through the wall, teasing my spine, my ass, the back of my head. It thumps and throbs, almost as loud and frantic as my heart as I join up with the last guy in my band, the last man in Beauty in Lies to take his girlfriend in an alley.

A smile steals across my lips as the flash of my orgasm fades away and I enjoy my last few minutes with Cope, his body finally slaking some of that burning desire inside of me, taking that flame and dousing it until it's just a slow-burning ember.

At any moment, it might light up and flare to life, but for just a brief second there, I feel satisfied.

I hold him close as he finishes inside of me and I rub his back in small circles.

"You're wicked," he whispers to me as he steps back, but we're both still smiling.

I put my breasts back in my bra, push my shirt-dress down … and then the venue door opens.

"It's about that time," Octavia says, her lips pursed slightly, eyes locked onto my flushed face, dilated pupils, and swollen lips.

"I should go back to the bus and shower," I whisper, but Ransom is grabbing me by the arm.

"After that, you *have* to see us play," he says, mouth twisted to the side in a crooked smile as he tugs me into his arms, against the soft sweet smelling fabric of his sweatshirt. "Don't you think you deserve a good show after all that work?"

"I'm …" I swallow a little and reach back to play with my hair. It's a little tangled from the wind … maybe from rubbing up against the wall, too. "Well, I don't think boys quite get how *messy* sex is for girls."

"Oh, it's messy for us, too," Pax says, his wicked smirk hot enough to burn. Even after all that, I can barely look at him. Hell, it's kind of hard to look at *any* of them. I mean, I just went and had sex with five men in a row, one after the other.

And I loved it.

Mine.

My rockstars.

"Fuck, fine," I say, following them inside and letting them each go with a kiss to the cheek before I stop in the bathroom and clean up as best as I can. When I step out, Octavia's waiting for me and I can hear the sound of the crowd cheering along to the animated video that always plays before the boys' set.

"Miss Goode," she says, her brown hair in a single braid down her back, those pale eyes locked on my face. They're the color of wet sand, a light brown that would be pretty if she didn't look so pissed off all the time.

"Ms. Warris," I say, trying to smile. After all, what's the point of giving her a second chance if I'm just going to act like a bitch? "Is there something I can help you with? I was actually hoping to catch the show tonight."

"Why him?" she asks me, but her voice isn't cruel or mean right now, just … hurt. I think she *really* liked Paxton. I feel bad for her because so do I. Despite that cold cruelness, the mean things he says, he's got a big heart inside of him. Maybe Octavia can see it, too? "You … I don't know what you're doing with the rest of them, but can't you just let him go?"

She's pleading with me right now, her tablet and clipboard tucked up against her chest. She really is a pretty girl when she's not scowling and throwing daggers at me with narrow eyed glares.

"Octavia," I say, hoping she doesn't mind me using her first name. I can hear the voiceover announcing the guys now. "It's not about me letting him go. It's not like that. I …" I try to figure out how to phrase this, some way that might make her understand. "Paxton and I, we need each other."

"You just met," she says, her voice rising an octave. "I've been working with him for a long goddamn time. How can you need each other after a week?"

"Have you ever lost someone you cared about?" I ask her, looking into her eyes, searching those depths for that empty flicker of pain that signifies true loss. I've been acquainted with that particular emotion for a good part of my life; we're almost friends, she and I. Grief. The best friend I never wanted.

"Not really, no," she says, but at least she says it carefully, respectfully, like she realizes this is a sensitive subject for me.

"Then I'm happy for you, really," I say with a deep breath, looking her straight in the face, trying not to squirm with the vivid carnal memories of what just took place outside. I fucked five guys. I took them all, made them mine, *owned* them with my body. "But that's why you and Paxton would never work. He's carrying around a lot of pain, and he looks for it in everyone he surrounds himself with. He'd ruin you if you ever got together. He needs to be around people that … are missing as many pieces as he is."

"That doesn't make any sense," Octavia says as I hear the lyrics from onstage leaking back to us, Pax's powerful voice carrying them like the storm tonight carried in the rain, thunder and lightning.

"*Look into his eyes and say goodbye; never let another day go by; don't miss the quiet moments in between; never love and never leave again.*"

It's the song. My song. The one I heard in the car right after I got the text about my dad dying.

"It makes perfect sense," I whisper, my hands shaking suddenly as I look up at the dark ceiling above us. "A happy person, a whole person, keeps all their pieces, holds the complete puzzle of their life in their hands. A broken person tries to give those pieces away because they don't like what they see. They fill in all those missing spots on the broken people around them, and in turn, they take some of those people's pieces." I look back down at the confused expression on her face. But I don't have time to explain it further. I *need* to see Beauty in Lies perform this song. And then I need to find out why Pax has it tattooed on his chest with some of the words changed. "They'll never be whole, but at least their pictures will change, until maybe they see something they like a little better than they had before. I have to go, I'm sorry."

I push past her and sprint down the front steps, flash my badge at the security guards, and find myself alone in front of the stage, between the security fence and guards, and the raised wooden platform above me.

"*A message from the afterlife, this curse burned deep inside my heart,*" Pax sings, his hands wrapped around the mic, this vintage silver microphone that I've never seen before. It must be a prop for this particular song, the one he has literally etched into his skin. "*I'm sorry for all my words of strife, the way our sins ripped us both apart.*"

Cope spins his drumsticks in his hand and then pummels his kit like a drummer in an old-fashioned marching band, sending this rapid-fire beat into the crowd that seems almost at odds with the softness of Paxton's words.

"*Those days we spent together fade away, but the hurt, that part is the thing that stays. Set me free, God, don't you see? All of this heartache is bloody murdering me.*"

Pax curls his hand in front of his chest, eyes closed as he lets the words echo with this surreal static through the old mic. The age of the technology seems to change the way he sounds, hollows his voice out a little, but in a good way. It's very artistic, the whole setup, the way he truly *sounds* like he's singing to this fucking ghost from beyond the grave.

And then I see his grey eyes flick over to Ransom again, and I start to wonder.

This song … it's tattooed on his chest as *look into her eyes.* But he sings it as *his* eyes.

Her and his.

Chloe and Ransom.

That's when it first clicks together for me.

Michael is going to be a serious bitch to work with. It's only been a few days and I can already see that.

We're at the sushi place I picked out, seated around a table in the back corner behind a six-panel *byōbu* aka a Japanese folding screen. This one's got a scene of five warriors fighting over a beautiful woman in a kimono.

How ironic is that shite?

I stare across the table at Lilith sitting on Michael's lap, catch his eyes as they slide over to me, and smirk at him. That bloody wanker. Who the hell does he think he is? Popping into the game at this stage and acting like he already has the highest score.

"Come on, Ran," Muse is saying, trying to get the hooded fucker to eat a spicy tuna, crab, and avocado roll. "How do you know you won't like it unless you try it?"

"I'm not eating raw fish," Ransom whispers from inside his hood, his dark eyes focused on the weird cocktails we all ordered. A *vanilla avocado martini.* It's absolutely atrocious, but I tossed mine back anyway. Alcohol is alcohol, right? "Thanks but no thanks."

Muse chuckles and pops the food into his mouth, a sea of tiny white plates covering the black tablecloth in front of him. About half are empty.

"Well, enjoy your *teriyaki chicken* then," he says, sliding his gaze over to Lilith as she examines the spread from the safety of Mikey's lap.

I fold my hands together behind my head and lean back in my chair for a moment.

"You don't even have to do raw," Cope says, lifting up his own plate. "Start in the shallows and have a California roll or something with chicken in it. I think you'll like it if you just try it. You used to eat those little dried seaweed flakes at lunch back in school."

"I always ate what my mom packed—even if I didn't like it." Ransom smiles sharply, the expression this deep dark thing just carved raggedly into the scarred planes of his face. I stare at him for a really long time, this strange gaping emptiness inside of me that I blame all the hell over Lilith. How can I just sit here and watch some crying, blushing grieving girl and not feel her tears loosen up the glue that's holding me together?

I've been a right git, I think, this uneasy feeling taking over my body. *I've been a rancid prick.*

Ransom … Jesus bleeding Christ.

I look away again and find Lilith staring at me, her eyes like two dark emeralds surrounded by thick black lashes.

"Can I ask you a question?" she says and I feel my mouth twist up to the side in a smirk. It's my go-to expression, that smirk. I can wear it morning, noon, and night, and get away with whatever I want. The only people who could get me to smile for real were Chloe, Harper, and Ransom. Two of the fuckers on that list are dead and gone, and the other …

I'm done staring at that arsehole right now. Fuck him.

"About?" I ask, because there are a lot of questions I

don't want to answer, not even for my new girlfriend. Hmm. My girlfriend. This is certainly an unexpected development. I must be completely mental to not only *date* some girl I just met, but to share her with my fucking mates. Somehow though, that makes this easier, not harder, like the pressure's not just on me.

And the sex?

Well, shit. I haven't met many girls who could satisfy me by themselves let alone me and four other guys without batting a lash. When she's fucking us all, she gets this wild look in her eyes, like she's not entirely human. I love that, that feral gleam.

I can't wait for her to meet my fiancée.

That uptight English twat is going to flip her lid when she sees curvy, redheaded Lilith Tempest Goode standing on my parents' doorstep with me. Because that's exactly what's going to happen. When we head to London for the concert, I've got three nights set aside to take a little detour and visit my parents' place just outside of York. I haven't told anyone else about it yet, but that's what's happening.

Won't that be fun?

"That song you opened the show with tonight, what's the name of it?"

"*After All There's Us,*" I say, sitting back up and grabbing a pair of chopsticks with my right hand, tapping them against the surface of the table as I return Lilith's stare and pray that that's the end of this conversation. I don't want to fucking talk about my music, any of it. It's all too personal, too full of pain, too rife with meaning.

"The song says *his* eyes, but your chest says *hers,*" she continues and I feel my breath escape in a rush. I pluck some crab sashimi from a plate and pop it into my mouth, trying not to grit my teeth or clench my jaw. "Is it about Ransom and Chloe?" she whispers, leaning forward across the table.

The other three guys are talking, but I bet Mikey can hear her.

"This is a bloody boring conversation," I say as I feel my heartbeat start to pick up inside my chest. Sure, maybe Lilith is right? Okay, fuck, she definitely is right. That song is about Ransom *and* Chloe, the betrayal I felt when they confessed their attraction to each other … and the pain I felt that night when I essentially lost them both. "Why don't we talk about your dead dad instead?" I ask and Michael narrows his eyes at me and scowls.

"Goddamn it, Paxton, what the fuck is your problem?"

"Leave us the hell alone," I say, pointing at him with the chopsticks, thinking how ridiculous he looks with his tattoos and eyeliner in the middle of this sleek white and silver restaurant. I'm the only one dressed for the occasion, in my fucking suit. "She's not just your girlfriend, Mikey, and you don't control my interactions with her."

"And you don't get to be a complete and utter prick whenever the hell you feel like it, so step off," he says, and I have to really resist the urge to chuck a plate at him. First off, it'll probably hit Lilith instead, and second, I refuse to let either of them see how damn emotional I am right now.

I lean back in the chair again and smirk.

The more I smirk, the less I feel.

"Hey, Ran," I say, looking back at him and seeing his gaze lift slowly from his food to my face. Both Cope and Muse pause their conversation to listen. "*After All There's Us,* who's that song about?"

He just stares at me, his stupid hands trembling as he

adjusts his grip on his fork. Like who the hell eats with a fork at a Japanese restaurant?

My lips purse as we continue to stare at each other, and I can't help but think of that kiss. That damn kiss. That fucking stupid arse kiss. God, I've kissed a lot of people in my life—girls, obviously—but I've never, *never* kissed anyone that sad, that empty, that fucked-up. Ransom is a mess, a scarred up, messed up, twisted nightmare of a man.

What the hell's happened to him? To that guy who came to my house with his hair slicked back, a confident smile on his face, a yellow t-shirt on. He stood there and slipped his hands in his pockets, looking like some kind of charmed hipster asshole. Then he told me he was in love with my high school sweetheart, that she was in love with him. We got into an epic row … and the rest is history.

Ransom was friends with my little sister, too. So … he lost her that night, he lost the girl he was in love with, and he lost me.

Then, he found Kortney, fell in love … and I took her from him. Just because I could. Because I wanted to punish him. Because he needed to suffer the way I was suffering.

But goddamn, the world has certainly given Ransom Wilder Riggs suffering in generous spades.

"Is it about me?" he asks, half like he hopes it is, half like he's praying it's not.

His eyes, they're the same color as the dried blood on Harper's pink jacket, the one she was wearing when I identified her body in the morgue.

I try to hold onto my anger, but it just slips away and I turn back to the food.

"That's the beautiful thing about art, isn't it, Miss Lilith Tempest Goode?" I ask as I pick up a piece of yellowtail nigiri and stare at it clutched between the two glossy black chopsticks. "It can be interpreted in so many different ways. There's no one meaning, is there?"

"No, but usually the artist has some sort of idea in mind when he creates the piece, doesn't he?"

"Sometimes the artist is as baffled by his work as his audience," I say, putting the food between my lips and looking over at Lilith, at the way her wavy red hair falls over her shoulder when she leans forward to grab her drink, sitting back on Michael's lap like she was meant to be there. She looks like a fucking queen presiding over her court.

"Paxton," she starts as I study her curvy body cloaked in that scribbled shirt-dress, my hands tingling with the memory of her heavy breasts trapped inside her lace bra, the slickness of her cunt, the strength of her muscles when she came wrapped around me. "What's your middle name?"

I pause and then set my chopsticks down, my body shaking with a burst of laughter.

"Cheeky bitch," I say and then lift my chin, meeting her hardened stare with one of my own.

"You said you didn't give your name to strangers. I'm not a stranger anymore. I want to know what it is."

She sips her drink with those full lips of hers, bruised from Michael's brutal kisses.

I tilt my head to the side and lick my lips.

"It's Charles," I say, smiling slightly. "And yes, I'm aware that my name is English as fuck, thank you very much."

"You're welcome," she says, and then she stands up, walks around the table and sits on my lap.

I can't even begin to figure out why I'm so goddamn pleased by that.

I've never much liked museums, probably because the houses I grew up in were like museums themselves. Cold. Impersonal. Stuffy. My parents' own art collection is worth as much as everything in this building—and that's in their *summer home.*

What I do like is seeing Miss Lily's reactions to the art pieces, seeing the way her big eyes get even bigger, her lashes fluttering as she takes in pots, paintings, sculptures, dresses, and murals with a child's sense of wonder.

"Do you see the careful intensity in those brushstrokes?" she asks, clutching at my sleeve as we pause in front of a dark painting featuring a girl in a hat with a briefcase held tightly in her pale hands. "It's like each and every single one was made with … with this fucking crazy amount of passion."

Lilith lets go of me and stands up, leaning as far over the red velvet rope as the security guard will allow. They've already asked her to step back three or four times, and I swear, I thought about beating the shit out of them. How can they interrupt somebody that looks that damn eager?

"Can you even imagine the love and the pain it would take to do something that intricate?"

"I can take a wild guess," I say, feeling my heartbeat speed up again. Even now, her eyes shiny and lips parted, Lilith is fucking with my emotions. I stare at her—how could I not?—and feel my cock get hard inside my slacks. I haven't had a chance to wash up since our encounter in the alley and I swear, I can still feel her juices covering me, soaking my balls, the inside of my pants.

"What do you think, Ran?" she asks, drawing him away from a life-size painting of a man in a white suit, and over to where we're standing. Derek, Cope, and Michael are engaged with the proprietor that's giving us our private tour of the building. I wonder how much Muse had to drop for the privilege?

"It's … kind of tragic, doll baby," he whispers, keeping his voice at that frustratingly low pitch that demands attention. If you don't give it your fuckin' all, you can't hear a damn thing the man says anymore.

"You think so?" she asks, leaning into him when he slides his arms around her and closes his eyes, breathing in the scent of her hair as I watch, feeling my skin prickle with want. I want to touch them, get in there and see what happens between the three of us.

And yet, I'm supposed to hate the man, aren't I?

But every damn day that Lilith is on our bus, she makes it harder and harder for me to do that. I swipe my hand down my face and look up at the painting, Ransom's words echoing sharply in my skull.

"*At some point, you're just going to have to accept that you fucked up, sweetheart. But you won't, will you? Because if you do, you'll have to accept that Chloe and Harper died in an* accident, *that you have no right to make me the enemy anymore. And* then *you'll have to accept that you kicked me when I was down for no goddamn good reason at all.*"

Hell, I'm drowning in pride, in hubris, in a nightmare of my own making.

I turn away from the two of them and wander out the door and into another wing, this one filled with more ancient paintings, from times and worlds so far away from here that I can barely fathom them. My education demands that I recognize the styles, the time periods, oftentimes the painters, the names of the paintings themselves, but my apathy refuses to care about any of it.

"Pax, wait up," Lilith says, jogging to catch up to me in the empty quiet of the museum. The marble floors echo with the sound of her heels as she walks alongside of me. "Are you okay? You seem a little off tonight?"

"Off?" I ask, pausing and turning to look at her, loving the shape of her mouth and her eyes and her face. "How would you know? We barely know each other."

"That's not fair," she says, her voice softening as she studies me with eyes the color of the English countryside, green and vibrant and alive. I should probably tell her that my parents have been calling me nonstop, driving me up the damn well. They want me to quit the band, come home, and marry the girl they picked out for me when I was seven.

Fuck them, and fuck her.

"Aren't we dating now?" she asks and she smiles so sweet when she says it that I get the urge to kiss her. I grab her chin with my fingers, probably a little harder than I should, and drop my mouth to hers. My tongue pushes between Lilith's lips, draws this small fervid sound from her throat. It makes me want to be crueler, rougher, take her into me and fuck away all my worries.

“Hey, the tour's moving on,” Ran says from beside us, his voice as distant and dark as a ghost's.

“Shit,” Lilith says, wiping her mouth, her cheeks slightly flushed with desire. “I don't want to miss anything. Which room did they go into?”

“Straight ahead, to the left,” Ran tells her and she takes off back the way she came, leaving the two of us alone together in the empty hall, the dead smiles of portraits staring back at us from the white walls. “Don't tell Lilith, but I think it's totally creepy in here,” he says.

I almost smile at that.

Almost.

“Not an art connoisseur, are you?” I ask as we walk back in the direction Lilith went, my Barker Blacks loud against the floors, Ransom's boots soft, almost shuffling. “That would require some level of class, wouldn't it?”

His mouth twists down at the sides and he tucks his hands into his pockets, smelling like cigarettes and that fucking violet perfume he never stops wearing.

“Now that Lilith's here …” he starts, taking a deep breath, pushing his hood off his dark brown hair. It's a trust move, when he does that, bares his face. Ransom looks over at me, that jagged length of scar marring what was once a picture-perfect expression. “I was hoping we could figure out some way to be friends again.”

“And why would Miss Lily change anything between us?” I ask.

Of course, that's bullshit.

Lilith is changing everything between us.

Just like her name implies, she's a tempest tearing into our bullshit and our hurt, cutting it up into smaller, more manageable pieces.

"We're in this together, Paxton," he says, still looking at me, sharing one of the longest looks we've had since that awful fucking night. There've been times over the years where I've wanted to give up my vendetta, tell him that I'm sorry, try to get back what we had before. Ransom's the reason I'm a musician in the first place. I mean, my parents raised me to sing, to play piano, cello, violin … but it was Ransom Riggs that taught me the ugly beauty of rock, the aching agony of a metal riff. He encouraged me to explore my feelings in song, to write my own music, to start my own band. "If we both want to be with Lilith, we'll have to find some way to get along."

"And how's that? I just forgive you for murdering my sister and my old girlfriend so we can share a new one?"

Ran grits his teeth, but he just takes a deep breath and keeps calm. Good for him. He's a better man than me. That much I'm sure of.

"I want you to listen to me, Paxton. I know I've said this a hundred times, but I'll say it again: Chloe and I never had sex. Never. We wouldn't do that to you, Pax."

"And why not? She was going to leave me for you, wasn't she? You were going to take her away? Why the fuck should I believe that you cared how I felt?"

"Because we both loved you, Pax. Both of us," he says, almost pleading, turning to look at me full-on. I keep his gaze, even though it makes my blood boil, my hands curl into fists by my sides. I've spent so many damn years being gutted by his betrayal, hating him with every cell in my body, I'm not sure I know how to get past that. "We loved you; we didn't want to hurt you. I swear on my *life* that we never meant to cause you any pain."

"Well, you did. A million times over. You stole

everything from me that night, Ransom."

"But I didn't," he says, his voice cracking, pressing his palms to the sides of his face. "It was an accident what happened to those girls. You think I wanted that?"

"Are we done with this conversation?" I ask, getting out a cigarette and then spotting the narrowed eyes of a security guard down the hall—not one of ours, one of the museum's. I tuck the fag back in the pack and shove it in my slacks pocket.

This is all getting too heavy for me …

"We're not done," Ransom says, his face pained, his voice weak and thready. "Pax, I lost just as much as you did that night. But you know what the worst part of it all was? The hardest part? As much as I loved Chloe and Harper, I loved you more. You're my best friend." A pause as my heart thunders and I grit my teeth in … anger? Frustration? Fear? Fear that I'll be pushed to a place I'm not comfortable with, a reality that I won't like … or that I might end up loving. That'd be worse though, wouldn't it? Ending up with something I'd be beyond terrified to lose. "*Were* my best friend," Ransom corrects. "But you've surely proven to me that there's nothing so awful and bitter as love turned to hate."

"I don't hate you," I say, and even though my gut instinct is to just tear into this man, say the worst shite I can think of, I simply fucking stand there and wait, breathing hard, shaking slightly.

"The worst part of everything that's happened to me is losing you," Ransom says again, and I feel some strange tearing sensation inside my chest, this horrible wrenching ache that makes me sick to my stomach. "I wish … if I could go back in time, I'd just ignore the feelings between me and Chloe. I'd watch you guys be together and I'd be happy for you instead. I don't want anything like that to happen again, with us and Lilith. I want you … *us* to try and be happy." He pauses and licks his lips, dropping his hands at his sides and glancing away. "I really like her, Paxton."

"More than Kortney?" I ask, and I don't know why I'm even bringing her up.

Ransom looks back over at me.

"Maybe you did me a favor by getting rid of Kortney. If she was willing to cheat on me, then she clearly didn't care about me in the first place. Besides, you freed me up to get with Lilith, right?"

He takes several long, deep breaths and tries to *smile* at me.

Jesus bloody Christ, he really is taking this seriously, isn't he?

"Fuck you, Ransom," I say, and then I turn and storm down the hall.

It takes him a few seconds to follow after me, catch up, grab me by the arm.

"Goddamn it, Paxton, *please.* Please. I need this to be over. I need it so fucking bad that it's *killing* me inside. Don't you see it? That you're fucking *killing* me?"

I look over at him, shaking and trembling again, his hood thrown back up, his face lost in the strange shadows of the museum. Somebody flicks off the lights accidentally in the wing we're standing in. Now the only glow comes from the individual bulbs aimed at the paintings.

I don't know what the hell comes over me, but … I lean forward and grab Ransom Riggs by the mouth. And then I kiss the fuck out of him.

I push between his lips with my tongue, kiss him as hard

and deep as I did Lilith a few moments ago, and I taste all of that cascading pain, that dreadful terrifying emptiness.

After a moment, he kisses me back, his palms pressed flat against the front of my suit.

When I press forward, he takes a step away, bumping into the railing at the edge of the room. Down below, I can vaguely hear voices. I think everyone else has gone downstairs.

They've gone down … and I'm kissing Ran for … some goddamn reason.

In that second though, it's not for Lilith's pleasure, is it?

Ran tries to break away, and I kiss him harder, take his mouth and push him against the railing. If he can feel the hardness of my cock, I don't care. It was for Lilith anyway, wasn't it? I just haven't stopped being hard is all, not even kissing that dirty awful mouth of his.

Just before I pull away, I drop a hand and feel Ransom's cock, stiff inside his jeans.

The lights flicker back on and I pull away, swiping an arm across my mouth.

But I can't even look at him.

I just can't fucking look at him.

There's a strangeness perfuming the air when we get back to the bus, this unfamiliar tension wound around the entire group but stemming from two people in particular.

Paxton and Ransom.

I mean, not that there *wasn't* tension between them before, but it's different now, shifting, morphing and changing like the storm outside the bus' windows. Thunder rumbles, shaking the glass, sending chills down my spine. There's violence in the air, the promise of nature's wrath. I might be kind of excited about it if I wasn't so sure there was another storm going on *inside* the bus.

"Are you alright?" I ask Ransom once we're all inside and Pax has stormed into the hallway and slammed the door. Ran's shaking, but his expression isn't … completely awful. I'm confused. "Did something happen with Pax?"

Ran pauses, his flirty scent sweeping me up, making me lean into him. As soon as I do, I can feel his arousal, pressing at the fly of his jeans, making my body go up in flames. And the way he looks down at me … My heart is in my throat, my sex silken and slick.

"Come with me, baby?" he asks and I nod, loving the warm curl of his fingers around my wrist as he drags me away from the other boys, down the hall and past the beam of light leaking underneath the bathroom door. We head into the Bat Cave and Ransom kicks the mess of clothes away from the door so he can close it.

I think that's the first time it's been closed since we started sleeping back here as a group of five—now six, of course.

I swallow past a suddenly dry throat as Ransom shrugs off his mesh hoodie, his tank, and then climbs up on the bed next to me. Sitting there, in front of his scarred but still beautiful body, I feel a little nervous.

"Is everything okay, Ransom?" I ask again, but he doesn't look at me, crawling through the dark shadows of the room as lightning flashes and highlights the rectangular shapes of the windows.

"I'm not sure, sweet thing," he says, voice dripping with lavish shadows and luxurious twilight. The sound of it … each syllable is like a Lucullan kiss, scrumptious and decadent, like I can feel the weight of his words against my mouth. "But will you help me figure it out?"

"Figure what out?" I ask as he flicks the switch for one of the red shaded lights that are attached to the headboard. The silver and grey stripes on the wall seem to glow, and the bat headboard grins down at me with its spindled mouth, making me shiver.

Ransom opens one of the drawers on the headboard and digs around for a moment, coming up with a length of silky red rope, the color of freshly spilled blood.

Blood.

Why does that color, that thought, make me think of my dad? He didn't die in blood. But my sister did … I shake those thoughts off, determined to make it through to New

York without having a breakdown. I don't need to have a breakdown, not with a whole host of scintillating rockstars to fall in love with.

Ransom sits back down and kicks his boots off the end of the bed, glancing over at me with eyes that for once aren't half-lidded or bedroom-dark, but open, surprised, slightly confused.

"Paxton … kissed me," he says and I raise one red brow.

"When?" He can't be talking about the two occasions I already know about.

"At the museum," he tells me, his voice even lower and harder to hear than usual. But god, it's worth it to lean in, to wait for it, to let that sensual silken sound slide across my eardrums. "We were talking through our shit and then … Fuck, Lilith, I don't know what's going on."

Ransom looks back at me and then lifts the bundle of rope up with a slight smile. I try to keep my eyes on his face, but I can't help my wandering gaze as it darts down to the sculpted perfection of his chest, his tummy, the scars that make him even more beautiful. I pause briefly when I catch the eyes of his mother's portrait, tattooed onto his bicep.

"You said you wanted to see what else was in these drawers. Are you game?"

"Who do you want to tie up?" I ask, blinking long lashes at him. "Me or Pax?"

It's supposed to be a joke, but it comes out a little … breathy. Fuck. I'm not trying to turn their kiss into an act for my own pleasure, but I have to admit that the thought makes me feel an intense libidinal hunger that burns and aches in my lower belly.

"God, darling, I don't know," he says as he looks over at me, chocolate brown hair kissing his forehead, his mouth slightly parted, the most adorable expression on his face. Yes, he's confused, but I think he's also a little bit excited? I could be wrong. "I don't think I'm bisexual. I've never looked at another guy and thought, like, I wanted to fuck him."

He runs his palms down his face as I close the distance between us and curl myself up in his lap, laying my head against his chest and listening to the clangorous rhythm of his heart.

"Maybe you're not bi …" I start, running my palm up the hard curves of Ransom's arm. Let's just say this: Kevin did not have arms with swoops and valleys like this. Being with a man who's filled out, who actually *looks* like a man, that's exciting. Kevin was soft and doughy, and honestly, at the time I thought I was in love so he was beautiful to me. But now that I look at him without rose-colored glasses? There's nothing attractive about the man. "Maybe you just like Paxton in particular? Sometimes gender is irrelevant. Love comes whether you want it to or not, and with love, sexual attraction builds. Somebody you never thought you'd find attractive becomes the sexiest human being alive."

"Well, I think *you're* the sexiest human being alive," Ran whispers as I look up and find the sensual glimmer of his eyes looking down at me. It's like being cast in moonlight, in starlight, in all the glamorous magic that lights up the night. "But … shit, I don't know."

He fingers the rope in his hand, trailing one end up the inside of my arm. The sensation makes me shiver.

"I feel like I'm out of control," he says softly, the words swirling my hair around as he speaks with his lips pressed to my scalp. "I want to get back in control."

"Do whatever you want to me," I tell him and feel his

body stiffen around mine. I mean, it was already stiff in the place that counts, but Ransom's muscles get taut, pulled like a bowstring. "I trust you, Ran."

I close my eyes as he lifts a hand up and curls his fingers gently around the front of my throat, pulling me back against him so he can lean forward and kiss my mouth with hot wanton lips. I let my body go pliant in Ransom's strong arms as he drags one of his big hands over my breast, kneading the tender mound with a measure of controlled strength that gets my heart pumping violently inside my chest.

"You might not believe this," Ransom whispers, his voice making me swallow hard against a lump of tears. There's just something so raw about him, about the way he speaks low and quiet, like he's afraid if he shouts, he'll start screaming and never stop. That raw emotionality rakes over me, drags me across the hot coals of my own past, my own detritus of a backstory. "But this is all because of you, the fact that Paxton is even speaking to me like I'm a human being half the time."

"What have I done?" I ask and then gasp as he drops his calloused hand under the shirt-dress and pulls it up and over my head, exposing my lacy black bra, my ruined crotchless panties. I was planning on changing them after the show, but I got swept up in the excitement of the concert and forgot all about it.

"That's the thing, doll face. You haven't really *done* anything. It's just you, your presence. You have this … way of being open, of having a conversation with reality that isn't one-sided. You're cracking all our shells with your fresh hurt, baby."

"I'm sorry," I whisper but Ransom shushes me, undoing the clasp on my bra, letting my breasts tumble free into the hazy red darkness of the Bat Cave.

"No, don't be. It's better to live wet and bleeding, wearing your hurt like a badge of pride than it is to live numb and empty, inside a shell separate from the world."

Ran clutches me to him, slips his hand down the front of my belly and into my panties, teasing me with his hand, making me writhe. The rough feel of his scars against my back send goose bumps shivering down my spine as I dig the thin black heels of my shoes into the sheets and arch into his touch.

A second later, the door opens and Michael's standing there, panting.

"Are you okay?" I ask, my own body trembling as Ransom dips his fingers inside of me and I gasp. He doesn't stop for Michael's benefit, fucking me slow and sensual and easy, as languid and luxurious as the sound of his voice, his scent.

"I don't know how to do this," Michael admits, slipping inside, leaning against the wall in that small, tight space at the end of the bed, watching us with eyes that would put Elizabeth Taylor to shame. She may have been famous for having purple eyes, but Michael's … they're the color of the irises in my mother's garden, vibrant and rich and saturated. "Stand out there and just …"

"Sit down," Ransom says, his voice gentle but firm. He's not like Paxton in that he needs to be in charge all the time, but right now … this is what he wants. "Watch me fuck her," he whispers against my ear, his breath hot, making me bite my lip at the sensation of it curling around my ear.

Michael watches me for a long moment, putting his hands on his hips and taking a deep breath. This is not easy for him, I can see that. He's going to have to do a lot of adjusting if he wants to make this work.

"Fuck," he whispers, but he tears his shirt over his head and tosses it aside, kicking off his shoes, socks, and pants and joining us in nothing but a pair of black boxer briefs. The slick material does nothing to hide the generous bulge beneath it. "I must be losing my damn mind."

"Minds can get complicated," I say and make a funny little chirp of a gasp, blushing at the sound. Ransom's hands are … well, they're magic. All that time fingering his bass has taught him how to tease the most intimate parts of a woman and make her sing. "Sometimes it's a good thing to lose one."

My eyelids droop as Ran draws me easily into an orgasm, this one the color of starlight on a forest floor, dappled and patterned, bright in some places and dark in others. That's us right now, a gentle mess, but a beautiful one.

"Lay on your side, darling," Ransom tells me, glancing up briefly to meet Michael's eyes. He's leaning against a mountain of pillows propped in front of the headboard, chest rising and falling with rapid, panting breaths. It almost looks like the firebird tattooed on his chest is flying.

"I've never done anything like this before," I say, and it's not a line. It's true. I've never been tied up during sex. Half of me is terrified. But the other half? That part's *ecstatic.*

"I've got you, wonderful," he breathes and I feel my mouth curve into a smile. Wonderful. Now *that* is a cute pet name.

I do as Ransom asked, facing Michael, watching him watching me.

My breath hitches as Ran curls his fingers under my panties and drags them down my legs and off, throwing them to the floor. He takes the length of rope in his hand and unravels it.

"I'm not an expert or anything," he prefaces, his own lips curving into a small smile as I glance back at him, once again struck by the color of his eyes. They're not *just* brown. They're as pretty as Pax's grey ones, Muse's hazel ones, Cope's turquoise and Michael's purple. They're rich and deep, like there's an old soul buried inside that young body of his. "I just like the idea of losing control … of taking it. If you get uncomfortable with anything, you just let me know, sweetheart."

"Okay," I whisper back, unable to raise my voice any higher when he manages to sound so delicious at such a low volume. My heart flutters like a wild butterfly, seeking out nectar from all the blooming flowers of spring. Only … my flowers are five rock-hard beautiful musicians with pasts as dark or darker than my own.

One day, our storms would clear and we'd all stand together staring up at the seamless blue of a cloudless sky, rays of golden sunshine warming our collective faces. One day … but today, there's thunder and lightning outside, Pax kissed Ransom again, and I'm about to be tied up.

I can't say I'm unhappy in this particular storm. At least the driving rain and the grey clouds of today are blocking out the pain of last week, hiding my father's death from me for a few more precious days. Once we get to New York, I won't be able to close my eyes any longer. I'll have to open them wide and see it all, let it really sink in, accept that things will never be the same again.

But not right now, not right here.

I put my hands in a prayer position and lay my head atop them, looking at Michael's shuttered gaze and parted lips. He looks so tense, almost battle ready. Our gazes meet, my body naked but for my heels, my charm bracelet … and the pair of necklaces that he gave me. I wonder if I'll ever take them off or if they'll become as much a part of my skin as the bracelet my mother once wore.

Ransom takes my leg in his hands, sliding his palms down the long sweaty surface, making my lids flutter and my breathing ache. That's a strange thought, an aching breath. But that's exactly what it is. My lungs are so tight, filled with too much emotion to leave room for oxygen. Each inhale makes my body tremble, my throat constrict.

Ransom takes the silky red rope and starts to wrap it around my leg in a complicated pattern, crisscrossing it against my pale skin, the splash of bright color almost startling. He ties me up like a spider weaving a web, starting at the crease between my hip and thigh and working his way down to my toes. He points them like a ballerina's and then weaves the magic of his rope to keep them that way.

My body thrills at the different sensations—the heat of his breath, the rough graze of fingertips, the gentle kiss of satiny rope.

I keep my eyes closed through most of it, too overwhelmed by texture and mixed stimuli to look at Michael. When I finally do open them, I'm glad I didn't do it sooner. The sight of that man with his sleeves of jewel toned tattoos, his vibrant chest piece, with his hand inside his boxer briefs, stroking and caressing the hidden length of his shaft … it almost sends me over the edge.

I let out a gasp as my eyes flick up to Ransom and find him threading the end of the rope through a small silver ring in the ceiling, one I hadn't noticed before. He uses a thick knot to tie my foot to it, suspending my leg in the air, the other lying flat on the bed, my foot between Ransom's knees.

The bedroom door opens again, spilling warm air into the room. The current curls around my naked flesh, teasing the slick swollen heat of my cunt. It's as bare and exposed as it could possibly get, almost put on display. I like that, knowing that the boys are getting a good look at the center of my sensual power. I take pride in the wetness of my core, the scorching heat of my desire. I think … I was never *ashamed* of it before, but I didn't know how to take ownership of it.

I feel like I'm taking ownership of it now.

"Come in," I tell the surprised face at the door. It's Derek, standing there with his mouth slightly ajar, his shirt missing (as usual), an apple clutched in his left hand. "And get Copeland."

"You want an audience, honey?" Ransom asks, kissing the naked spaces of flesh between the ropes, making me squirm.

"And Paxton. Get Pax, too," I tell Muse and feel Ran stiffen up a little.

"Yeah, yeah, gotcha," Muse says, touching the slicked curve of his silver-black mohawk with a shaking hand. "Fuck."

He turns quickly and disappears down the hall as I feel the bed moving, Ransom sliding around behind me. He opens another drawer and takes out a new length of red rope. I start to move, to glance back at him, but he gently pushes me back into the bed with a hand on my shoulder.

Being topped by Ransom Riggs … it's soothing, safe, but also … I can taste the dark twisted perfume of his grief and anger in the air. It adds this slight edge to the satin of his touch, this enigmatic mystery to the feel of his fingertip dragging down my spine.

"Stay right where you are," he tells me, but his hands are trembling now. Because of Pax? It must be. It has to be.

I keep looking at Michael Luxe, my lips inadvertently whispering his name, teasing the air with the sweet sound of it. Michael Luxe. Luxe, Luxe, Luxe. That's how he looks right now: luxe. Expensive … no, no *priceless.* A rough and unpolished jewel covered in tattoos and dark razored hair that hits at the shoulders, arm muscles decorated with esoteric intricacies.

As I stare at him, Ransom reaches over me and tugs my praying hands out from under my head, wrapping them up in knots that tie me up, but feel like one big long hug. He binds my palms together, my wrists, all the way down to the elbows and then lets me lay my head back on them.

Michael's shoving his underwear off now, throwing the bunched fabric to the floor. The big thick length of his cock is held in a tight grip as he grits his teeth and stares at Ransom and me with that fucking intensity of his, that vibrant interactive gaze that demands attention.

"Orders dispensed and received," Muse says, slipping back into the room and crawling up on the bed, lying on his side in front of Michael so that we're at eye level. "Who *are* you?" he asks, reaching out to lay a palm on the side of my face. "That you have the power to do this to me?"

"It was Ransom that did this," I whisper, but Muse just leans forward and kisses me, that strange break in his expression still intriguing me, begging me to dig deeper, but right now, I can do nothing but surrender to the warmth and touch of my mates.

My wildcat purrs her assent.

Muse takes my mouth apart with his tongue, kisses me so deep and long that I hardly notice Ransom straddling my left leg, positioning the hard head of his shaft to the aching bareness of my opening. He drives into me and I scream—purely in pleasure, of course—right against Muse's lips, making him groan and dig his fingertips into my face.

My eyes close, my body trying to acclimate to such wildly violent pleasure. It tears through me the same way Muse's kiss just took over my mouth, making me tremble wildly, groan and arch and wiggle.

Vaguely, I recognize movement behind me, the soft gentle touch of a boyfriend's sweet hands.

That's Copeland, has to be.

He trails kisses across my shoulders, up the back of my neck to my hairline. He touches me reverently, respectfully, as if being in here with me is some sort of privilege. Ransom though … Ransom holds my hip with one hand, his other curled around my bound leg, and he just fucks hard and fast and desperate, burying himself in me with long agonizing thrusts.

I can feel him bumping the end of me, almost too long with my legs spread wide like this.

Almost.

I feel every emotion that he's feeling in his thrusts, all of that fucked-up strangeness with Paxton, the years of fighting, the anger, the rage, the unfairness of it all.

"It's a bloody party in here, isn't it?"

The words come from behind me, next to Ransom, and his thrusts slow, still, my aching cunt gripping him, rippling in pleasure.

Muse and I break our kiss briefly to glance back at the two men.

They're looking at each other now, Ransom's face hard, that shield up and in place, firmly held against whatever cruelty Paxton might throw his way. But the man with the cold, cruel gaze says nothing. Instead, he shrugs out of his navy suit jacket and tosses it on the floor, takes his tie off and leaves it hanging around his neck as he unbuttons his white shirt with terrifying slowness.

"Give me something that vibrates, Derek," he says, his British accent thick and intoxicating to my GenAm ears, the dulcet tones making me quiver with desire. As if I wasn't feeling enough of that, like there's a natural disaster happening inside my body, too many storms colliding into one.

Muse pulls away from me and sits up, digging around in the drawers and coming up with a curved blue silicone cock with a grey and yellow knob on the end. He twists it experimentally and its ridged length starts to vibrate.

"Will this do?"

He hands it over to Pax as Copeland cups my ass with his longer fingers, kneads the flesh and scoots close to me, pressing his erection tight against the excruciating rawness of my body.

Paxton Charles Blackwell, the English prick with the beautiful storm grey eyes, he takes the cock and slips it between his lips, still vibrating. When he pulls it out, he looks at Ransom and then scoots forward a few inches, putting their bodies ridiculously close together.

The sight of them side by side like that makes my breath catch sharply, almost painfully.

The two men lock eyes as Pax teases my clit with the slick vibrating toy, making me buck against Ransom, making him grit his teeth as my body pleasures his in its ecstasy.

"What are you doing, Pax?" Ran asks, but I'm pretty sure he's asking about more than just this moment.

Paxton ignores him, Cope going still behind me, Michael freezing with his fingers wrapped around his shaft, Muse staring at the two of them with a curious expression.

Pax touches the tightness of my opening with the toy, still looking at Ransom, and then slowly, slowly, slowly, he eases it into me.

I gasp as my body stretches to accommodate so much … almost too much.

"You okay, baby doll?" Ransom asks, breaking Pax's intense stare to look down at me. His body shakes and trembles as the vibrations course through me, rocket into him. "You …"

He can't even get the words out, and neither can I. I melt into the heavy feeling of fullness, that stretched tight and filled up in all the right ways sensation. It makes me surrender completely, go liquid on that bed amongst all those boys.

Paxton fucks Ransom and me both with the vibrator, taking that control that Ran wanted so badly and wrestling it back.

My second orgasm that night is like the sound of the thunder outside the bus, an all-consuming, earthshaking noise that manifests physically, rocking the windows, breaking the silence of the early morning with a wild growl.

Sweat pours down my body, but I've become this insatiable thing, this vessel of emotions and wants and needs. My grief is a far away ship, sailing in the distance, silhouetted against a pregnant moon, but irrelevant at this point and time.

I can't think about anything but my boys.

Mine.

All five of them.

Paxton switches off the vibe and withdraws it, pushing Ransom aside.

They trade places, Pax freeing his shaft from his slacks, looking down at me with that whiplike smirk cutting into his face. He slips his body into mine, still staring at me. He doesn't break that gaze until Ransom makes him do it, turning Pax's face with fingers under the chin.

They stare at each other and then … they kiss again. Their mouths move with long, slow movements, tongues tangling, Pax's hands tightening on my hips as he drives into me, my leg still wrapped in red silk rope and hooked to the low ceiling of the Bat Cave.

"Oh, Cutie," Muse says, drawing my attention back to him, kissing me again before he moves to my breasts, sucking and licking the nipples with all the slow sensuality that's missing from the wild thrusting between my thighs.

Michael is cursing, watching with barely restrained need while behind me, I can feel Cope pushing his pants down, freeing his own shaft.

Suddenly, I wish my hands weren't bound, that I could touch and stroke and kiss them all.

Instead, I let my eyes linger on Ransom and Paxton, on Pax's cruel fingers taking hold of Ran's shaft, stroking and working him with easy confidence, making him hard again, as if he hadn't already come inside of me.

I keep watching them as I listen to Cope's heavy breathing behind me, Michael's rapid panting to my left, Muse's lips suckling my nipples.

They don't look like they're just kissing for me this time. They almost look like … lovers?

I cry out as Pax drives into me with force, our bodies colliding as he pulls away from Ransom's lips. He stays buried deep inside of me and then … slides out, leaving me gasping and trembling.

"What the fuck is going on?" Ran asks, fisting a hand in his own hair and closing his eyes for a moment. "Paxton …"

Pax gets up and buttons his slacks, running away just like he did that first night—*exactly* the same way.

"Fuck this," Ran says, reaching up and rapidly untying my leg from the hook in the ceiling. He moves up between me and Muse, tearing the bindings from my arms and freeing me. He pauses briefly to lay a hot kiss against my mouth, one that tastes like bourbon and cigarettes. Like Paxton Blackwell. "Are you okay if … ?"

"Go," I say, waving him away and watching as he shrugs his jeans on and disappears down the hall, making sure to close the Bat Cave door behind him.

I sit up, finally getting a chance to look down at Cope, shirtless and confused as hell behind me.

"What the … fuck are they doing?" he whispers, but I don't have an answer to that.

What I do have are three men with thick, aching shafts and a body that refuses to quit, even after two orgasms.

"Give them a minute," I say, my leg still encased in a red web of rope, my nipples hard, almost painful, slick from Muse's tongue. "Just … give them some time."

I sit up and straddle Derek, loving the easygoing smile he gives me. *I'm getting everything I want right now,* that look tells me. *Everything.* I start to wonder then if his past really matters, if I even need to know it. Clearly, it's not something he wants to talk about. And right now, he looks so … peaceful. Well, *horny* and peaceful.

"God, you're like a silver screen goddess," he tells me as I straddle his shaft and slip down it with my silken cunt. The moan that escapes his mouth is swallowed by my own as Cope finds his way over to us, kissing along the back of my neck again.

"Fuck me like I'm your girlfriend," I whisper and he makes this … this sound that's half pain, half ecstasy.

"Lilith," Cope says, the siren song of his voice calling to my heart, soothing it. I feel that urge again, that breaking up of all my thoughts into words that seem to belong to him, to his comforting touch, gentle hands. He uses one of those gentle hands to tease my ass, slipping a few fingers inside to make sure I'm ready.

Michael … he needs some direction.

I hold my hand out to him and he stares at it a long moment before reaching out to take it.

He's so fucking sexy right now, nude and beautiful and slicked with sweat. I kiss him at the same moment Cope switches his fingers out for his cock, filling me up and sharing my body with Derek. I let him guide our movements since he's so good at it, good at taking control without being aggressive or dominant or dickish (like Pax).

My palms tease Michael's hard nipples, warm him up before I drop one down and take control of his shaft. I stroke him with my fist, slipping my palm over the liquid pre-cum slicking up the end of his cock. He thrusts into my grip, those same ragged bestial moans falling from his lips. I work him into such a frenzy that he ends up grabbing my hair and pushing my face down to his shaft.

I'm more than happy to take him between my tender lips, suck and kiss and caress him while my body rides wave after wave of pleasure.

Muse's confident touch, Copeland's loving warmth, Michael's violent need.

I let it all sweep around me until my body breaks into pieces again.

My third orgasm that night tastes as fresh as the rain pounding the metal walls of the bus, wild and clean, washing over me, drenching me with a deep-seated feeling of satisfaction.

And love.

Lots and lots of hot sweaty bodies, hands, cocks … and emotion.

The six of us … we had that shit in *spades.*

"What the fuck, Paxton?" I ask, letting the storm slam the bus door closed behind me.

He tries to leave me behind, heading for one of the staff trailers, but I stop him with a firm grip on his arm, making him turn and face me.

Rain lashes my hot, sweaty skin, tearing across my bare chest, soaking my hair and dragging errant strands into my face. I really miss my hoodie right fucking now.

Pax turns to look at me, wrenching his arm from my grip, his eyes narrowed, his blonde hair dark with rainwater.

"Leave me the hell alone, Ransom," he snarls, letting cold, cruel anger lace his words, mouth tight, jaw clenched.

"Why should I? I've been leaving you alone for four years and it hasn't done shit, sweetheart. No, sorry, man, but I'm fucking finished with that crap. Let's do this, here and now. If you need to break my wrist again, so be it."

I stare at him, standing in the middle of a rainstorm, lightning cracking the sky in half, lighting up the night. All around us, the parking lot is empty but for the sounds and sights of the storm, the faint whir of generators. It's too loud out here for me to whisper, so I end up screaming and it feels kind of … I don't know, liberating or something.

In a few hours, the rumbling engines of the buses, the staff RVs, and the trucks towing trailers will roar to life and we'll be off to Pittsburgh for our next show. But for now, it's just me and Pax, like it was when we were kids, trolling the Seattle underground, trying to be cool together, to find our way in the world.

"There must be *something* you want to say to me, after all that," I shout, my voice too loud, still hard to hear with the wind whipping through the parking lot. I'm standing barefoot in a half inch of cold water, shaking, staring at the carved lines of Pax's face, the tattoos on his neck, chest, hands. His white button-up is plastered to his skin, completely see-through. But at least *he* still has his shoes on. "I mean, where the hell are you even going right now? Why did you leave like that if there's nothing going on?"

He shoves me hard in the chest with both palms and I stumble back, sweeping wet hair off my forehead, my breath coming in rapid-fire pants. I'm … Jesus, I'm all twisted up inside. That, and my body is stretched taut, my cock a diamond rod inside my jeans, my nipples hard enough to cut. Because of Lilith, obviously, and … Pax? Am I into Paxton or something?

God, I don't know. I'm so confused right now. But I can't do anything about it, can't figure this out unless Pax talks to me.

"Go ahead, honey. Hit me again if that's what it takes."

"What is your bloody problem?" he screams, some of that polished perfection of his cracking like the night sky. "Are you a glutton for punishment or something? Can't I have a damn minute to myself?"

"Not after what just happened in there … at the museum. Pax, you kissed me and it wasn't for Lilith. Are you … dude, are you into me?"

"You think I'm gay for you?" he asks with a mean laugh, sliding a smoke from his pocket and then staring at the wet soggy length of it between his fingers. He tosses it to the ground with a snarl. "Please. Get over yourself, Riggs."

"No, I know you're not gay—not that it would matter to me if you were. But I've seen you with Lilith. Shit, I've seen you with a hundred different girls, honey. That's not what I'm saying."

Paxton shoves his tattooed hands in his pockets and drops his head for a moment, closing his grey eyes against the storm. He looks about *this* fucking close to having a complete breakdown. But hell if he's not overdue for one. Paxton spends all his time making sure his suits are pressed and perfect, his hair slicked back, his expressions like ice sculptures, just caricatures of real human emotions.

But that's not all he is. I've known him for too long to believe that he's just some cruel, heartless asshole. Sorry, but I'm not buying what he's selling.

"Then what *are* you saying, Ransom? Tell me." He lifts his head and looks up at me, beads of moisture catching on his lower lip. I stare at his mouth, still breathing hard, and then lift my eyes to his gaze. If it wasn't pouring rain out, I might think he was crying. Shit, maybe he is?

"I miss her, too," I tell him, the trembling in my body from more than just the cold. "Chloe."

"I don't miss Chloe," Paxton snarls, lifting his chin in cold defiance of my statement. "Fuck that bitch. She deserved what she got for what she did to Harper."

"Just because she made a mistake in the end, that doesn't change the person she was or the way you felt about her. I miss her every goddamn day. Every day. You *know* that if

I'd had any idea of what would happen that night, I'd have packed up and left for good, never spoken to her again. I didn't go over there to fight with you."

"Don't you think I know that?!" Pax screams back at me. "There, I said it. I said it. It was an *accident.* That doesn't make Harper any less dead, now does it?"

"It doesn't make you miss Chloe any less either," I whisper and Paxton just … drops to his knees. He falls to the pavement in front of me and sits there, breathing hard, staring at nothing. I follow him down, squatting in front of him, watching the expression on his face shift from anger to pain to regret.

"Bleeding hell," he says, closing his eyes and running his palm over his face. "Fucking bollocking cocksucking bloody hell. This is all that *girl's* fault, that weeping, blushing redhead …"

"Maybe," I say, my voice back to the low, soft tones I adopted after my mother's death. "But, sweetie, you *need* to stop hiding from your emotions. You need to stop fucking blaming me for everything that's gone wrong in the last four years."

"Your mother …" Paxton starts, still not looking at me. He knew my mom well, spent a lot of time at my house over the years. And then Chloe and Harper, Kortney, all that stuff happened, and he didn't see her even once the last three years of her life. I imagine he regrets that now. I know I do. "I should've been there. You needed me, and I left you to rot. How does a person get over something like that?"

He looks up at me, the rain dragging his blonde hair into his face. In his suits with his cigarettes and his cocky swagger, he always comes across as older, put together, sophisticated. Right now, Paxton Blackwell looks like a lost and damaged kid.

"Why don't you let me worry about that part?" I ask, curling my fingers around my knees, waiting patiently. I've got heaps of that shit, patience. "Stop wondering what I might do or how I might handle things and just … god, just *forgive* me, Pax, so we can move on."

"There's nothing to forgive you for," he says, sliding his hands down his face and dropping them into his wet lap. "Nothing. I'm the one that needs to be fucking forgiven, Ran."

"Then I forgive you," I say and Pax scowls at me.

"Can't you for one goddamn second just get angry with me?" he snaps, but I don't react. What's the point in that? It gets me nowhere with him and at this point, I'm done fighting. There are so many awful people in this world, so many awful things, why on earth would I waste my energy on somebody that I actually give two shits about? I just won't do it anymore.

"No, I won't."

"Fuck you, Ransom."

"Is that what you want to do?" I ask. "Because you *were* just stroking my cock."

Paxton shoves to his feet and I rise up with him. But now, he won't even look at me.

After a few seconds of standing comatose in the rain, he turns like he's going to walk away again and I grab him, spin him back to me … and kiss him.

And ah, it's a little weird. It is, I won't lie. Like I told Lilith, I don't think I'm gay or even really bisexual, but … I don't know. Fuck it. Does it matter *what* label I slap on this? Will it change anything?

Paxton stiffens up, but I don't let him pull away, fisting

my hands in his soggy button-up, kissing him long and hard and deep until he finally fucking lets go. His hands come up, tattooed fingers curling around my forearms. My tongue slides into his mouth, slicking against his when he tries to fight back, take over. But like I said, I want to be in control of this tonight. I need to, to make sense of everything.

I turn us both slowly until his back is to the wall of our bus, and then I slam Paxton into it, pressing my body against his. I can feel his cock, just as stiff and desperate as my own. Still kissing me, I open his slacks and take his shaft into my hand. It's warm, wet from the rain, and for a second there I almost panic because I don't know what to do with this shit … But I'm a guy, too, so I do what I'd do to myself, gripping him with firm fingers, sliding my fist slowly along his length.

Our kissing amps up, mouths fighting for control, waves of fire sweeping over me, making me forget for a little while that this is all new to me, that Pax and I have been sworn enemies for years, that I'm standing outside in a thunderstorm. I'm just a man kissing somebody that I've loved for a long time. I don't know that the love I felt for him was ever like this before, but … with Lilith and this arrangement of ours, maybe this is something that could actually work?

Paxton undoes the button and zipper on my jeans, takes my cock into his hand like he did on the bus. He strokes me with fiendish fingers, his touch burning straight through me, lines of fire shooting from my dick and straight up through my chest.

I gasp and pull away for a second, still panting, still trembling.

"Fuck," I say, but Paxton just leans his head back against

the metal wall of the bus and closes his eyes. I push his hand away and slick my own fingers through my hair. *I'm going fucking crazy here,* I think, but before I can stop myself, I do what I'd do if it were Lilith wet and shaking out here with me.

Kneeling down, I curl my fingers back around Paxton's shaft and slip him into my mouth the way I did that dildo I used on Lilith, my tongue swirling around the head of his cock like she did for me that same morning. I've barely had a chance to get used to the idea of Paxton's fingers in my hair, the hot hard thickness of his shaft between my lips, when the door to the bus opens and Lilith appears.

She's slipped a short white nightgown on, but as soon as the rain hits it, it turns the whole thing transparent, the fabric clinging to her curves in a way that's criminal. *Jesus.* I slide Paxton's dick from my mouth, breathing hot against the tip as he bucks his hips toward my face with wanton need.

"Are you guys okay?" she calls out, but there's a slight smile in her voice that says she already knows the answer to that question. I wait until she walks over to us, bare feet splashing in the water that covers the parking lot like a lake.

"I have no idea what I'm doing, gorgeous," I tell her, those ripe lips of hers catching the rain when she smiles at me.

"Oh, Ransom," she says, and then she's kissing Pax, this long, deep tonguing that draws my attention, makes my heart hammer in my chest. When she pulls away, she kneels down next to me, that purple-red hair of hers darkening to a bloodred burgundy in the rain. Without speaking, she looks me in the face with her emerald green eyes and curls her fingers around my own where they're wrapped around the base of Paxton's dick.

She leans in, mouth parting, and kisses the head of his cock, reaching out and taking hold of my hair, pulling me forward to join her. We touch mouths, our tongues sliding out to tease his skin as we go through all the motions of kissing each other with him in between us. Even with the rain and the thunder, I can hear the deep, almost guttural sounds of pleasure escaping Pax's lips.

It doesn't take long to push him to the edge, one of his hands fisted in my hair, the other in Lilith's.

"He's going to finish if we don't stop …" she whispers to me, our eyes still locked as we pause for a moment. "I'd rather he finished in me," she says, "with you."

My throat gets tight and I swear, *I* almost finish in my pants.

Lilith and I both stand up. She takes Pax's and my hands in her small, warm ones and tugs us back to the bus and up the steps. The living room is empty, so the others must be in the Bat Cave.

"Fucking storm," Pax snaps, tearing off his wet shirt, kicking off his shoes, peeling off his socks. "I have half a mind to go out there and rip Mother Nature a new one."

"Don't change the subject," Lilith says, peeling her wet nightie over her head and tossing the soggy fabric into a heap on the floor. Naked and pale and wet, she looks like some sort of primeval witch, some ancient feminine goddess that could shove her hand into my chest and tear out my beating heart while still looking ethereally beautiful.

That, and I'd probably smile as I bled to death in front of her.

I shed my wet jeans by the door and wait as Lilith drags Pax to the couch, pushing him down on the sofa and straddling his lap. Normally, he's fucking obsessed with being in charge of everything. Right now, he looks completely broken and resigned to whatever fate Lilith and I want to assign him, his head pillowed against the couch arm, legs stretched out along the length of the cushions.

I don't have to ask what she wants to do as she straddles him, climbing up to join them both on the wet leather surface of the sofa. I take my place behind Lilith as she slides the scalding pink heat of her pussy down Paxton's shaft.

"Miss Lily," he whispers, his voice as ethereal as wet smoke, his hands lifting to cup her breasts. I suck in a deep breath of my own as I take Lilith by the hips and position the already slick length of my cock against her ass. When I enter her, I can hear Paxton sucking in a sharp breath, already prepared to crash through the wall of pleasure and collapse on the other side.

"I got you," I whisper as I start to move—and I'm not just talking to Lil.

Slowly, carefully, I fuck them both with long, deep thrusts, feeling Pax's shaft pressing against the soft tissue of Lilith's body, teasing my own with its hardness. My wet hands stay on her hips, but my eyes … they find Paxton's grey stare and hold there.

Shit, tomorrow … is going to be one *hell* of a morning after.

I move faster, encouraged by the rocking motion of Lilith's hips, bringing Pax to orgasm relatively quickly, the sharp sounds escaping his mouth completely new and different, like maybe something really *has* changed in him tonight.

I'm fucking *praying* for it.

"Oh, baby," I whisper as Lilith casts a glance over her shoulder, red hair spilling across the fine line of freckles across her shoulders, covering up the small sunburn on her neck. “Oh, god, honey.”

My head drops back as the orgasm hits me, tearing through my body like a tornado. It rips me to pieces, leaving me this panting, awful mess.

“That orgasm …” Lilith says, drawing my head back up, opening my eyes. “That one felt … like the sun peeking through the clouds.”

I have no idea what she means by that, but by the time we arrange ourselves into some sort of semi-comfortable pile on the sofa, I'm already asleep and too far gone to think much about it.

"Dude, it's time to get up."

A hand gently slaps the side of my face and I groan, lifting my head to find Muse staring at me through the thick lenses of his glasses, a stupid silly half-smile on his face. His silver-black mohawk is already styled up into spikes on the top of his head, a shiny black cuff wrapped around his ear, leather bracelets lining his arms.

"It's time to get ready," he says as he stares at my sleep dazed face. "Up and at 'em."

Blinking, I sit up and realize that I'm completely entangled with Lilith and Paxton, my muscles aching from sleeping in such a strange position. Pax is still on his back, Lil between his legs, her head pillowed on his stomach. I was basically draped on top of the both of them, still naked but covered in the black afghan we usually keep folded over the back of the sofa.

"Jesus," I say, popping a knee up and leaning my elbow on it as I cradle my head in my hand. I feel like a have a hangover which is fucking impossible since I barely drank last night. I had maybe two weird cocktails at the sushi place and that was it. Maybe it's an emotional hangover or something?

Lilith groans and stretches, her green eyes fluttering open and coming to rest immediately on mine.

A thousand unspoken words pass between us.

"Anyone want some tea?" Muse asks, padding back into the kitchen and taking the whistling teapot off the stove. "Because I've got some killer fucking oolong that is just like, ugh, to *die* for."

Neither of us answers him, but that's okay. He'll probably make us all cups anyway.

"Are you okay?" Lilith asks quietly, Paxton breathing slow and deep beneath her. I'm pretty sure he's still asleep.

"I'm fine, sweetie," I say as I rub a hand over my face and go to throw up my hood … only I can't because I'm naked.

"Here."

Michael tosses a black zip-up hoodie and some sweats in my direction. I glance at him, but I'm having a hard time reading the expression on his face. I feel bad; there's been a lot of tension between us since Pax and I started fighting. Yet another shitty outcome from our toxic bullshit. Michael and I have never had a reason to fight with each other except for the fact that he always defends Pax. I never understood that before, but I think I might now.

As tough as he looks, as cocky as he acts, Paxton is hurting deep inside. Maybe Michael's seen him for what he truly is all along? A man as fucked-up and sad as the rest of us.

"Thanks," I say, slipping into the hoodie first, leaving it unzipped but tossing the fabric up over my head. I feel safest like that, better, like I'm hiding cloaked in shadows and memory. Things might be looking up around here, but Lilith isn't an instant cure-all for our problems. I still need my security blanket.

"What happened last night?" Cope asks, also already dressed in a red tank with a white bird silhouette on the front, his hair styled into a ridge, eyeliner around his turquoise eyes.

"It's complicated," I start and then catch Lilith's gaze again as she sits up and scoots closer to me. "And I think Pax and I … well, we kissed and I sucked his dick."

"You … fucking *what?!*" Michael asks, blinking down at us like he thinks I've finally lost my goddamn mind. "What the … shit …"

"Oh, don't get your knickers in a twist, Mikey," Pax mumbles, turning on his side, still wearing his unzipped slacks. He tucks his junk away and buttons them up, grey eyes flicking up to look at Michael. "If you're jealous, we can always work something out."

"Are you two, like … did you make up?" he asks, shaking his head like he can't quite believe what he just heard. I can't either, come to think about it. Me and Pax. Me and Pax … dating? Shit, I don't know. Weren't we already dating since we're both with Lilith? I mean, group sex—even if it's completely focused on our girl—does require a certain level of intimacy.

Paxton doesn't respond to Michael, dragging himself into a sitting position and looking over at Lilith, wrapped in the black blanket, the darkness of the fabric stark against the whiteness of her skin.

He stares at her for a second and then he looks at me.

"We talked," he says, his voice neutral, hard to read.

"What'd you talk about?" Muse asks, overreaching as usual. But at least he brings us cups of tea. The first two he hands over to me and Lilith, but I refuse mine with a palm up and he gives it to Pax instead.

"What the hell do you think we talked about?" Pax drawls, draping his tattooed body back against the couch arm, sipping carefully from the steaming black cup in his hands. "Harper, Chloe, Kortney."

"And somehow that ended with Ransom sucking your dick?" Michael asks, pinching the bridge of his nose and sighing. "Sorry if I don't quite understand the transition."

"I think we might be into each other, hon," I say quietly, my voice hoarse from screaming in the storm last night. I accept the next cup of tea that Muse brings over and clutch it in sweatshirt covered hands, my sleeves pulled low.

"You *think*?" Michael asks, a fucking bulldog as usual. Once he latches onto something, he just fucking refuses to let go. "What the hell does that mean? You two wanted to murder each other yesterday and now you're, like, boyfriends or something?"

"Does it really matter?" Lilith asks, closing her eyes and savoring her drink in a way that makes me want to kiss the fragrant heat of tea from her lips. "I said you guys could do whatever you wanted with each other."

I don't think any of us misses the smile that steals across her mouth.

"Hey, if to *kiss and make up* you two need to literally kiss—and suck each other off—then I am down for it. Congratulations," Muse says, pushing his glasses up with two fingers and popping into the swivel chair across from me. He plays with the string of his tea bag, bobbing it up and down in his cup. "It's about time we worked on the male intimacy issues on this bus. So, are you guys good then?"

He flicks his eyes up to the three of us sitting on the couch, the color caught somewhere between a foggy morning and a sunny afternoon.

"You'll have to let Pax answer that one," I say as I look back at him and find him staring at me again, mouth pursed, inked fingers stiff as they curl around his mug. "I've decided to let it all go. All of it. I've forgiven him, *and* I've apologized. As far as I'm concerned, all of that shit is water under the bridge."

"What do you think, dolly bird?" Pax asks, his attention moving to Lilith, naked and silent in between us.

Michael stays standing at the edge of the living room, but Cope gets himself a cup of coffee and joins us, sitting in the second swivel chair.

"I can't answer that for you, Paxton. It's up to you to decide—do you give your relationship with Ransom a second chance? Only you can decide to let go of the blame and hate. But I promise if you do, you'll feel a hell of a lot better."

"Trust me," I tell him, my voice quivering just a little, my hands shaking slightly. "Even if you don't do it for me, let the hate go. If you let it fester inside of you, it literally eats your soul from the inside out."

Lilith lays a hand on the knee of my sweats and the trembling subsides, just like that.

See, I fucking told you I wanted to marry this girl. There was a reason that I wanted her from the first instant I laid eyes on her. My darkness likes her darkness, but together, it's almost like they cancel each other out. When she touches me, all I can see is light.

"I *am* doing this for you," Paxton says, sitting up, nestling his cup in his lap and locking eyes with me. "You think I just snog any random bloke?" He drapes one arm over his knee and continues to meet my gaze, drinking his tea with a slow, practiced motion that honestly sort of scares the shit out of me. There's nothing regretful or angry in that expression of his. It's all steely determination and torrid resolution.

Fuck. What have I gotten myself into?

But hell if I don't miss Pax, if I haven't been missing him for four years. If he thinks his lack of sympathy during my mother's passing made me miss him less, he's dead wrong. No, losing her only showed me how fucking important it is to keep the people you love close, cherished.

"You think I've *ever* sucked anyone's dick before?" I retort, and Michael sighs from beside me.

"Just don't let this get out of control. Remember: the three of us"—he gestures to Cope, Muse, and himself—"saw the fucked-up spiral of bullshit you put yourselves through when you were *just* friends and had a falling-out. If you're going to do this, make sure you're goddamn serious about it."

"I'm serious," Pax says, still looking at me, taking a deep breath. "Fucking mad as a box of frogs, but serious."

I smile slightly, the tightness of the scar on my cheek pulling with the motion. With my entire body slathered in reminders of an event I'd rather forget, how could I say no to any small scrap of happiness?

"I'm serious," I say, feeling Lilith's fingers curl around my own.

When I look down, I see she's got one of Paxton's hands, too.

I'm not sure if I've ever felt as complete as I do right then.

I might not be able to heal the scars on my body, but maybe there's a chance for the ones decorating my heart?

"Lilith."

I'm sitting at a small bistro table behind a black metal fence with the other over twenty-ones in the audience, sipping some beer and enjoying my new vantage point from the back of the audience. I've seen almost all of the shows on the Broken Hearts and Twisted Souls Tour, but always from either a balcony, the very front, or backstage.

Right now, I truly feel like I'm part of the audience, the ambience, instead of an insider. It's kind of fun—although I wouldn't give up my connection to the band for anything.

I turn at the sound of my name and find Octavia Warris standing nearby, her tablet and clipboard conspicuously missing from her person. Her hair is in its usual ponytail, her typical uniform of a black t-shirt and jeans still holding strong.

"Yeah?" I ask, listening to the wild shrieks from Tipped by Tyrants' guitars. Their music is much heavier than Beauty in Lies', much angrier. Something about it calls to me though, the angry chant of the lead singer, her beautiful voice transitioning from animalistic growling to the sweet sound of angels in a heartbeat.

"Do you mind if I sit for a moment?"

"Not at all," I say, grabbing the extra cup the waiter handed me when he brought over the pitcher of beer that I ordered. I guess since I was sitting at a table for two, all dressed up, he assumed I was on a date or something. I didn't bother to correct him although if I were on a date … I'd need four more cups to make it right.

"I can only stay a second," she says, but she doesn't have to explain. I get it. The guys are backstage, waiting for their set. As much as I wanted to hang out with them, today's venue afforded me the perfect opportunity to watch the entire performance from start to finish, out in the midst of the audience, just another rock 'n' roll fan out on the town.

Of course, when I think of Pax and Ran getting it on in the rain, I get these crazy butterflies and a ridiculous urge to squeal and run backstage, just to make sure I don't miss anything between them. I think the only thing hotter than watching them kiss each other is seeing them work their way back to the strong friendship they had before. Obviously I wasn't around to see it personally, but it's not something you can miss, not if you spend any significant time with them in the same room.

Octavia takes a seat and surprisingly also takes the beer that I offer her. I pour a big frothy glass of some local lager and wait while she takes a big gulp of it.

"I know I shouldn't drink on the job," she says, on the tail end of a long sigh, her pale brown eyes lifting up to the pink haired woman onstage as she throws her head back and lets out a scream worthy of hell's craziest demons. "But I guess at this point it doesn't matter much, does it?"

"I'm sorry, Octavia," I say, but I'm not sure what else to offer. At this point she hasn't made any effort to make amends for what she did to me. I don't hate her, but I also can't imagine being a champion on her behalf either. "I wish that wasn't the case."

"You won't be glad to be rid of me?" she asks, but not with any real anger in her voice, just a question. I keep my gaze on the show, on the big metal building with the protruding stage. Our Pittsburgh stop is an outdoor amphitheater with room for almost six thousand crazy concertgoers. The excitement perfuming the cool evening air is palpable, almost tangible enough to reach out and touch. I imagine that if I did, it would feel like vibrant heat against my palm, and it would pulse, too, like a heart in motion.

I suck in a sharp breath, thinking of last night, of riding Paxton, of feeling Ransom slide in behind me. Tucked between them both, I could feel their pulses, the rapid hammer of their hearts. They were definitely both *in motion* last night, and I don't just mean physically.

I sip my beer. It's a little bitter, but that's okay. I'm here to taste local flavor. I think this stuff is called *Iron City Beer* from the Pittsburgh Brewing Company. I'm not much of a beer person, but Octavia seems to really like it. She raises her brows during her second sip and then gulps down a third.

"Why would I be glad of that, Octavia? You seemed to have a decent working relationship with the boys. And I feel bad for you, I do. It's obvious you have a lot of passion for your job."

"This is all I've ever wanted to do, work in this industry," she says, her voice strained, almost sad. She finishes off her drink and grabs the pitcher to pour some more.

"You can't have imagined that kicking me off the tour with a lie and insulting me straight to my face would go over well, could you?"

"You've been in love before, haven't you?" she asks, but that question's getting harder and harder to answer. Now that I've spent all this time with Beauty in Lies, I don't think that I actually loved Kevin at all. I think I got comfortable with him, got lazy, became complacent. I don't know if I'd say I was in *love* with all the boys yet, but … I can see myself getting there. I can *feel* myself getting there. And quick.

It's a little scary, I won't lie.

What would you think, Dad? I wonder, the pain of his passing still fresh in my heart. The boys, this tour, those are my bandages, wrapped tight around the bloody mess of my soul, keeping me together. And their pain does make for a pretty brilliant distraction. But I haven't forgotten my daddy, my brave beautiful father who volunteered as a firefighter, who fixed his neighbors' cars for free when they couldn't afford to pay for labor. I miss his deep voice, his unfettered laugh, his big hands holding mine on the way to the pink and yellow building that housed my elementary school.

I decide that as unconventional as my situation is with the guys, that dad would be happy for me as long as I was happy. It's all he ever really wanted for me.

"I have," I reply carefully, because … it feels like a lie to say anything else.

"Then you know what it does to you. It makes you do stupid things. Even if it's not real. Just that false promise is enough to make a person feel desperate." Octavia puts her beer down and rubs her eyes, pausing for a moment to press a button on her headset. "I'll be back in a moment. Give him a VIP pass and a free t-shirt."

She lets go of the headset and opens her pale brown eyes to look at me.

I think of Ransom and Paxton, how shitty their situation

ended up because of love, romance, attraction. Whatever it was that happened between them and Chloe, them and Kortney.

"Some asshole tripped on a cord and is threatening to sue the bands *and* the venue. Clearly he has no case, but sometimes it's best to put fires out when they're still just sparks."

I smile, taking a long drink and letting the slight buzz of alcohol warm me up between sets. Tipped by Tyrants is leaving the stage to raucous applause; Rivers of Concrete will be up next.

"Anyway," Octavia continues, closing her eyes again, taking several deep breaths. "I'm sorry for what I said to you. And frankly," she opens her eyes to look at me, "I'm a little surprised by your reaction. I'm not sure I know anyone else that would've reacted the way you did. So, thank you."

She stands up and then reaches into her pocket, putting a twenty on the table.

"For the drinks," she say, but I'm already trying to hand it back to her. "No, please, just take it. I'm sure the boys paid for this, but it doesn't matter. Give it to Muse or whoever's card is on your tab."

My smile gets a little wider. It is, in fact, Muse's credit card that's on file with the bar.

"Octavia," I say as she starts to walk away, pausing for a second to glance back at me. "I forgive you. Just … next time, try to remember that women need to stick together, okay? We should be helping each other up, not pushing each other down."

She smiles, a little tightly, but at least the expression's there.

"I should get backstage before Paxton or Michael find

something else to make a lawsuit out of." She lifts her hand in farewell and disappears through the crowd, leaving me to order another pitcher of lager and enjoy the concert, one lone girl in the middle of thousands.

I smooth my hands down the front of my short red dress, yet another one of Muse's picks from the Chicago mall, and clap with the audience to welcome Rivers of Concrete to the stage.

Their set is the perfect transition between Tipped by Tyrants' angry music and Beauty in Lies' heartfelt rock. I find myself singing along to songs I wasn't even aware that I knew. And as soon as the last note of their last long plays, I feel it. The crowd's love for my boys is palpable.

That's when I stand up, finish off my drink and dig my way into their midst.

Confetti cannons fire from either side of the stage and even from all the way back here, I'm showered in tiny pink and red hearts. The animated short plays on the white curtain, lifting up to reveal my boys dressed in their concert best.

They open to a horde of admirers with arguably one of the best lines out of all their songs.

"*We fight and we cry and we fuck and we bleed, but it's when we give our hearts away that we find what we need.*"

There's nothing sexier than five sweaty rockstars piling onto one bus, their scents mixing into this toxic confection that heats my entire body from head to toe. Violets, pomegranates, new denim, smoky incense, and the sharpness of expensive cologne. Plus, I know old sweat is gross, but fresh sweat … there are literal pheromones in it that supposedly excite the human libido.

It seems to be working on mine.

"That crowd was electric," I tell the boys, smoothing my hands down the front of the pencil skirt portion of my dress. The top is a built-in corset with real boning, and the fabric is as rich and red as the apple Muse picks up from a small bowl on the counter. "Do you guys feel that when you're up onstage?"

"It's impossible to miss," Cope says with a soft smile, looking at me with his tropical blue eyes, his expression laced with … affection. My heart pitter-patters and I feel myself wetting my lips, anticipating one of those perfect kisses of his. It's interesting how each one of the guys kisses in a completely different way. If they were to blindfold me again and kiss me one by one, I'd have no problem telling them apart. "When someone—when a lot of people—

connect with your art, there's this …" Cope twists the fabric of his red tank in his long fingers and lets his smile soften slightly. "I don't know, undeniable response from deep down, this satisfaction of being understood by other human beings. It's almost indescribable."

"If you ever actually showed us any of your art, then maybe you'd feel it, too?" Paxton says, his accent sweeping against my ear along with the warmth of his breath, making me shiver. I turn and watch him shrugging out of his red suit jacket. Yes, *red* today. I wonder if he was trying to match me or if he just felt bold as fuck after his night with Ransom.

I purse my lips a little and then let out a long breath.

"Are we going out tonight?" I ask, feeling slightly disappointed that we slept through most of our day here. If I'd managed to pry myself out from between Ran's and Pax's naked bodies, I'd have dragged the boys to the Carnegie Museum of Natural History. They have dinosaurs there—*dinosaurs.* I'm a big sucker for fossils of any kind. I don't know why, something about seeing a piece of frozen history just fascinates me.

"Can't," Muse says, biting into his apple, his face an entirely different canvas without his glasses on. Personally, I think I actually prefer them to his contacts, although he's beautiful either way. "The buses leave at midnight for Philly."

"Okay then," I say as I take another deep breath, tucking some loose hair behind my ear as I catch Michael's gaze. "If you don't mind me using your laptop again, I … guess I can show you some of my work."

"You can have the laptop if you want it," he tells me and I feel my lips part in surprise. His computer is nice, a lot nicer even than the one Kevin took from me when we broke up. I play with the charm bracelet on my wrist and try not to touch the necklaces at my throat. I seem to do that a lot when I'm looking at Michael, and it makes me blush every time. "For your art."

"Hey," Ran says, coming up behind me, sliding his arms around me and breathing me in. I do the same to him, loving the flirty scent of his mother's perfume, the animalistic allure of his sweat. My sex gets wet just standing in the circle of his arms like this, my body a candlewick and each one of these boys a flame. It doesn't take much to ignite me these days. "Since we're getting into Philadelphia so early, do you want to find an art store or something and pick up some supplies?"

My heart skitters and jumps at the idea of creating something new again. Other than a few random sketches, I haven't committed any time to my art since I left Kevin.

"*Your paintings, Lily, they make this empty heart of mine feel full. I see Davina in every line you make, every color you choose. You're your mother's daughter, that's for sure.*"

Dad's words hit me like a brick, and I have to blink past a sudden rush of tears.

"Are you okay, gorgeous?" Ransom asks me, reaching up a thumb to brush a single droplet away from my eye. His fingertip comes away smudged with a bit of silver eyeshadow and some black liner.

"I'm sorry. I just … I'm thinking of my dad again."

"You don't have to be sorry, darling," he says, his voice the color of sensuality, this indescribable shade of lust and romance, like layers of chocolate silk sheets and glasses of expensive wine in sweaty, sex scented hands. "Grief doesn't have an expiration date; love doesn't have a prerequisite."

"Are you saying you're in love with me?" I joke, but

Ransom doesn't answer and the entire room just gets … I don't know, *charged.* "Hand me the laptop and I'll show you what I can do," I say, trying to get my voice above a whisper as I glance back and meet Ransom's eyes, watching him push his hood off his head as he studies me.

Personally, I'm waiting for him and Pax to … I don't know, sneak off to the Bat Cave or something, but all they do is gather around me when I sit on the couch and pop the lid to Michael's computer.

I log into the cloud drive and then stare at the sea of folders.

"I want to see *Sex and Sensuality,*" Muse says, making my cheeks color slightly.

"Of course you do," Copeland says and the two of them make tight stupid smiles at each other.

"I told you, I wasn't really in touch with my—"

"Hogwash," Pax snorts, clicking the folder by reaching over my shoulder to steal the keypad. "Excuses, excuses."

The folder opens and a flood of digital paintings emerges, most of them unrecognizable colors and splotches, feelings that I didn't know how to express trying to escape the best way they knew how at the time.

"I like that one," Ran says quietly, pointing at a long narrow canvas, its dimensions making it look like a bookmark from afar. I double click it, my heart thundering, my skin warm with a hot flush of embarrassment. I never really showed my art to anyone before—just my mom, my dad, and my sister. The only pieces Kevin ever really saw were the physical ones I hung on the wall of our apartment. He didn't have much interest in any of it.

"*Orgasm,*" Michael reads from the filename. "Is that what your orgasms used to look like?"

The canvas is dark, a shadowy grey with speckles of silver and the smallest splatter of white in one corner. Studying it now, as abstract as it is, it's a little sad to look at.

"I don't think I'd actually had a real one until I climbed on this bus," I say and there's a sort of collective silence around me that makes my blush ten times worse. "If I were to paint it again now, it wouldn't look like that."

"Would it look like the sun peeking through the clouds?" Ransom asks and I glance back to see Michael making a face behind him.

"What the hell does that mean?" he says as I bite my lip and glance away suddenly, scrolling through the digital art, and then moving over to the folders that hold photographs of my real stuff, those big soaring canvases I covered in gobs of thick oil or acrylic or watercolor. They're all gone now, but at least there's proof that they once existed.

"I can't take anything like this on a plane, but if we could stop somewhere and pick up a digital drawing tablet, maybe a sketchbook and some pencils, that would be … fuck, that would be nice." I pause for a moment because it hits me again how poor I actually am. They'll have to pay for everything—including the very expensive computer programs that I'll need to do my work. I can't ask for that …

"Don't hold back," Muse says, giving my shoulder a squeeze as he stands up and slips off the denim hoodie he was wearing, the one covered in pins and patches. "If you need something, you have to ask. You promised, remember?"

"I promised not to put my art on the back burner to take care of you," I say with a smile fighting to bloom its way across my cherry glossed lips.

"What kind of idiot wanker made you promise that?"

Paxton asks, sliding into Muse's place next to me.

"So what else do you need?" he asks as he stands in front of me with his hands on his hips, his pants sagging low, flashing enough flat perfect skin that I've got a pretty good idea that he's not actually wearing any underwear today. "I'll get it for you."

"I've got it this time," Ransom says, smiling one of those sad, dripping smiles of his. They're so tragically beautiful that they make my heart ache inside my chest. "I want to do this, get the art supplies."

"Okay, Ran," he says, still smiling, that crack still visible down the center of his face. Damn it, but I have no idea how to crawl in there. I'm starting to think that I'll have to wait for an explicit invitation, something I'm not sure he's ready to give. "Since, you know, I got to buy those *amazing* crotchless panties that we all seemed to like so much."

"I'll need to download some programs," I say, trying to distract the guys from the subject of crotchless underwear—not an easy task, I'll tell you that. "Adobe Photoshop, most importantly. But a handful of other things, too. If I have that, a good mouse, a digital pad, and a few physical art supplies, I can do my work anywhere."

"Then that's exactly what I want you to do," Muse says, pointing at me and wiggling his black painted fingernail in my direction. "I want you to fucking just … *create.* Make shit. Whatever you need. Consider us patrons of the arts. We'll give you grants to continue your work."

"Even if I do happen to make anything worth looking at, I don't know what to do with it."

"You find your niche and then you blow it wide open," Pax says, leaning back into the couch and looking up at the ceiling of the bus like he's thinking back on something important. It's got to be about Beauty in Lies, about starting the band, seeking out men with as much or more pain than he had. I bet it would've been exciting, to be around them at the beginning, watch them rise from virtual obscurity into serious up-and-comers in the rock world. "Tenacity and drive, that's what's most important." His mouth quirks into a sideways smile. "Just pretend you're Mikey with a serious vendetta and latch on tight."

Michael sighs, and I smile.

"Why does it bother you so much when he calls you Mikey?" I ask, leaning into Ransom's warmth and letting the thick folds of his hoodie envelop me.

"It's what my parents used to call me," Michael says with another sigh. "It was *their* name for me, not his or Tim's or Vanessa's."

"And yet I've been calling you Mikey for years, imagine that," Paxton says, looking smug as hell.

"Mikey is a cute nickname," I say, leaning my head back so I can look at him when I talk. "And you *are* the only person here without one." I start listing them off. "Ran, Pax, Cope, Lil, *Muse.*"

"Jesus," Michael breathes, looking down at me, "you're too goddamn beautiful. I don't want to say no."

"Is it cuter when I say *Mikey* than when Pax says it?" I ask as Michael reaches down and lifts my chin with his fingers, burning my lips up with a scorching kiss, one that makes my toes curl against the bottoms of the black high-heeled booties I'm wearing.

"Maybe not for Ransom," he says, and for a second there, I'm afraid the joke will push the two fragile men on either side of me too far. But it doesn't. Ransom chuckles and when I glance back to look at Pax, I see him sitting there with his eyes still closed, smiling.

"Do you think you guys are going to seriously pursue a romantic relationship?" Muse asks, still working on his apple, surveying everyone in the room, gauging their moods. He's almost too good at it. He seems to have zero problem being a background character, putting the other guys' needs above his own. I can't let him keep doing that.

"I have no idea," Ransom says I look up at his face, his eyes flicking in Pax's direction. "But I don't feel like I need to have an answer to that yet. We're both with Lilith, so what does it matter?"

"Are you going to pursue a more sexual relationship?" Muse continues and Paxton snorts.

"Are you asking us if we're going to fuck each other? Christ, Derek, don't you have any propriety whatsoever?"

"Not a lot, no," Muse says, sitting back down in the swivel chair across from Ransom.

"Are you interested because you want in on it?" Pax jokes, but Muse doesn't answer, just sits there and takes another bite of his apple, juice shining on his lower lip.

"I think it's time for a subject change," I say, closing the lid on the computer and taking a deep breath. "Let's do something together, all six of us."

"You mean like get naked?" Cope asks, smiling at me, his red hair still sweaty and tousled from the show, sticking to his forehead.

"I mean something *other* than sex," I correct as I curl my fingers around the laptop and feel my heart start to beat like one of Cope's drums. Right now, I don't have to worry about selling my car, finding a place to live, seeing if I can grab a minimum wage job that I'll hate just to make ends meet. No, I get to sit here and think about all the art I want to create, the world I get to see, the boys I get to fall in love with.

I don't think about how close we are to New York. I don't want to. Did Cinderella think about the chores she'd have to do after the ball? The lonely years of living in a house with family that wasn't family? No. She danced with the prince and enjoyed the ball; she lived in the moment.

That's what I'm going to do.

"You mean like that movie the other night?" Cope says, his voice flirty enough that I can't keep my smile from growing at least three shades brighter.

"I mean …" I start, leaning forward and grabbing the front of the coffee table, using the built-in mechanisms on the sides to push the top back and reveal an entire sea of board games hiding away underneath. "Something interactive, like a game. Do you guys want to play Scrabble?"

"Strip Scrabble?" Ransoms asks, his low chuckle like a dark chocolate truffle melting against my tongue. I shiver and he wraps his arms tighter around me.

"No, not *strip* Scrabble, regular Scrabble," I say, but the box is already being lifted out by Pax, the coffee table lowered, the board set in place. I sigh. "Okay, fine, strip Scrabble. But only because you guys turned me on at the mention of art supplies."

"If that's the case," Paxton says, glancing sidelong at me … maybe saving a little of that heated gaze for Ransom? Or maybe that's just wishful thinking … "Then I'm buying you bouquets of paintbrushes instead of roses."

"I'd love you forever," I say and the room goes briefly quiet.

Love you forever.

That's what I'd like to do. But can a situation like this

one, drenched in rock 'n' roll and glitter, really last a lifetime?

I didn't know it then, but the answer was a resounding *yes.*

I'm still exhausted from 'strip Scrabble' and all the things that came after it when we hit the town the next morning, using one of the label's trucks—the same hideous purple one with the black flames that Michael drove to breakfast with Vanessa—to get to a local art store.

Lilith is like a kid in a candy shop, her eyes so big they look like cool forest pools, the water reflecting back the green of the trees above it, deep and full of wonder. I swear, she makes three passes around the shop before she decides on anything at all. I mean, even an *eraser* is a big deal to this girl.

"That brand smudges," she tells Paxton, plucking the square white rectangle from his fingers and setting it back in the basket on the shelf. I smile softly, trying to imagine that she's looking at drumsticks or cymbals or snare drums instead of pencils, paper, and erasers. When I do that, her obsession and eye for detail makes perfect sense to me.

"One rubber's the same as the next, isn't it?" he asks and Lilith giggles. "What?"

"Rubber is slang for condom," she says, flicking red hair over her shoulder flirtatiously, glancing my direction to smile brightly. Apparently art supplies *are* a big turn-on for my new girlfriend. "Right? Have you ever used the word *rubber* in place of condom?"

"All the time," I say and we both grin.

Paxton just rolls his eyes and digs a smoke from his pocket.

"Well, then, Yanks, enjoy picking out an *eraser* together. This expat is out the doors to have himself a *fag,*" he says, dressed in a light grey suit that matches the color of his eyes. With the exception of casual loungewear on the bus, I've literally never seen Paxton Blackwell in anything but a well tailored suit.

"You know," I start, wondering if Muse has already thought about what I'm going to suggest. Knowing him, he definitely has. "If there's anything you want that you can't take on the plane with you, pick it out and have them ship it to us back home. Or hell, order it from Amazon or something and have it delivered."

"Back home?" Lilith asks, pausing with her hand tucked into a basket of pink erasers. Her green eyes lift up to find mine, widening slightly in surprise.

"Yeah," I say, stepping around the corner of the white metal shelves to stand beside her, reaching over to finger the frilly lace sleeve of her purple dress. It's the color of Michael's eyes, and it hugs her body like it was made for it, draping those curves with the same elegance that Paxton's custom suits drape his. Lilith is a seriously gorgeous girl, but I'm not sure that she's at all aware of it. "To Seattle."

"Seattle," she whispers, like the thought hasn't occurred to her. But it's occurred to Muse (obviously), to me. That's why I got so serious about this dating thing. I'm not playing around here. This tour—even with the world portion—is only going to last three more weeks. And then what? All five of us live in Seattle.

I own a nice suburban three bedroom that my mom lives in; Muse has a downtown apartment; Ransom lives in an old purple Victorian; and Michael and Paxton share a fancy as fuck condo.

With Lilith dating all of us … we might have to come up with some other arrangement.

Unfortunately, she can't live with me, not yet. My mom is … she's not fucking well. If I brought a girl home to live with us, she'd either make my life a living hell or drive Lilith off for good. That much I'm sure of.

"The tour won't last forever, Lil," I whisper, sliding my fingers through the rich mahogany strands of her hair. My eyes trace the slight brush of freckles across her nose as I watch her process the idea of what's really going on here. "Just a few weeks and then we'll be back in Seattle. As soon as we get there, we're starting work on a new album. We'll probably record a few singles, shoot some music videos, and then eventually we'll be back on tour again."

She looks up at me, taking a handful of the pink erasers in her palm and dropping them into the red plastic shopping basket I'm holding for her.

"Where will I live?" she asks, but more like she's trying to puzzle out the answer for herself than she's really asking me.

I feel fucking awful though when I hear that question because the only answer I want to give is *with me.* But I can't offer that, I can't. Maybe if my mom and Lilith meet, if things go well with the new medication Mom started before I left on the tour … there are too many fucking *ifs.*

"You can live with us," Michael says, strolling down the aisle with his hands in the pockets of his black jeans, a leather belt with silver bullets stuck through the loops. "Pax and me. We have a nice two bedroom near Pike Place. We have a spectacular fucking view of Elliott Bay."

Lilith looks up at him, breathing hard, the rise and fall of her chest hard to look away from. The dress she's wearing has a sweetheart neckline, emphasizing the pale white mounds of flesh that it frames in with dark purple fabric.

I glance at Michael and realize I'm not the only one that's noticed.

"Or," I start, thinking about her story, about Kevin and the apartment she shared with him, how her whole adult life she's been the girlfriend with the successful lover, the one without any real power in the relationship, "we could all pitch in and get you a place of your own."

"I can't ask you to do that," she says, but Michael's already shaking his head, threading his fingers through his raven-dark hair.

"You're not asking. We're offering. Fuck, we could start looking at places now, online. If there's something that stands out to you, I could send some friends to look at it, give us a video tour with their phones or something."

Lilith bites her lip, shiny with pink gloss, the faintest breath of roses wafting from her smooth skin.

"Maybe if you could help me with the security deposit, I could get a job and take over the rent."

"I wasn't talking about renting," I say, looking up at Michael. Our eyes meet and I see that we're on the same page here. "We've made a lot of money, Lilith. Between the five of us, it wouldn't really be that extravagant of a gift."

"You can't …" she says, closing her eyes and taking a long, slow breath. "No, you can't buy me a house. You've only known me for two weeks."

"Why do you think I was so serious about agreeing to this?" I ask her, my voice almost as low as Ransom's usually is. I close what little distance there is left between Lilith and me, raising her head by putting my fingertips gently against the sides of her throat. From here, I can feel her heart thundering.

There was only so much he could say with words. The rest of his feelings—all of those deep, rich murmurs inside his heart—he had to say those with a kiss. How else could he explain the strength of his emotions to her? They'd just met and already, he couldn't imagine life without her.

I blink against the black and white text in my head, the words of some long forgotten book burned so perfectly in my brain that I could recite them drunk and not miss a single syllable.

"You don't have to decide now," I tell her, breathing in the pomegranate spice scent of her hair. I drop my mouth to hers, closing my eyes, feeling the moist strawberry glazed perfection of her lips press up against mine. That urge to care for her, to make sure that her every fucking need is met, satisfied, exceeded … as scared as I was of having a new relationship, I still can't shake that feeling. All I want to do is make Lilith Goode happy.

Our kiss mimics the one we had in the bookstore last week, soft at first, quickly heading into the same territory that strip Scrabble took us last night.

When we break apart, I find myself gasping for breath, my cock throbbing inside my blue jeans.

"Hey Cope," Lilith starts, her gaze focused low, on my wrist it looks like. She raises her face to look at me. "Do you think we have time to fit in a tattoo?"

"A tattoo?" I ask, surprised, looking up to exchange a

glance with Michael. His lips are already quirked in a slight smirk. "You're afraid of committing to a house, but you want a tattoo?"

I laugh.

"I … a house is too big of a deal, too much money. I can't accept a gift like that. It's not really the permanence that scares me, Cope. I just don't want you guys to commit to something that might not last."

"And why wouldn't it last?" I whisper, still holding her by the neck, my thumbs stroking over her rapidly beating pulse.

"One day you guys might want wives, houses, kids …"

"Not me," I say, still smiling, even as my chest gets tight at the idea of never having children. "And we all already own our own places. None of us rents."

"What part of this arrangement would prevent us from having kids anyway?" Michael asks, stepping in close. Lilith's body tenses up slightly, her nipples pebbling beneath her dress. If we were back on the bus, this situation would definitely take a turn towards the torrid. "Stop thinking so hard about this. Fuck. You and I both know how shitty traditional relationships can be. Either one of us could have easily gotten married, bought a house, had some kids and lived a typical life with our exes. But that's not where fate sent us, Lilith."

"No, it's not, is it, Mikey?" she whispers, her glossy mouth curving into a smile.

"I like the tattoo idea though," he says, running his palm over his inked hand. "What did you want to get?"

My eyes meet Lilith's again.

"I think we should get something together, all of us. Matching tattoos. No matter what happens, I want to remember this moment. I want to remember being connected to all of you."

"Stop talking like we're doomed for failure," I say with a smile, kissing her again, loving the feel of her fingers curling in the fabric of my pale green t-shirt. "I'd much rather talk about getting new ink."

"I have no fucking clue what I'd get," she says with a self-deprecating laugh. I slide my thumbs down the sides of her throat, across the perfect whiteness of her skin.

"Can I make a suggestion?" I ask, my mouth curving up into another smile.

"Shoot," she says, eyes locked on mine as I pull my hands reluctantly away from her warm skin and point out the tattoos on either of my forearms. I have bass clef hearts on one side, and eighth notes arranged into stars on the other.

"We could do something like this, a design made up of notes." I shiver as Lilith lifts her hands up and slides her palms down my multicolored tattoos. "Maybe a circle of bass clefs with treble clefs in the center? If we did six of them, it'd make a perfect loop."

"Six of them," she says, her mouth twitching. "I like that. Would you do it with me?"

"I'd fucking do it," I tell her because goddamn, her excitement is infectious.

"Michael?" she asks, turning to him, chuckling at his loose shrug.

"Ink is ink," he says, running his palm up his arm. "I'm always down for more."

"Oh my god, then let's do this," Lilith says, lighting up, her green eyes sparkling. "My first tattoo. I want full sleeves," she says, pointing at the bare skin of her arms.

I can't help the warm laugh that bubbles from my throat.

"Full sleeves would look good on you, but maybe we should grab your art supplies first?" I ask, taking her in my arms again and giving her a kiss that thrills me all the way to my fucking toes. Holding her like this, I am totally and completely convinced that I made the right choice by giving this a try.

"Art supplies," Lilith says, licking her lips, "and then ink."

Sounds like a plan to me.

There's no shortage of tattoo studios in Philadelphia—and no shortage of artists willing to go out of their way to make room for Beauty in Lies. And Beauty in Lies' collective girlfriend.

After the art store, I leave with a heavy glossy black bag and a heart aching with questions and affection both.

Seattle.

I haven't given a single thought to what might happen *after* the tour. Being here with the boys, living in the moment, it feels like this is it, my whole life. Travel, music, sex, the Bat Cave. I wouldn't mind sleeping in that giant bed for the rest of my life.

I'm moving to Seattle, Washington.

I try to let that thought sink in as the guys and I head to lunch, browsing tattoo artist portfolios on our phones until we find one that we all like. A quick phone call from Michael and that's that; we've got ourselves an appointment with one of the best artists in the city. I have no idea what other work the man had lined up for today, but having a multiplatinum selling rock band in his portfolio has got to be priceless.

On our way to the tattoo studio, we stop briefly at another

store so I can pick up a drawing tablet. Of course, I try to go for a cheap one, something under a hundred bucks, but Ransom, Muse, and Cope somehow end up talking me in a circle and getting me to admit what my dream tablet would be. I wind up with a piece of technology that's worth more than my car with a glass display that I can draw on directly with a stylus, watch my art translate into the digital world in crisp HD.

"You guys are going to spoil me," I say, trying to still the frantic whisper of my heart in my chest, the one that keeps saying things like *Dad is only four and a half hours away from here* and *what's going to happen when we get to Seattle?* On the bus, we're all trapped together in a small space, sleeping together, fucking together, eating together. But in Washington, the guys all have their own places, their own lives.

Frankly, I'm a little terrified.

"Hey," Muse says, sitting in the back row with me and Cope. "I got a message from the auto body shop where we sent your car." He sips the brightly colored bubble tea he bought from the place next door to the Philly cheesesteak shop we visited for lunch (what else did you think we were going to eat in Philadelphia?). His eyes look down at his phone and then flick back up to my face. "The guy says it's worth about ten grand in good condition, but the damage is extensive. To get it back into prime shape the work estimate is around six thousand. If we ignore all the body damage and just go for getting it into working shape, it's about a thousand."

I feel this flicker of fear trace across my skin. Wow. What the fuck would I have done if I'd taken that plane trip back to Phoenix? Even if I had been able to beg my old job back, where would I have gotten the money to fix the car? I would've just had to let it go for whatever amount I could get for something with no windows, no tires, a busted trunk, and extensive water damage.

"What do you want to do?" Muse asks, still looking right at me, still not wearing a damn shirt. Today's outfit is a sleeveless silver hoodie with black lining, the colors a perfect mimicry of his hair. "Obviously I'll pay—"

"*We'll* pay," Michael corrects, glancing up in the rearview mirror as he drives us toward the tattoo studio. "We will pay for whatever you want to do."

"I can't keep taking your money like this," I say, wishing I didn't feel the need to protest so much. I almost wish I could just let them lavish gifts on me and smile my way through it all with nothing but a thank you. But I can't. I'm not too prideful to accept some things—this drawing tablet could change my entire life … and I really needed those new pairs of underwear—but my car, a house, that's just too much. I grew up lower middle class, with everything we needed but nothing we didn't, my dad a hardworking man who enjoyed providing for his family and a mother that chased her dreams until the very end, even if those dreams didn't exactly bring in a lot of cash.

"Why not?" Muse asks, raising his pierced brow at me, his tattooed hand covered in bats still clutching his phone. "We have plenty of money and you have none. It just makes sense. There's nothing else to it."

"Besides, Paxton is distantly related to the royal family. His parents are beyond loaded," Cope says with a slight smile, watching to see if he's going to get a reaction out of Pax.

"Beyond distantly related," he drawls in that panty

melting accent of his, waving his hand dismissively. But when he glances over his shoulder at me, he looks smug as hell. "It's hardly worth mentioning at all."

"Oh, please," Ransom snorts from beside him, his hood actually resting on the back of his shoulders and not his head for once. Oh, and he's sitting *next* to Pax. I keep hoping I'll catch them gazing into each other's eyes or holding hands or stealing secret kisses, but I guess they're taking it slow. I haven't seen anything like that. Yet. "The first thing you told me when we met was that you had royal blood."

"No, I'm certain that was the second thing I told you. I'm almost positive that the first thing I mentioned was that I was rich." There's a slight pause in his humorous tone, like he's just remembered something that makes him uncomfortable. I bet it has to do with the constant calls and texts to his phone. Thankfully, mine have stopped completely. I forgot to re-block Kevin's number after Michael's call and still, I haven't received any new insults or threats. "Or that I had a massive cock and a great big pair of bollocks."

"If you said that," Ransom tells him, putting his hands behind his head and leaning back into the center seat of the front row, "then I'm sure I blocked it out."

I smile, tucking my lower lip in my mouth and glancing down at the shopping bags near my feet.

"The guy at the auto body shop, he said it was worth ten in good shape. Do you think he'd be interested in taking it off my hands?" I look back up at Muse and manage to catch a surprised expression on his face.

"I can text him back and ask," he says and I nod.

"Yes, please." I take a deep breath, trying not to get too sentimental, to think about how that was my mom's car, how it's one of the last few things I have left from that time in my life. The car is in Arizona, and it's trashed, and even if Muse pays to fix it, how the hell am I going to get it if I'm flying right back to Seattle with the boys at the end of this tour? No, I think it's just easiest at this point to let it go. "And have him deduct whatever shipping costs he needs to mail me the rest of the stuff that was left inside."

"I can do that," Muse says, dark brows raised, looking slightly impressed at my decision. "You're positive about this though?" he confirms, lifting his green-blue-grey eyes to stare at me.

"I'm positive," I repeat and watch as he types out a message with his thumbs.

In the background, the radio starts playing a Beauty in Lies song and I get the chills all over.

"It's still weird to hear us just come on like that," Cope says as I turn to look at him, leaning forward, his hands pressed to the back of Michael's seat, his cheek against his knuckles. "I'm not sure if I'll ever get used to it."

"Do you remember the first time you ever heard yourself on the radio?"

"I was in a Target buying tampons for my mom," Cope says with a wrinkled nose and half-smile. He's trying to make a joke out of it, but I can already tell that anything having to do with his mom is dead serious. Oddly enough, I kind of want to meet her. I just want to see what she's like. She can't be all bad with a son like Cope, right? I think about his face when we started talking about Seattle. Unlike Michael, he didn't offer for me to come and live with him. I'm guessing his mom already does?

"I was at the dentist," Ransom whispers with a small cringe, like even the thought of having his teeth looked at is abhorrent.

"A friend's wedding," Michael says.

"An online ad for a streaming music service," Derek says, sipping more bubble tea through his straw and pulling his gaze from his phone for a moment to look at me.

"What about you, Pax?" I ask, wondering if it's any weirder for him since it's his voice that's on display. A little bit of Ransom, too, in the background, but all those clear, sharp notes that take front and center, those are Paxton's.

"In a car with my parents," he says, sounding frustrated. The edge in his voice gives me another small clue. Obviously, a lot of Paxton's issues stem from Chloe, Harper, Kortney, and Ransom. I get that. But Beauty in Lies was started *before* any of that happened. If he was already in pain then, already seeking out other lost souls then there was something else that gave him his initial scars, started him down the pathway of rock 'n' roll in the first place.

His parents.

There's definitely an issue there.

"You don't get along with them, I take it?" I ask, wondering how far he'll let me go before he shuts me down again. This week has been a lot for Pax, and he's already prone to running away and trying to hide his emotions with anger. I actually don't expect him to answer at all.

"My dad's a dodgy git, and my mum's an arse licking sycophant."

I have to blink several times to process that one.

"Wow," I say as Michael parks our borrowed truck on the street in front of a tall brick building. Bricks. The color of the stones, the imagined texture … I can't help the slight flush that crawls across my skin as I think about our raunchy alley sex. "That's heavy, Pax."

"Yeah, well," he starts, getting a cigarette out and

shoving open the door, "you'll see what I mean when you meet 'em."

He lights up and climbs out, leaving me with a pounding heart and butterflies in my tummy.

Meet Paxton's parents? Holy shit. I hadn't even really thought about that, about meeting the boys' families. I mean, I guess I already got to meet Michael's brother, Tim, but I wasn't dating him at the time.

It hits me then that I don't have any family left for the guys to meet.

"You okay?" Muse asks gently, drawing my attention back to him. He's looking at me like he did that day on the bus when he first invited me to stay, when he compared our souls to lonely travelers, when he bared his heart to me and admitted considering suicide once upon a time.

"I have no family left for you guys to meet," I say and Muse's smile softens, saddens.

"Neither do I," he says and then pauses, glancing away for a brief moment, tapping his cell on his knee. "To tell you the truth though, that's not such a bad thing in my case."

His cell pings with a message and before I can ask about that cryptic statement, he's checking it and turning the screen around for my perusal.

"Guy says he'll give you four thousand for it."

"That's fine," I say, more concerned with the strange expression on Muse's face than I am with the money. Then again, at least I'll have a decent nest egg of my own to start a new life in Seattle. Maybe I can actually get my *own* place without having to take more money from my boys?

"I'll tell him five and it's a deal," Muse says, leaving me with that little nugget from his past, no elaboration. "And I'll give him my address to ship your stuff to. You can make whatever other decisions you want about living arrangements later."

"Thank you," I say, watching him do what he does best, take care of all the practical shit. I want to see him be impractical for a moment, let passion take over logic, let himself get swept away in something great. Maybe we could do it together?

I climb out onto the street next to Cope as Muse sends off another text to the auto body shop, and then gets out on his own side.

The six of us gather on the sidewalk and head up a small cement ramp into the front doors of the brick building, a huge metal sign attached to the wall next to us that reads *Brotherly Love Tattoo and Piercing.*

"The City of Brotherly Love," I whisper, a smile stealing across my mouth as I recite one of Philadelphia's nicknames, looking around at the five guys surrounding me. What an appropriate title. Well, except for maybe Paxton and Ransom. I'm not sure that it's *brotherly* love that they're feeling toward each other.

We head inside to polished concrete floors and exposed brick and ductwork, the air a lot warmer in here than it was outside.

Michael walks right up to the silver desk and taps on the bell, not at all shy or embarrassed or tentative. I stand next to him with Copeland and Muse next to me, Ransom and Pax behind us. Standing like this, I get that feeling of being protected, watched over. There's a sense of belonging in being with the boys that I'm not sure that I've *ever* felt before, like I'm part of a club or something … part of a *band.* My instrument is sex, my tool for making beautiful music with my boys.

I smile and glance up at the high ceilings, the artwork on the walls, the glass cases full of jewelry.

"I can't believe we're getting a group tattoo," Paxton says with a cruel edge to his voice. "Now I'm sure everyone will think we're all poofs."

"Who cares what everyone thinks?" Ransom whispers, and I glance back to find them staring at each other. Paxton shakes his head first, ruffling his blonde hair with fingers covered in a tattooed skyline, the trees black silhouettes, the sky a blue washed gradient, the stars negative spaces carved out of the color.

"Bloody hell," he murmurs, pausing when the owner of the shop appears and introduces himself and his apprentice. There's a lot of gushing, praise, some serious fanboy moments happening as the man shows off his Beauty in Lies tattoo—based off that same artwork that plays during the animated short at the concerts. It occurs to me then that I have no idea where that comes from.

"What's with the art on the album, the stuff that plays on the curtain?" I ask, turning to Pax and Ran, breaking apart another charged stare between them. They both turn slowly to look at me, blinking like they're coming up for air. Wow. Intense. I have to really fight not to smile; I'm afraid if I do, I'll spook them both. "Does it mean anything?"

"It's all based on sketches, darling," Ransom says, his voice black velvet and merlot. "From Harper's notebook." He looks like he's about to start sweating buckets when he says this, slipping his hood up over his head.

Paxton goes still for a moment and then reaches up, tugging the hood back down from Ransom's mussy chocolate brown hair.

"We found it in her stuff after she died, in her purse.

Even buried in there, it somehow had blood on it," Pax says, his face stoic, grey eyes the same color as the polished cement beneath my black leather booties. "But she was an artist, too. Kind of like you, Miss Lily," Pax says, moving away and walking around the edge of the shop in his sharp suit, tattoos peeking from the starched collar of his shirt.

"I'm sorry," I say to Ransom, watching his eyes follow his … friend? Are they friends again? Or are they going to be lovers? Personally, I don't mind either way. "I shouldn't have brought that up."

"There's no way to know unless you ask," Ran says, eyes half-lidded when he turns them on me and smiles. He almost looks like a different person without his hood on. "Where are you thinking of putting your first tat, honey?"

"On my wrist," I say, adjusting my mother's charm bracelet and turning my bare arms over. "But I can't decide left or right."

"I'd say if you want to do your art," Ransom starts, stepping forward and taking both my hands in his, rubbing his thumbs over the pulse points in my wrists, sending my heartbeat racing, my eyes taking in the dark lusty haze of his expression. "Then get it on your left wrist. Tattoos take time to heal. It'll be sore and swollen for a while; that might make it hard to use that fancy new tablet of yours."

"Hey guys, you want to come take a look at this?" Cope asks, drawing my attention away from Ransom—it takes a *lot* of effort for me to extract my hands from his—and over to the sketch on the metal surface of the counter. Ran steps up behind me to look and my nose fills with the bright scent of violets, taking over the ink and iodine smell of the shop.

On the piece of paper in front of me, I see a circle made up of six bass clefs, connected together in the center, each sloped form peppered with a pair of dots on the outside curve. Also arranged in a circle are six treble clefs, each one situated in the little wedge of space between bass clefs. Just glancing at it, the whole design looks kind of like a flower or a fancy asterisk.

It's subtle, simple, but the meaning is there. Six parts. Six people. Music and connectivity.

"I fucking love it," I say as I touch a pink painted fingernail to the center of the design. "This is perfect."

"I'm glad you like it," Cope says, his voice soft, his eyes the color of sea glass when the sun hits it just right. He taps his long fingers on the counter and grins at me. "So, you want to go first?"

"Absolutely," I say, following the shop's owner over to a black leather chair and taking a seat, heart racing, a little nervous but fucking excited, too. "I can't believe I'm losing my ink virginity today," I say and Cope chuckles, sitting in the chair next to mine in his perfectly fitting jeans, his t-shirt the color of mint ice cream.

"It's just the first prick that hurts," Paxton drawls, taking a seat next to Cope and playing with his silver cuff links, these ones in the shape of tiny butterflies with intricate designs on their wings.

"Gee, thanks for that," I say, taking a deep breath to calm my nerves as Michael, Muse, and Ransom gather on the other side of me, behind the tattoo artist.

"Where did you want the design?" the guy asks me, taking my hand in his. Unlike when Ransom touched me, I feel nothing. *Sorry, Dad,* I think as I point at my left wrist. He was never a fan of tattoos. But he's not here anymore, and I am. I have to make my own decisions.

"Right here," I say, unhooking my charm bracelet for the

first time since Mom passed away. The feel of it slipping from my skin sends cold chills down my spine. But maybe this, too, is a good thing? I'm not taking it off obviously, just moving it, but the fact that it's been in one place for so long makes me wonder if I've ever really moved on from mother's and sister's deaths.

This fresh start I'm trying to make … maybe it's not *just* about my father?

It's my entire past that's drenched in tragedy. I don't want to swim in those waters anymore.

Cope leans forward to help me clasp the bracelet onto my other wrist, the sensation of his fingers dancing across my skin takes my breath away, the gentleness of his touch soothing my nerves a little as I wait for the tattoo artist to transfer the sketch to a translucent sheet of paper.

He sizes it for my wrist and then cleans my skin off, slathering a clear gel across the surface and then pressing the design against it. When he peels the paper off, the bass and treble clefs are sitting in sharp black relief against the white paleness of my flesh.

"How does that look?" he asks, giving me a moment to study the position.

I let the boys check it out, get their approval, and then decide it's got mine, too.

"Let's do this," I say, looking up and into the mirror, finding the deep forest green of my eyes staring back at me, long wavy tendrils of red curling past my cheeks, over my shoulders. The purple dress I'm wearing brings out the violet highlights in my hair, making the color look like something out of a box instead of what I was born with. Freckles dance across my nose, just above the full glossed pink of my lips.

All around me, my boys sit or stand, each one his own

shade of unique, his own brand of beautiful. The way I'm sitting, it's like I'm perched on a throne, the five of them arranged around me like worshippers.

I smile.

At least until the needle is touching my skin for the first time. But Pax is mostly right—it's just the first *few* pricks that hurt, a couple minutes of pain until my body relaxes and I get used to it, closing my eyes for a moment and breathing deep.

Two concerts left, and then … Upstate New York. Gloversville. My childhood home.

Dad's ashes.

When I open my eyes finally, I glance down to find the design inked permanently into my skin. It's all done in crisp, black ink with a few random splotches of watercolor behind it, like drops of rain mid-splatter, the sun reflecting off the liquid and making a rainbow effect.

"That's some hot fucking ink," Michael says, putting a hand on my head, leaning over to take a closer look. "It suits you," he says, and I smile.

"So it does."

I guess the number six just looks good on me—on *us*.

My hand slides up and over my shoulder, close to the aching discomfort of my new tattoo. But I'm an old fucking pro at this, and I don't touch it. I see Muse doing the same, teasing the red edges of skin around the black design at his right hip. His pants are so low-slung they don't touch the damn thing, and he's still wearing just an unzipped silver hoodie and nothing else on top.

My fellow guitarist is definitely an interesting person. To tell the truth, I'm a little shocked at *how* interesting, how nice he turned out, considering his background. Just thinking about it makes me feel lucky that all I had to deal with were two dead parents and a resentful asshole brother.

Fucking Tim.

I check my phone with one hand, smoke my cigarette with the other, and keep an eye out for Lilith in the backstage melee. She slipped away to the bathroom a few minutes ago, and I can't stop myself from getting these sharp little thrills of excitement as I wait for her to come back.

Jesus, I've never fallen this hard for a girl before—not even Vanessa. Just thinking about Lilith turns my cock to granite, makes me sweat, speeds my heart rate up until I feel dizzy. I can't help but feel a little jealous when I see her with the other guys, her body gyrating them to orgasm, the necklaces I bought her swinging with the motion of her hips. At the same time though, I kind of like it, too. I like seeing Paxton fucking *smile* for once. I like seeing Ransom without his hood on. Cope needs to get over Cara and be a goddamn boyfriend again since that's what he's so damn good at. And Muse … Muse needs Lilith more than anyone.

Van broke up with me.

I put a pause on my Lilith obsession for a second to reread that text from Tim.

Huh.

How am I not fucking surprised?

What did you expect, Timmy? An HEA?

Mikey, call me, is what he sends back followed with: *what's an HEA?*

I sigh and pocket my phone. It's the first time I've texted him back since I left the hotel. I don't intend to make a habit of it. What the hell did he think would happen when I found out he was screwing the girl I'd been waiting for for an entire year? The girl I held while she cried for her lost baby, the one I thought was mine? I mean, come the fuck on. If Tim thinks *we're* going to get our HEA—*happily ever after*—he's dead wrong on that front, too.

I'm goddamn done with him.

"Mikey."

I pull my cigarette from my lips and glance over, my cock thickening at the sight of Lilith standing next to me in a pair of tight jeans, pink and white Chucks, and a tank top with a big black heart on it, made out of an alto clef turned on its side and a 'V'.

"You know," I tell her as I ash my cigarette against the wall and then flick it into a nearby trash can, "that nickname doesn't sound so god-awful when you say it."

"Good," she says, the tattoo on her wrist catching my attention. All of our designs are in black with a few random color splotches making up the background. Lilith's look like rainbows while mine are in the same jewel tones as the rest of my work. Cope's are as vibrant and neon as the tattoos on his forearms while Muse's are in varying shades of red, and Paxton's are all shades of grey.

I try really hard not to think of that last one as ironic.

"Because I like having a nickname for you," Lilith continues, reaching up to brush strands of hair from my forehead. It feels so goddamn good to be touched that I let my eyes drift shut for a moment, the sight of roadies in denim and sweatshirts and band tees fading away. "Besides, at this point it seems like you should probably just give up on trying to get Paxton to stop calling you that. I'm not sure that I've actually ever heard him say *Michael* before."

Lilith's body drapes over the front of mine, her hands sliding around my neck, just above the new tattoo between my shoulder blades. I open my eyes for a split second before her lips touch mine, kissing me, igniting that violent fucking hunger that I can't seem to shake. I keep telling myself it's because I spent a year not having sex, but in reality, I think it might just be Lilith.

My hands settle on her hips, my cock pressing against the inside of my jeans, pushed up tight to her belly. I feel this surge of triumph as I get to make out with her the way I saw Paxton doing that night, the night when she wore the glittering green dress and got tossed out of the venue. It feels fucking *great.*

We pull apart after a few minutes, when my heart feels like it just might make a break and tear out of my rib cage, our gazes locked, her lips looking as swollen as mine feel.

"Thank you for the offer, about Seattle and all that," she says, leaning back a little, putting some space between us. I notice she doesn't take her palms off the front of my hunter green t-shirt, the same color as those gorgeous eyes of hers.

"You're welcome," I tell her, wanting her to move in with me and Pax, share my bedroom, share my *bed.* Pretty crazy thoughts to have about a girl I met two weeks, but fuck if I can help it. I don't know if it's some magic in that rosewater perfume she spritzes all over herself, or the way her red hair tumbles down her back in glistening ruby waves, or the feel of her hot tight cunt wrapped around my shaft, gripping and milking and working me until I come … but I can't get enough of her. "By the time this tour is done, I'll have convinced you to move in with me, so maybe you should just start thanking me for that, too?"

"Wow, cocky, much?" she asks, the others standing close to us, but staying out of the conversation. Or maybe they just can't hear for shit because it's so damn loud back here? "You have zero confidence, Mikey. None at all."

"That's me," I tell her, my own version of a smirk working its way across my face. I might not have that royal British swagger that Pax has got, but I know how to make a woman swoon.

"Can you do me a favor?" she asks, and I sense this is the real reason she came over here and buttered me up with a cock hardening kiss.

"Sure thing, Lil. What's up?"

I don't say it aloud, but in my head, I hear the words: *I'd do anything for you.*

How stupid is that? I keep a goddamn lid on that shit.

"Do you think you could borrow that truck we used today

and drive me over to Gloversville on the way to Montréal? It won't add any extra time to the trip except for whatever actual time we spend there."

Her breath catches a little as she talks, her mood shifting despite the obvious push to make herself smile.

"Fuck, Lil," I say, reaching out to touch the side of her face with my tattooed hand, loving the contrast between the dark designs on my skin and the pink freshness of hers. I knew she wanted to stop in and see her childhood home one more time, pick up her father's ashes, but I guess I just hadn't given much thought to how we'd go about it. "Of course. I'll talk to Octavia about it later."

And by talk, I mean basically tell her what we're planning on doing. There's no way in hell she or the record label is putting a stop to this little side trip.

"Did you want it to be just us?" I ask, wondering as the words come out if that's what I want, to spend time together with just her. But no. I actually stand there and *hope* she asks to bring her other lovers—*my* friends. My family, really, since the only person in this world that I'm actually related to is a liar and a fucking thief. *Who also happens to be the man that raised you,* my mind adds, but I'm not going there, not right now. I'll officially deal with Tim once we're back in Seattle.

"I think we should all go," Lilith says, glancing over at the guys. They're all standing behind us, fresh tattoos peeking out from the back of Cope's neck, Ransom's elbow, Muse's hip. Paxton's is hidden beneath the folds of his grey suit, charcoal button-up, and pale pink tie. It was a hell of a lot harder to figure out where to put his than it was for even me. Pax's tattoos basically cover him from head to toe. But Lilith managed to pick out this one, single blank spot on his chest, just above his heart. It even seems to compliment the lyrics written out below it, from his neck all the way down to his hips.

"You guys are up in just a minute," Octavia says, shouting a little to be heard over the backstage din. "One minute." She holds up a single finger and I pause to press one last kiss to Lilith's mouth.

"Break a leg," she tells me, giving the other guys kisses on the lips, one after the other. But it doesn't just look like she's going through the motions. The way she kisses each one of us is different, her mouth as hungry for Muse as it is for Cope, Ran, Pax. Me. "Good luck!"

We make our way onstage, picking up our instruments, getting ready for the second to last show stateside. Well, okay, so we're also playing Montréal, but technically that's in Canada, so it counts as world tour destination number one.

I slip my Gibson's strap over my shoulder and slide a purple guitar pick from my pocket. My fretting hand finds the neck, one thumb resting on the backside, my knuckles bent. My upper right arm rests along the body of the guitar, my strumming hand floating over the sound hole. This particular guitar is *ocean burst green.* To me, it looks like the exact shade of Lilith's eyes.

I'm so deep in Lily fucking la-la land that I can't remember what song we're supposed to start with, so I take a small step back and glance at the set list taped to the floor. Ah. Shit. This song is perfect.

I dig the purple and black bandana out of my other pocket and tie it around my forehead, using it to pull my long dark hair back. That first night that Lilith and I got together, I was so pumped to play for her, picking at my guitar strings like in incubus intent on seduction. But she didn't get to hear me then, so I'm going to make this count tonight. Obviously she's seen a bunch of shows between now and then, but tomorrow's going to be a hard day for her. I want to make it just that much easier.

Our animated video nears its end as Pax tilts his head back and takes a deep breath.

"You guys ready?" he asks as Muse hefts a black and white guitar into his hands, Ransom clutches his jet-black base, and Copeland twirls his drumsticks around in his hands.

"We're ready," I say as the curtain starts to lift up.

"Congratulations, Philly," Paxton says, when it's still just our shoes that are visible, my black motorcycle boots, his fancy custom Beatle-boot-meets-biker-boot Barker Blacks, Muse's red Chucks covered in black Sharpie graffiti. "You've got Beauty in Lies in town tonight. My name is Paxton Blackwell, and this is a song my friend, Michael Luxe, over here wrote when he was desperate to fall in love."

The crowd roars, the sound caught somewhere between an earthquake and a tornado. Definite destruction. Tonight's venue is this massive industrial building with exposed ductwork and two long metal balconies that run the whole length of the space. Two intricate chandeliers drip their glittering crystal forms over the dark mass below us, looking oddly out of place amongst all the steel and chrome.

"He, uh," Pax continues, tapping the heel of his boot on the stage and shaking his blonde head with a sly smile, "was sleeping with any groupie he could get his hands on." *I am going to fucking kill him after this,* I think as I look to my left and spy Lilith watching us from the edge of the stage. Our eyes meet and she smiles. "Even though he had a girlfriend at the time …" The audience groans as I roll my eyes to my friend's back and seriously think about stabbing him in it. "Even though he *did,*" Pax goes on, "he was lonely as fuck. This song is dedicated to the new woman in his life, and it's called *Hey You, Everything.*"

The room goes completely nuts as I curse under my breath and someone releases a sea of balloons from the ceiling in white, pink, and black. They fall from the net between the chandeliers and drench the crowd, bouncing and dancing as I reach down and start to finger my guitar. I'd rather I was fingering Lilith, but I'll take what I can get.

It's just me and my guitar for a few seconds, Copeland joining me next. Muse and Ransom don't drop in until Paxton starts singing.

"*Hey you, is your life everything you thought it'd be when it began?*" he croons in the dulcet tones of a lover's bedroom voice. "*Mine's not shaping up the way that I'd dreamed. The blood inside my veins tells me I need a different plan. Our eyes met; you bled me dry. Now I guess I just don't understand. You, for me, you're everything. Just the two of us until world's end.*"

Ransom steps in for the screaming/growling portion of the song, blowing my mind as he usually does when he's onstage. How somebody who speaks every word in a whisper can crack the sound barrier like that just fucking baffles me.

"*YOU MIGHT NOT KNOW THAT I FEEL THIS WAY! YOU MIGHT NOT UNDERSTAND THE THINGS MY LIPS DON'T SAY! WELL, SHIT IF I'M LETTING IT END THIS WAY!*"

"*If I asked you for your hand, just what would you say?*" Paxton sings, carrying his notes through another round of Ransom's hoarse screams, the two competing sounds cutting across one another in a way that's still somehow harmonious. Listening to them sing together like this … I guess I can kind of see some connection I might've missed before.

Jesus. Pax and Ran as lovers? Lilith Goode, what have you done to this band?

"*Tell me, what would you say?*" he continues, sliding his hand down the front of his pink tie. I know he'd never cop to it, but I think he wore it for Lilith. Pink seems to be her favorite color. "*Maybe you can't tell how twisted these feelings make me? Hey you, everything, my plan's not anything I ever really planned. My love for you is now just a quivering plea. Why can't I just say it? What the hell is wrong with me? My life was nothing until I saw your perfect face. Hiding all of this deep inside just makes the aching feel real ugly.*"

Ransom's screaming portion of the song comes back around, repeating the same lines a few times as he strums his bass with relaxed, easy motions, buried inside a purple and black striped hoodie, the slight darkness of stubble on his face.

I cut him off with the raunchy guitar portion of the song, inviting Muse up to the center mic as Paxton steps back and lets us have the limelight. You'd think with his personality that he'd be one greedy motherfucker when it comes to attention, but he's not. For a kid that grew up rich as fuck, as *royalty,* he's not as pretentious as you might think. I wouldn't be sharing a condo with him if he were.

Muse and I line up together, thrashing the stage as Paxton moves into place beside Ransom for the next few lines, barely audible over our frantic strumming. If I had to describe the sounds we're making together, I'd have to compare it to the wail of a banshee, a dark faerie that calls out a person's death just before they lose their life. But this, maybe it's worse than that because it's not about dying, it's about never living, never finding a person you truly love. Or fuck, even shittier than that—finding them and not letting them know how you feel. That's what this is about.

"*Hey you, can you hear my blood singing your name? My heartbeat, my lips, my body just waiting to live? Hey you, can you tell I feel all of these gloriously awful things?*"

Muse and I break for a moment, letting Ransom use his fingers to claw out a deep, sad sound, one that reminds me of a dirty, throbbing heartbeat. We start back up again a few seconds later, Copeland right behind us, chasing our asses with these sick clattering beats that churn up the crowd … even Lilith.

I can see her from the corner of my eye, moving with the music, not at all ashamed to be dancing alone on the side of the stage by herself.

As our guitar solo winds to an end, I start to move back, catching sight of Ran and Pax, sharing the microphone for the next verse, their lips … intriguingly fucking close.

Dear god, can they just fuck already?

As the lighter instrumental portion of the song comes up, I wait for Paxton to take center stage again, distract the crowd by tossing and catching his microphone, taking off his tie, unbuttoning his shirt.

Instead … Ransom and Paxton start to kiss at the mic.

Like, *really* kiss.

The crowd goes batshit as I improvise for the next line of missing lyrics, dancing my fingers across my guitar for a little extra thrill, putting my own lips to the center microphone. I'm no Pax, no Ransom, but with Muse and Cope joining me for backup vocals, we sound alright.

"Hey you, I know you're not the one to blame. You can't read the shape of my mouth or my breathless sigh. Why would I play this stupid game? There's not a thing in my life that makes sense with you missing. This isn't the way I wanted this wild ardor tamed. So, you, my everything, do you have all the things you need? If there's something missing, just remember my name. Hey you, goodbye and sorry it had to end this way."

The three of us finish off the song without a bassist or a lead singer, the last few notes of the song echoing around the roaring, shaking, quivering room. The whole thing sounds like a collective gasp of breath or a stuttering heartbeat.

Ran and Pax … still kissing.

Sweat drips down my face as I tilt the mic to my lips.

"You want to meet the girl?" I ask, briefly distracting the masses. "The one I was playing for tonight?"

Before Lilith can even think to run away, I'm jogging over to her and taking her by the hand, pulling her into the spotlight with me, over to the center mic.

I … Jesus fuck. There are no words to describe how beautiful she looks standing there with the colored lights flickering across the liquid fire wash of her hair, the priceless glimmer of her eyes.

Behind me, the roadies pull out a set of stools for one of our acoustic pieces, trading Muse's electric guitar out for an acoustic one.

Glancing back, I see Paxton's long cruel tattooed fingers on the mic, Ransom's hand dressed in a fingerless black glove curled around his tie. They look … almost relieved to be making out onstage.

"We got this," Muse whispers as the crowd starts to murmur, and we trade places.

Lilith looks confused as hell—and admittedly kind of excited—as I have her take a seat on one of the stools. Muse stands at the center mic, looking back at Copeland and giving him a brief nod as he comes down the dais steps and grabs a small drum from one of the roadies' hands, taking a seat and letting them adjust another mic near his hands.

"Hey, Lil," I whisper, handing her a tambourine. "Can you find the beat with us?"

"I can try," she says, biting her lower lip, cheeks flushed with excitement.

"Just hit this against your leg in time with the song. It should come pretty naturally."

I take a deep breath and sit down with the guitar.

Obviously, Pax is supposed to sing this one while Muse plays the acoustic guitar. I actually use the fucking tambourine, and Ransom does backup vocals; Cope taps out the easy beat on his drum.

I see Octavia sneaking around behind Cope's drum dais, but I ignore her as I pluck the first note.

"This one's got a long name," Muse begins, shoving his hands into the pockets of his unzipped hoodie as the crowd cheers. They already know where this is going. "It's called *Keep Your Friends Close, Your Enemies Closer, And Your Friends Will Help You Bury their Bodies.*"

He clears his throat and closes his eyes for a moment, the crest of his mohawk catching the light from above.

"You ready?" I ask Lilith and she nods, glancing back at Ran and Pax briefly, her lips curling into a grin that's half amused and half embarrassed. Fuck, she should be; those are her goddamn boyfriends messing up the show.

I smile, too, and shake my head.

"*Tiptoeing past that closed door,*" Muse sings in this

disturbingly gentle voice, trying to capture the irony of the song the way Paxton does. He's nowhere close, but he's not half-bad either. I know I sure as hell couldn't hold half these notes; I give him mad props. "*We made it down to the bottom floor. Exchanging looks and half-smiles, we know there's a reason that for each other we'd travel more than a thousand grueling miles.*"

Muse takes a deep breath as Cope pounds the drum with soft easy smacks of his open palms. I strum the guitar with my bare fingers and watch as Lilith starts to tap the tambourine against her denim clad leg, sharing a secret smile with me.

I hope she's not pissed about me dragging her out here. That, and I'm kind of curious to see what all the media hype says tomorrow when news of Pax and Ran's make out session mixes with the reveal of my redheaded girlfriend, the same one that Cope was kissing in that picture from last week.

Should be interesting.

But frankly, I don't give a shit whether they like any of this or not.

I just spent two years of my life living for somebody else. I don't need to keep doing that. I won't bow down to please anybody—not even the world.

"*Blee-ding,*" Muse sings, dragging the word out with two, long unbroken sounds. This part in particular is hard as hell, and we both look relieved with Paxton steps up next to him and helps finish out the line. "*But my friend, they really had it coming. In the whole world, you guys are the only ones who'd stand with me. The ones who sent my enemies running.*"

Ransom steps up beside me and takes the last empty seat,

the one with a mic tilted low for backup vocals. His face is streaked with sweat and he's shaking like hell, but it's a different sort of tremble from his usual. He doesn't look like he's about to have a breakdown right now. Although his cheeks and forehead *are* the same color as Lilith's hair.

"*They told me I could never love my friends this way,*" Paxton, Muse, and Ransom sing together. Pax breaks off at the end to send a vibrating chuckle through the microphone and into the crowd.

"Not like that," he inserts, pointing at Ransom and making the room laugh along with him.

"*They told me to keep them close, but keep my enemies closer. In the backyard, that's where we'll make their graves. You didn't think I'd sing about something as simple as friendship devotees. No, my demons are the ones they helped me leave dead and buried.*"

I hope the crowd gets that the song's a metaphor for hard feelings and shitty pasts, not actual people, but if they're not getting it, I guess murder works, too. After all, Copeland basically helped Ransom bury the body of his mother's rapist. When the police came, he told them he'd seen the man following Ran, seen the fight get started, and ran to get his cellphone from his car. For me that story was obviously bullshit—Copeland would never leave Ran alone in a fight—but the fact that Ransom was stalking the guy, that he attacked him first, nobody would ever have to know about that.

"*There's no way for anyone to know what we've done. You guys, you scrubbed all of the blood until it was good and gone. Listen to me and follow me outside into the pouring rain. If you need me, I'll be there by your side, the next time something else awful needs to lie down and die. Just like that patch of dirt beneath my favorite tree.*"

The chorus repeats, the three voices blending together seamlessly, Paxton covering up any missteps that Muse might make. Lilith and I share another glance, her pale hand moving the tambourine, my fingers teasing the guitar.

"*You have no idea how awful it was to wake up alone at night. Before you guys came into my life, there were nightmares at both ends of sleep. I didn't know if I had it left inside of me to fight. Killing my demons and saying goodbye to my scars. My friends so close. Oh yes. Fuck my enemies; I just want my friends closer.*"

As the crowd explodes into raucous applause, Lilith leans over and puts her lips to my ear.

"Who wrote that one?" she asks. "Ransom?"

"No," I reply, sweeping red hair back from her ear, "that one's all Muse."

"Don't say a bloody thing," Pax says before we're all even on the bus. "Not one bloody thing!" he shouts as I climb up the metal steps after him and try to suppress a stupid girlish urge to hop up and down and squeal.

Paxton and Ransom.

I'm definitely into that.

In the back of my mind, Muse's song keeps playing, adding more shiny gold nuggets to my chest of clues. What could possibly be so awful in his past that's worse than mine, Paxton's, *Ransom's*? I don't let myself imagine anything because the places my mind wants to go are dark and terrifying. I won't go there unless that's where Muse takes me.

"What the fuck was all of that?" Michael asks, sounding pissed off. But I don't think he really is. I think he's just passionate about everything he says. "Who the hell kissed who back there?"

"I can't believe I just did that," Ransom says, slouching against the counter and lighting up a cigarette with shaking hands. "That was weird, wasn't it? It was seriously fucking weird."

"What the hell did Octavia have to say?" Cope asks and

Pax snorts, pushing past him and yanking the fridge open to grab a beer.

"Who the hell cares?" Paxton says, grinning wickedly as he ruffles up his blonde hair and meets my gaze. There's a hunger there—and not just for Ransom. The way Pax is looking at me now, I'm not at all worried that he and Ransom might be more interested in doing their own thing than they are in me. I mean, I have no idea if they'll ever want to have sex alone together, but as far as a relationship, I don't see them breaking us up over their attraction to each other. "Come Montréal, she's done and gone."

"She was actually pretty nice about it," Ransom whispers, smoking his cigarette with the hood on his black and purple sweatshirt up, a quirky smile playing on his lips. For whatever reason, his mouth looks extra sexy with the surrounding stubble. "Although I can't remember what she said."

"No, you were too busy listening to me butcher my own song," Muse says with a laugh. It's cheerful and easygoing as usual. He's got that smile on, too, the one that says he gets everything he wants. But again, I'm seeing a total disconnect. Derek is laughing, grinning, but he's not letting the truth of that song rise to the surface. There was a lot of fucking pain there—and a lot of love, too, for his friends.

"You were great, sweetie," Ransom says, turning that quirky smile on for Muse … and then looking over at me.

"You guys don't need my approval to … go into the Bat Cave alone or anything," I say as I put my hands on my hips, the soreness at my wrist a pleasant reminder of the way we spent our afternoon. From where I'm standing, I can see Copeland's tattoo on the back of his neck, beneath his auburn hair. Considering Muse is hardly wearing any clothing, I can see his too, right on his hip. "I already said I'm okay with it."

Ransom laughs, the sound as smoky and hazy as the white curls drifting up from the lit tip of his cigarette.

"Only if you come with us, baby," he says, the darkness of his voice an irresistible invitation.

"You don't have to ask me twice," I say as Ransom raises his dark brows and then chucks his cigarette into the ashtray on the countertop. Slowly, so slowly that I'm almost positive that it's a come-on, Paxton locks his eyes with mine and tilts his beer bottle to his lips.

Mesmerized, I watch his throat as he swallows.

"Yeah, alright," he says when he's finished drinking, setting his beer aside. "I didn't just kiss some bloke onstage to pretend like it didn't happen, now did I? Although, it was fucking bloody Ran that kissed *me.*"

"Yeah, maybe," Ran says with a shake of his head, like he can't even believe this is happening. He runs a palm down his face and then reaches out to take my right hand, the slide of my mother's charm bracelet both foreign and familiar now that it's on the opposite arm. "I mean, it probably *was* me."

I take one last look at the other three boys, and Muse waves at me with that cheerful smile still firmly stuck in place.

Down the hall, into the Bat Cave.

I climb right up onto the bed. Muse and I changed the sheets this morning, so everything is crisp and fresh and smelling of laundry detergent as I kick my shoes and socks off, peel my jeans down my legs and toss them aside.

My panties are white and lacy, covered in pink hearts. Both boys notice them right away.

"Nope," Pax says as he takes his tie off and stuffs it into the pocket of his slacks. "I am not fucking gay." He climbs up next to me without waiting for Ransom, his butterfly cuff links shimmering as he takes my knees and gently pries them apart.

Me, I want to talk about what happened onstage, see if I can get a dialogue going between these guys. Kissing and blowing each other off won't solve years of hurt and pain and frustration. But they're men, so I guess we're starting with the sex stuff.

With a mellifluous sigh, I lean back into the pillows and grasp two handfuls of Paxton's dirty blonde hair. His mouth presses against the silken surface of my underwear, and I can't help but wonder if he's still got the taste of Ransom's lips lingering on his.

"You played that tambourine like a pro," Ransom whispers in my ear, sucking my lobe into his mouth and making me shiver. My toes curl into the black duvet cover as Paxton kisses and teases my cunt through the thin layer of fabric. "Thanks for covering for us, darling," he adds, the sound of his voice almost enough to bring my tortured body to orgasm.

When Ransom leans in to kiss me, the stubble on his face brushes against the smoothness of my own, teasing me with a slightly rough edge that makes my heart tremble in my chest. I slip my hands inside his hoodie, feeling the warmth of his body through the tank underneath. The armholes are cut so low that I can easily slip my fingers beneath it, too, touching his bare skin, his scars, his nipples.

"I want to see your tattoo," I breathe between scalding kisses, my body trembling from Paxton's mouth working against my core. He seems to be taking his time tonight, kissing me the way he kissed Ransom onstage. "Both of you," I whisper and Pax pauses, sitting up and looking every bit the supposedly royal asshole that he is.

"Do you now?" he drawls, slowly taking his cuff links off, placing them in his pocket. I swear, the man could make millions in the porn industry by simply undressing. He wouldn't even have to do anything else, just take off one of his handsome suits.

"Please," I say, popping the *P* sound off my glossed lips, leaning back on my elbows.

Paxton and Ransom exchange a look, shedding all their clothing from the waist up, two gorgeous specimens of masculinity bare and open for me to look at, admire, rake apart with my gaze. I wonder if there's another reason behind all their fighting, their love for the same woman, and then their sharing of another woman's bed. Was that coincidence? Or maybe they were meant to be together with one woman all along?

Fuck, but I want to be that woman.

I study the tattoo on Ransom's elbow, the way the circle of bass and treble clefs surrounds the fine point at the end of his arm, taking up what little space was left there. His black and grey tattoos—including the one of his mother—surround it, draping the thick muscular width of his arm in art. Maybe as an artist I appreciate their bodies for what they are? Fucking *canvases.*

Paxton perches himself on the edge of the bed and proceeds to remove his leather boots in a way that should probably be rated X, the new tattoo on his chest almost invisible in the sea of ink that cascades down his chiseled form.

The way I compared Michael to a werewolf before, and

Paxton to a vampire, that still holds true. He moves so slowly, so carefully, his cruelty this fine cover for his emotions, like a glittering black masquerade mask, so beautiful to look at. Paxton's movements are practiced, perfect, each fluid contraction of his muscles exacted with deadly efficiency.

Watching Pax and then glancing over at Ransom as he yanks his bulky buckled boots off, I'd have to call him … some kind of demon. A dark one, one whose exterior doesn't match the beautiful lightness of its heart. He has this feral grace, but it's controlled. It's not bestial or animalistic like Michael's just … dangerous. Deep. Capable of cutting until it leaves nothing but blood and an aching heart, still beating for the whisper of his shadowy wings.

Carefully, moving like I'm in the middle of two predators, I take my shirt off, Michael's necklaces jingling as they clink together against my chest. My bra is new, a perfect match to my panties. I decide to leave it on. It feels sexy and feminine, a soft but powerful beauty in the midst of all this masculine energy.

"Will you kiss for me again?" I ask, but I'm not sure that I even need to ask. The two of them are watching each other, moving back to the pillows. At first, I'm not sure who's going to start kissing who, but then Paxton pushes Ransom down next to me, a palm on either side of his head, and he moves until their mouths are pressed together.

From this view, I can see that both their cocks are hard, straining against their pants, brushing against one another as they move, hands roaming experimentally but not tentatively. Whatever sparked to life between them tonight, it's at least temporarily burned away their fear.

My hand slides down my belly and under the lacy

waistband of my underwear, touching the silken heat of my sex, fingers slippery with the proof of my desire. My eyes take in the sight of those two muscular bodies rubbing together, nipples hard, sweat dripping down their chiseled frames.

Ransom's moans are low and deep, as velvety as his voice. Paxton's are wicked, as ferocious and sinful as always. I gasp as he curls his hands through Ran's, tattooed fingers pressing the other man into the bed. My fingers start to move more quickly, rubbing my aching clitoris in circles.

The sight of them kissing turns me on so much that I find myself moaning shamelessly, lost in the erotic sights and sounds that drench the Bat Cave in sex. Our only source of light is from the moon, dripping in through the open curtains. From down the hallway, I hear jovial laughter, but I don't have it in me to pay much attention.

My eyes squeeze shut as I arch my hips, bringing myself to climax with just my fingers on my clit. The groans that escape past my lips draw the attention of the boys, breaking their focus on each other.

"Don't worry about me," I pant, wanting them to keep going, exploring, finding out what it is that they see in each other. But they come to me anyway, Paxton covering my body with his, the same way he did Ransom.

"Do I look *worried*?" he asks me, kissing down my sweaty throat, kneading my breasts through the cute white and pink cups of my bra. "Stop fretting so damn much, Miss Lily."

Paxton reaches down and unbuttons his slacks, yanks down his zipper. He glances up at me, over at Ransom.

Before I can even figure out his next move, he's pushing aside my panties and shoving himself into me, making my head fall back, my body fall to pieces.

"At least now," he whispers, voice slightly ragged with pleasure, "you can *watch* me fuck your girlfriend."

"At least there's that," Ransom whispers, taking over Pax's mouth again, kissing him with all the passion and strength that he gives me. My body rocks with the hard push of Paxton's hips as he drives himself forward with merciless abandon.

I reach my hands up, touch them both, revel in the feel of their hard warm bodies beneath my palms. I decide in that split second that they were actually the ones in the right in this situation—this is so much better than talking. And haven't the six of us been using sex as a communication device all along? Since that first night I dragged myself wet and sad and tired onto their bus, haven't we been using it to fucking heal?

So Paxton and Ransom … whatever they are, whatever label they want to use, I decide that they need this, need to fuck each other, feel each other's heartbeats, taste each other's mouths.

"Fuck, I love you guys," Ransom says in that delicious dripping voice of his, making me shiver, making my mind race with the implications of that statement.

Paxton pauses, stills, freezes with his cock still buried inside of me. For a second, I think he's going to run away again—it does seem to be a habit of his.

Instead, he gestures with his chin at Ransom.

"Take your fucking knickers off and get your arse over here," he says, his eyes silver in the moonlight, ethereally beautiful, impossible to look away from.

Ransom does what he's asked, but slowly, baring his scarred lower half and shucking his jeans and boxers aside.

Completely nude, he looks like a statue, something I'd study in pursuit of my art.

I need to paint these guys, I think as the scene in the bedroom heats up, takes an interesting turn.

Ransom moves close to us, near my head where it's pillowed in black silk and feather stuffed cushions. He pauses there as Paxton leans forward and takes Ran's cock in his mouth. Seeing those tattooed fingers curl around Ransom's shaft does all sorts of things to me—especially since Pax picks up the movement of his hips.

I tease his blonde hair with one hand, play with the silken strands and wrap them around my fingers. I use the other to gently squeeze and caress Ransom's balls, feeling them tighten up as pleasure coils in his body and he comes with shuddering, gasping breaths. Paxton keeps his mouth wrapped around Ran's shaft, swallowing as he sits up and wipes his arm across his cruel mouth.

"Well, fuck, that was certainly easier than I thought," he says, looking down at me and then dropping his mouth to mine for a kiss. He tastes like Ransom's come, the smell of violets clinging to his lips. It's that sensation almost more than his driving shaft that draws my hips off the bed, yanks me to another climax and leaves me a sweating, quivering mess. "Now, what the hell are you two arseholes going to do for *me*?"

Ransom and I exchange a wordless look that speaks volumes.

Should I? he asks me with his eyes.

Oh, yes, you should, I respond with a slight tilt of my lips.

Paxton slides his thick, swollen cock out of me, shimmering with the satin silk of my cunt.

I sit up, using my hands on his shoulders to guide him around, kissing him until *he's* the one lying on his back. By the time he realizes what's happening, it's too fucking late.

"Oh, hell no," he says as Ransom slaps a handcuff on one wrist and hooks him to the spindles in the headboard bat's mouth. But he's got gravity working against him, so even though I'm guessing he and Ransom are at about the same level of strength, he can't fight Ran off when he grabs the other wrist and locks that up, too. "You bollocking prats," he growls as Ransom and I sit back and look down at him.

Somehow, he still manages to look like a dickish asshole with both hands bound above his head.

"After all the shit you've put me through over the years," Ran says, his voice even and steady, "the least you can do is put up with this."

I sit on my knees next to him as he pulls one of the drawers out, finally getting to look for myself and see what's inside.

"Oh," I breathe as I see leather paddles, nipple clamps, candles, rope, and dildos. There are straps I wouldn't know what to do with, as well as vibrators, lube, and plenty of condoms. "Can we bring some of this on the plane."

"Honey, you don't even have to ask me that," Ran says as he grabs a flogger, much like the one Paxton himself was wielding in the back room at the Silver Skull.

"He's got this shite stashed all over his house, too," Pax murmurs lazily, like he's not at all concerned at being tied up. Maybe he isn't? Hell, I bet he likes it. "You'll probably get tired of it before long."

Ransom shoves the drawer closed as I dig around in another, finding the cock ring that Copeland and I used together.

"Are you going to beat me senseless?" Pax asks as Ransom straddles his legs and drags the black and purple tails of the flogger down his chest, teasing his hardened nipples, sliding it over his erect cock.

"Not really, no," Ran says, continuing his exploration with this tortuous slowness that's fascinating to watch but which quickly drives Pax up the wall—especially when I turn the cock ring on and slip it in my mouth. I lean down, sweeping red hair across the tattooed song lyrics on Paxton's midsection, over his nipples, and then I start to kiss.

My lips press against his ear, the vibration strange and foreign on my tongue. I use it to lick a hot line down his inked throat, along his jawline, even to part his lips.

"Bleeding hell," he curses as I make my way lower, suck his nipples into my mouth and watch in satisfaction as his hips arch up off the bed. Ransom really does whip him then. And again. And again. The more times he does it—hitting Pax's tight, flat belly, his shaft, his balls—the deeper and more pained Paxton's moans become.

Ransom and I pause to make out, his hand teasing me, slipping two fingers under my panties and fingering me until I'm trembling again. Just before we pull apart, I slip the cock ring from under my tongue and into his mouth, and he hands me the flogger.

"What the fuck are you two doing?" Pax snaps as Ransom scoots down and starts to lick and suck Paxton's cock. I swear, his storm grey eyes roll back into his head with pleasure.

Me, I lay back on the bed, my cunt facing Paxton, and I slip the handled end of the flogger beneath my panties and inside the insatiable heat of my body.

"Damn it, Lily," he whispers, voice rough with pent-up

pleasure and need.

I keep myself propped on a single elbow, moving the toy slowly in and out, watching Paxton's grey gaze get heavy-lidded as Ransom services his cock.

The orgasm that hits him reminds me of an earthquake, breaking him in two, one half for me and one half for Ransom. That crack down the middle spills some of his old hurt and pain into the air, lets it drift away in the sex tainted haze of the night. He comes hard, right into Ransom's mouth as I finally lay back and finish myself with one hand on my clit, the other still thrusting the toy into me.

Afterwards, none of us moves for a long time.

Ransom has tilted his body so that his head is near mine, the rest of him draped horizontally across the bed, across Pax's legs.

We both leave him tied up while we recover.

"What are your parents going to think of the inevitable viral video of us making out?" Ransom asks after a good ten minutes has passed in silence.

"I guess we'll find out when we visit them," Paxton says, drawing Ran up and onto his elbows.

"You're visiting them?"

"When we play London, yeah. We all are."

"I'm meeting your parents?" I ask, surprised. I watch as Ransom moves up to the headboard and lets Paxton free. I guess he's not one to leave his lover tied up while he makes a run for it. I almost smile at that, but then … Pax's parents. Holy shit. "They're not going to like me, are they?" I ask as Ran groans.

"They've never liked me," he says, but not like it *really* matters to him. "I guess now they'll probably like me even less."

"I'm counting on it," Pax says, sitting up and stretching his arms above his head. "But forget about that. What about right now? We're staying the night here and leaving for New York tomorrow. That gives us plenty of time if you guys want to go out."

The door slides open and I look over my shoulder to see Copeland leaning against the doorframe.

"I think we'd rather stay in," he says, and then he slips into the room and onto the bed.

Michael and Muse aren't far behind him.

The next morning, I get up before anyone else is awake, bolstered by the fact that Ransom had zero nightmares last night. Zero.

I sneak down the hall and get my new digital drawing tablet out of the bag, opening the box and powering it on. Without a single scrap of clothing on, I climb back into bed and draw the tangled sheets and sweaty naked bodies of the men around me. All five of them are out completely, and all five of them are most assuredly one hundred percent nude—and most assuredly one hundred percent *male.*

The sprawling mess of masculine beauty around me makes for an interesting sketch, this charged image that I spend almost two hours on before I hear a faint knock at the door.

"I'll get it," Muse says, his face pressed into a pillow, but I just sweep some of his silver-black hair away from his face and give him a small peck on the lips.

"I can get it."

I throw on yet another random assortment of clothes from the mess on the floor—Cope's white linen pajama pants and Muse's zip-up sleeveless hoodie. He might like to wear it completely unzipped, but I drag the metal together all the way to the top, over the fullness of my breasts, and then head across the heated wood floors to answer the door.

It's Octavia.

"Good morning," I say softly, crossing my arms over my chest and leaning my shoulder into the wall of the bus, my feet planted on the metal stairs. "Do you need to talk to the boys?" I wonder if she's going to lecture Ran and Pax about last night, or maybe ask them questions, maybe ask *me* questions.

Instead, all she does is hold out a pair of keys.

"Michael asked me last night if he could borrow one of the label's trucks. We'll need to hook up the trailer and tow it later, and with that attached, there's all sorts of extra liability issues …" Octavia sucks in a deep breath, but she doesn't look directly at me as I reach out and scoop the keys from her palm. "Anyway, I rented a minivan. It's not as … impressive as the truck"—we both pause and look across the sun warmed pavement at the ugly truck with painted flames —"but you can use it to do … whatever you were planning on doing."

We both smile a little at the disparaging of the poor hideous truck.

"This is my official apology. I'm not very good with, well, this kind of stuff, so there you go."

Octavia turns like the conversation is over, as brisk and businesslike as usual.

"Don't you want to talk to Pax and Ran?" I ask, but she just shakes her head, ponytail bobbing.

"Do you?" she asks, looking back at me. I think I see her cheeks color slightly. "Weren't you dating one or both of them?"

I smile.

"I still am."

Octavia turns around at that and blinks several times, putting two fingers up to her temple.

"Do I want to know?"

"It's definitely a triple X rated story," I say, clutching the keys tightly in my hand, "but if you want to hear about it sometime, I can give you the modified version."

"Well, tonight's my last night. Tomorrow, my colleague, Tamasin Perez, will meet us in Montréal and take over management duties there. Don't worry though—I already made arrangements for you to travel with the band. You shouldn't have any problems from here on out."

"Does the label know why you're leaving?" I ask and Octavia lifts her chin slightly, clearly a prideful women. Maybe that's where some of that aggression comes from? From fighting so hard to get to the top, to stay at the top, from dealing with sexism and bullshit. I just wish she hadn't used all of that anger and vitriol on me.

"No. I just said we were having creative differences and that the boys would like a new manager. I have a friend in personnel who made the switch really easy for me. I don't know how you did it, but thank you for keeping Paxton from calling in a personal complaint. What I did to you … could've ended my career."

I tap my pink fingernails against the metal wall next to me.

"Is it too late to change your mind?" I ask, praying like hell that I'm not going to regret this.

My quest for forgiveness with Kevin got me into some serious trouble, but then again, the woman did rent me a minivan.

"Paxton will never let me live this down," she says, but

her voice has this quiver, and I swear, before she turns her head away from me, I see the slightest shimmer of tears at the edges of her eyes.

"Why don't you let me worry about Paxton?" I ask.

Octavia pauses for a long moment.

"Do you want to come have coffee with me?" she asks, shocking the hell out of me.

"Can I come, too?" Copeland asks, surprising me when he comes up behind me and puts his hands on my shoulders. I didn't even hear him come out of the hallway. "I'm dying for something besides whatever that canned shit is that Michael and Pax buy."

"Certainly," Octavia says, taking a deep breath, clutching her clipboard and tablet to her chest. "I hope you don't mind if I drive."

She walks away with that haughty swagger that bothered the hell out of me when I first met her. But her hands, where they were wrapped around the clipboard, those were trembling.

"She's so fucking lonely," Cope says as soon as Octavia stands up to grab her coffee from the counter. "That's got to be it, why she acts the way she does."

He leans that magazine worthy face of his on the palm of his hand, one elbow propped on the table, his smile soft and affectionate as he glances over at me.

"That's what I thought, too," I whisper as I tuck my own mug close and gaze at the intricate coffee foam design in front of me. It's almost too pretty to drink. Somebody at the counter got creative and drew a flower with six petals. Wouldn't it be nice to think that fate was looking out for me from the surface of my coffee? After all she's put me through, the bitch basically owes me. "That, and I think she's had to fight tooth and nail to get where she is. I think she might've felt threatened by me? I'm not sure."

"Do you really think asking her to stay is a good idea?" he asks with a slight nonjudgmental shrug. "I mean, what she did to you was seriously fucked-up. Anyway, she's one of very few women in my life that I haven't liked straight off."

I smile at him. His insatiable need to be the white knight is funny to me. On the one hand, it's who he is, what he lives for. On the other, it's the thing he's most afraid of because to him, success and failure are synonymous with life and death. With Cara, maybe even with his mom, that actually proved to be true. I just need him to know that I'm different.

"I think she's just one of those people you have to get to know first," I say as Cope looks down at his own foam design, a fairly intricate skull and crossbones. Now I hope *that* one isn't a message from fate. "Do you think Paxton will freak when he finds out I asked her to stay?"

I lift my gaze up, pan across the row of paintings on the wooden wall to our left. Apparently this is a café/art gallery. Cute idea. I guess I know why Copeland picked this place out.

He picked it for me.

I pick my coffee mug up and let my lips obliterate the foam design, drinking it slowly and savoring the deep rich notes of chocolate against the bitter background of freshly ground beans. It tastes a little bit like heaven, I won't lie. Only nowhere *near* as good as Pax's mouth after he'd swallowed Ransom's come.

"I don't know. Maybe. But he likes you, so you might just be able to convince him to get over it." Cope winks at me, running a hand over his auburn hair. The ring in his lower lip shines silver in the sunshine peeping through the window behind him. "If you really believe she deserves this second chance, I'll stand by you. Maybe now that she's given up her attachment to Pax, I'll get along with her better? She does always make fun of my books though. That could be the reason we never really clicked."

I grin at him, this crazy fluttering inside my chest that has nothing to do with the fact that we'll be leaving for New York City soon, that after the show tonight I'll be heading home.

Home.

To the place where Dad took his last breath, where his soul left the aching shell of his body for the last time, fled to greener pastures. I don't know what I believe in exactly, but if there's a heaven, he's there. If it's rebirth, then I hope he's a goddamn prince.

Right now, in this second, all my butterflies are for Copeland Park.

He's dressed in jeans—of course—with a loose black tank featuring some of Harper's art. This particular shirt has the convertible with the five guys in it, the sketch white instead of black this time. He's got those same black cord necklaces with the pewter charms on them, and white sweatbands with black sketched hearts.

“The convertible …” I start and Cope cringes.

“Paxton had just bought a brand-new Porsche Boxster,” he says, tapping at the side of his mug with one of those long fingers of his. “Chloe borrowed it that night to take Harper out.”

He doesn't have to say anything else. I'm done asking questions about the art.

Well, okay, maybe that's not true. I'm actually beyond curious to find out why the hell Paxton would want to use this stuff in his shows and as his album art when it represents one of the worst tragedies in his and Ransom's life.

“Sorry,” Octavia says, sitting down beside us with her drink. It's completely drenched in chocolate sprinkles. Like, I can't even see the whipped cream through the deluge of brown bits. “They served me the wrong drink and I had to have it remade.” She sweeps her hand over the slicked back surface of her brunette hair, looking almost naked without her signature headset on.

It's funny, seeing her sitting there complaining about her drink, and then witnessing the messy spray of chocolate sprinkles. I feel like I'm seeing a hidden side of Beauty in Lies' manager.

"While you two were getting dressed, I made some calls. Frankly, it'd be a lot easier if I just stuck around and continued my duties. If things don't work out by the end of the tour then I could work side by side with Tamasin in Seattle for a few weeks to get her up to speed and ready to work on the new album."

"I like that," I say, sliding my hand under the table and onto Cope's thigh. His jeans are holey as hell, so it's easy for me to dip my fingers into the denim and find his bare skin. He curls his hand around my wrist and gives me a comforting squeeze.

God, he's so fucking *easy* to be with. I really do feel like we've been dating forever.

"Like a trial period," I add as Octavia watches us with a sharp as hell gaze, like a hawk or something. At the same time, I feel like she doesn't quite get what's going on between Cope and me, like maybe she's never been with someone who took her breath away with a single smile. "I'm sure Pax can get used to the idea."

Octavia looks down at her drink and then picks up the spoon from the side of her plate, grabbing a heaping pile of whipped cream and sprinkles and putting it to her lips.

"I didn't know Paxton was gay," she starts and I laugh; I can't help it. Her pale brown eyes flick up sharply.

"He's not gay," I promise as my body flushes and I suck my lower lip into my mouth for a second, teasing Copeland's bare thigh and making my charm bracelet jingle. On my opposite wrist, the fresh burn of my tattoo reminds me that

I'm still here, that I'm still alive, and that I want to fucking *feel* it. "Him and Ran just … Well, how's the media handling the news?"

"Oh, they love it," she says, leaning back, taking another spoon of sprinkles with her. "They also liked seeing you onstage with Michael. You're all over the internet today."

"Thank god I haven't checked my phone then," I say as Cope sips his drink and watches me. It's like he can't take his eyes off me. I like that, especially considering I can barely pull my gaze from him. This little tingle starts in my belly as I imagine living in Seattle, going out to coffee with him, having tea in the mornings with Muse, going to dinner with Michael. The one thing I am going to miss though is having us all together. "I wonder if my stepmother's seen it yet?"

"Is that who you're going to see tonight?" Octavia asks, and it's like she's shot this arrow of ice into my heart without even meaning to.

"Actually, no. I'm going to pick up my dad's ashes from my empty childhood home." I hope I don't sound bitter when I say that. Although, to be honest, I am. I am a little fucking bitter that my stepmom cleared out several lifetime's worth of items without consulting me, dumped my shit in the living room, and then abandoned a sampling of my father's ashes like a punishment against my sexual sins.

"I'm sorry to hear that," Octavia says, and she sounds genuine about it, too.

Cope scoots his chair a little closer to me, slipping his arm around my shoulders and giving me one of his famous hugs before I even realized that I needed it. I reach up a tentative finger and find a few stray tears sneaking down my cheeks.

"Um," I start, clearing my throat, my mind, trying to emotionally prepare myself for what I know has to happen. The final goodbye I never got to have. The last visit home. An ending to an entire chapter of my life. "Why did you want to have coffee with me?" I ask finally, trying to get to the root of this visit.

"Because you said you wanted to be friends," Octavia says, looking up like she's a little surprised at my question. Her genuine reaction is what seals it for me. She did and said some horrible things, but so did Pax to Ransom. And look at them now, right? Octavia seems like she has everything under control, but there's a weird, slightly awkward person hiding inside of her just like there is in all the rest of us.

"I think that's a great reason," I tell her, leaning into Cope, closing my eyes and breathing in the sweet scent of freshly brewed coffee and new denim, the bright scent of laundry detergent.

"So," he starts, taking over the conversation for me, giving me a moment to breathe, "I saw the schedule you emailed out last night for the next leg of the tour. What are the three days of personal time penciled in after the London show?"

Oh. Shit. That's right.

We're all going to meet the Blackwells together.

If they're anything at all like their son, this should be interesting.

With light traffic, the drive from Philadelphia to New York is just over two hours. Factoring in time to get to the venue, park the buses and trailers, and set up the generators, it's still barely noon.

There's another package for me from Roger Monet—the crazy magic shop guy that I used to work for—that one of the roadies drops off at the bus door shortly after we park. He probably sent it a while ago, but all our mail for the last week was forwarded here to pick up today.

"Tea, tea, and more tea," I say, sipping a cup of organic peach rooibos with honey and watching Lilith sit in the sunshine with her new digital drawing tablet. The bus door is propped open to take advantage of the weather, a gentle breeze sneaking in along with the sounds of a city—people, traffic, construction, fucking *life* at large. "Most of this will have to go back to Seattle on the bus. I have no idea how tea and customs and all that shit works."

"You've never been out of the country?" Lilith asks, her eyes lifting briefly from her drawing to watch me. She's wearing a sundress today that I've never seen; I think she dug it out from one of her boxes. The fabric is white, covered in cherries, and there's a matching headband. All put together with a pair of burgundy velvet pumps I bought her in Chicago, and she looks like a fifties pinup/housewife—in the best possible way, of course.

My cock thickens and I lick my lip, turning back to the box and rummaging through crumpled newspaper to find a pair of red candles tied with twine, a pendulum crystal on a chain, and another book. This one's labelled *The Art of Perfect Sex: Using the Occult to Achieve Sensual Bliss.* Based on the last two weeks, I don't think any of us needs help in that department, but I grab it and toss it into the duffel bag on the floor, the one I'm taking on the plane out of Montréal.

"Nope. I take it you haven't either?"

"Not once," Lilith confirms. "I got that passport because Kevin promised me that when we got married—which was always *soon, soon, soon, relax, Lilith*—that we'd go on a fabulous whirlwind honeymoon around the entire globe." Her lips—slathered in this sumptuous deep red color—twitch invitingly. "I guess you guys get to take me on the honeymoon of my dreams, huh?"

Her red brows raise up, but she keeps her eyes locked on the screen, her charm bracelet jingling as she draws. Looking at her now, I am beyond fucking grateful that I went with my gut instinct and invited her along. If anything, I'm *more* intrigued now than I was in Atlanta.

"Like I said, my speciality is making dreams come true." I wink at her when she looks up at me, refusing to let the dark shadow of my past take over this moment. I feel like everyday since Atlanta it's been getting worse. I can't figure out if that's because I was so worried about Lilith that I started imagining the awful things that might've happened to her and then connected those to my own past … or maybe if it's just fucking time for me to face my demons.

I think of those hummingbirds again, the ones outside my bedroom window. Somehow, the beauty of those birds hasn't been tainted for me, not even when I was raped in that same room, looking at that same window, staring at those same birds.

“Hey,” I say abruptly, as much to catch Lilith's attention as to distract myself. “You want to do something? I mean, I know tonight's a big night for you, but we're in NYC, Cutie. It seems silly to just sit around here.”

Lilith sets the drawing tablet aside and turns to face me, leaning forward on the couch, hands curled around the edge of the leather cushions. She looks so eager, so excited. It makes me want to be eager and excited, too.

“I'm not ashamed of being a tourist,” she says with all due seriousness. “I will go to the Empire State Building, visit Times Square, go to the wax museum …”

“There's a fucking wax museum?” I ask and she nods, making me laugh.

I lean my head back for a moment and then drop my chin to look at her, pushing my glasses up my nose with two fingers.

“That,” I tell her with a flashy grin, “is what I want to do. Where is it? *What* is it?”

“It's called Madame Tussauds, and it's actually *in* Times Square. We could kill two birds with one stone and at least walk around a little so I can say I've been there. It's just a big building full of hyperrealistic wax figures modeled after real celebrities.” Lilith pauses and bites her lower lip, waggling her eyebrows at me. “Are you sure you guys aren't on display in there yet? I bet basically everyone that visited would take selfies with their hands on your junk.”

"Is my junk that impressive?" I ask with a flirty voice, setting my tea aside and leaning my palm against the counter.

"It is to me," she replies, and the air gets a little thick for a moment there.

We stare at each other for a long time, and I wonder how she's going to do, seeing her hometown, being reunited with her dad's ashes. I'm scared to see her fall apart; I don't want that for Lilith. She's an amazing young woman, and when I'm with her, I don't feel lonely. I mean, I always have the guys obviously, but … there's something in her spirit that calls to mine. She eases that awful ache inside of me.

Copeland pounds up the front steps in his running clothes, a white tank sticking to his body, sweat dripping down his muscular legs. It's his thing, to take a run in every city. He's been slacking a little lately, but I don't blame him. It's hard to want to go out when staying in is so much goddamn fun.

"Wax museum," I say and Cope's eyebrows lift in question as he grabs a white dishrag off the counter and runs it down his face. "You want to go?"

"Why the fuck not?" he asks, looking from me to Lilith. Michael's taking a shower and Ransom and Paxton are talking in the Bat Cave, but I'm sure they'll want to go. Sometime soon I'd like to take Lilith out on a date, just me and her—like when she went dancing with Cope—but for now, I like being in a group setting.

All of these people, all of these emotions running wild … it's easy for me to forget my own trauma for a while.

"You want to grab the others?" I ask Lilith as she stands up and moves over to me, the breeze playing with that gorgeous dress of hers. Without any explanation, she walks over and kisses me on the cheek, putting her mouth to my ear.

"I'm not wearing any panties underneath this dress," she says, and then pulls away to head down the hall.

Before we leave, I head into the bathroom to put my contacts in … and I make sure *I'm* not wearing any panties either.

The museum really is in the center of all the action, tucked in Times Square amongst all the flashing signs, the tourists, the shops. There's enough anonymity here that we can walk around without being recognized, our silent bodyguards blending into the crowd and escaping my notice as usual.

We stop for food and drinks at the Hard Rock Café—come on, we just *had* to—and then hit Madame Tussauds with a nice buzz. Frankly, I think that was a pretty brilliant decision.

"This place is totally creepy," I say with a grin, standing in the middle of a room meant to look like a swag Hollywood party. There's a red carpet, a faux fountain, backdrops of the city with flashing paparazzi cameras. Situated around the room are A-list stars in disturbingly realistic detail, down to freckles, eyelashes, and tiny eyebrow hairs that the visitor's booklet Lil bought at the front counter says were hand placed by the artists.

"This is great," Lilith says, giving a frozen statue of Taylor Lautner a fake kiss. I snap a picture with her phone and she grins at me, taking it and slipping it back into that pink leather purse of hers. One of the things I've noticed about Lil—and which I totally dig—is that she doesn't spend a lot of time staring at her phone.

She's not out and about to fill her social media pages or pretend like she's having a good time; she's serious about actually doing shit, living life, making memories. Yeah, she takes a picture every now and again as a memento, but then she puts the cell away and breaks out that smile of hers.

"I know we should do the floors in order," she says, examining the map as the rest of my bandmates cluster around us, "but I kind of want to skip straight to music and then backtrack."

"Whatever you want to do is fine with me," I say as Lilith rubs her thumb over the bathroom icon on the page and gives me a look. Like, the same look she gave me before we left. It still says *no fucking panties.* "Actually, yeah, let's do music next."

"I feel like I'm in a crazy taxidermist's shop," Ransom says, poking a grinning Anne Hathaway in the forehead as he walks by. "Or maybe like I'm in that old horror movie, the one they redid with Paris Hilton. Cope, you like horror movies. What's that one called?"

"*House of Wax,*" he says with a smile, pressing the button to call the elevator. "And yeah, those are based around a wax museum so you're on the right track. All we need is a fire and a creeper bent on vengeance and we could make the third incarnation of the film."

"Hey Michael," Lil says as we hustle into the elevator together, a few curious faces—real ones this time—craning to watch us go. I guess there really are a few people that recognize us here. "What kind of movies do you like?"

"Movies?" he asks, chewing his lower lip for a second in thought. "Sci-fi, fantasy, anything that gives me a break from reality."

"Reading works even better," Cope quips and Michael gives him a look.

"Sorry, man, but reading about fucking cowboys and CEOs and shit …. well, *fucking* just doesn't sound like a lot of fun to me."

"There are other genres of books besides romance," Cope says, but Michael's got his bad boy swagger on now, so there'll be no compromising. I grin as I watch them tease each other all the way down to the bottom floor. When you first get to the museum, they make you take the elevator up to the top and work your way down.

I guess we're just seriously unconventional up in here.

"You could even try reading comics, you know, so that there are some pictures."

Michael punches Cope gently in the arm as we pile out and into a room packed with more wax figures. As the guys disperse throughout the room, Lilith grabs me by the wrist and yanks me over to the bathroom, pulling me inside before any of the employees can catch us.

"I want a quickie," she says, breathless, cheeks flushed. "With you, right here."

"How long have you been planning this?" I ask as I grin and grab her by the hips, walking her backwards into the red stall at the end of the line. Luckily, the bathroom is currently empty.

"Since I got back from coffee this morning," she tells me, and I raise my pierced brow at her, locking the stall door behind us and using the bat tattoos on my left hand to caress the side of her face. "I didn't know if we were going anywhere today, but I figured I could at least get you to come outside into the parking lot with me."

"The parking lot? You are a naughty girl, Lilith Goode."

I lean in to kiss her and she stops me with a palm on my chest.

"What's your middle name?" she asks suddenly and I laugh.

"Micah," I say and then I'm kissing her, pressing her body against the—thankfully—clean looking white tile walls. My heart beats this insane fucking rhythm in my chest, this frantic quiver that makes me feel a little dizzy. "I was named after my uncle," I whisper, taking a slight break between kisses to give her a little more of my story. I want to give her all of it, but … sometimes even I can't remember.

I think to protect myself, my brain tore my own story into pieces. Sometimes it hides certain scenes or faces or moments from me. But my uncle, he was the only person in my family that cared about me, that treated me like I *was* family. When he was alive, I was safe. After he died … that was when everything started.

I don't need to go over that shit and process it or heal or whatever else that Michael is doing with Vanessa, Cope with Cara, Ransom and Paxton with each other. That's not what *I* need. What I do need is to get it out there, tell Lilith so that she knows. I just need her to understand, that's it. I think if I do that, I can stop dredging up these feelings, seeing these skeletons grinning at me from beyond the grave.

I cut my own thoughts off by kissing Lilith deeper, sweeping my tongue along hers, sliding my hand up to cup her full breasts through the fabric of her sundress. Her mouth tastes like roses and fucking sunshine to me, but maybe I'm just imagining that because I'm so attracted to her?

The fingers of my other hand curl in her red hair, falling

like spun rubies across my skin, making my cock that much harder as the silken strands tease the sensitive inner part of my wrist. Her hands end up curling around the waistband of my black and white striped skinny jeans. She grazes the sensitive skin of my new tattoo, but I don't mind. I just want her to touch me—*everywhere.*

The main door to the bathroom opens, the chatter of a few young girls coming along with it.

"Did you see that? That was Beauty in Lies out there."

"One of the figures?"

"No, like literally four of the five band members."

"No fucking way. You're so full of shit."

Lilith smiles against my mouth as I bite back a chuckle. I can't remember if we're in the ladies' room or a unisex bathroom, so I figure it's probably best to just keep my mouth shut.

The stall next to us opens, feet shuffling under the door.

Lilith lifts her eyes to mine, reaching down to undo my pants, sliding the quivering heat of my cock into her palm. I shove her skirts up around her hips, reach underneath her ass and lift her against the wall. It's just basic frigging biology from that point, my shaft pressing up against the scorching heat of her core, my hips thrusting, her body opening up to me.

Lilith buries her face against my neck. Shit, she even *bites* me in her attempt to keep quiet.

The sound of flushing toilets and running sinks drowns out any little sounds we might make as my pelvis grinds Lil into the wall, taking her hard and fast, giving her a quickie just like she asked.

And it's goddamn *fabulous.*

The sex we've been having lately is great, intricate,

sensual, complicated.

This? This is just two bodies fucking.

I revel in the moment, letting myself get all blah-blah bestial and male and all that shit. It feels good to claim my girlfriend, hold her in my arms, screw her with wild abandon.

I press our foreheads together, doing my best to keep our gazes locked. It makes those beautiful green eyes of hers a little blurry, but that's okay. I just want to look at her while I'm inside of her.

Lilith has this light that makes my darkness recede, this inner core of steel and strength.

For me, I think this girl is the companion that my lonely traveler was looking for.

"Oh, *Derek,*" she groans, her velvet heels locked behind my back, her sex silken and slick, drenching me with wet heat. The sound of her voice in my ear makes me come so hard that I can't breathe, that I almost drop her when she squeezes my cock tight, spills me into her heat with a ragged cry of release.

"Oh, *Lilith,*" I correct with a slight smile, holding her there for several long moments, just because she feels so damn good, because I need to be inside of her, because I like her so fucking much.

The bathroom door opens again.

"You guys in here?" Michael asks as I pull back and set Lil gently on the floor, fix her skirts, fix my pants.

"Yeah," I call back, still breathing hard, still struggling to look away, "we're in here."

As if he can sense that we need another moment alone, Michael leaves without a word and Lilith and me … we share a breathless kiss that rocks the heavens, shakes up hell, and leaves me a rapturous worshipper wrapped in sin and bent on penance.

I intend to find all of it—my damnation and my rapture—with the woman standing in front of me.

My hands are shaking as I lean in close to the mirror and try to finish my makeup without smudging what I've already done. Part of me feels like I'm being ridiculous … the rest of me is fucking terrified.

This is Cinderella at the stroke of midnight, still sitting in her carriage, still dressed in her gown, but racing back toward her stepmother's manor, terrified that the prince might see her for what she is—a broken, sad girl with no father, just a gaping empty spot in her heart that used to house him.

Still, Cinderella got her slipper back after the fact, didn't she? And she married the prince and lived happily ever after. I'd like for my ending to be a little more forward thinking, a little more progressive. Of course, I don't mind marrying the prince*s* at the end of my story (okay, we're not there yet but I'm speaking metaphorically), but I want something for myself, too.

I want to forge my own path.

And these guys, these young cocky stupidly rich rockstars are helping put me on that road.

The very fact that Muse is concerned I might lose myself in another relationship the way I did the last one shows me that this is about more than just sex. Between him and me … between all of us.

"I want you to come with me," Michael says, standing in the doorway. I smile because he's the last one on the bus, afraid to leave me here like he did in Atlanta, afraid that the clock might strike twelve and I'll disappear.

"I'm coming," I say, rising to my feet, my dress short and black and covered with skulls and crossbones. It might seem ironic to wear symbols of death on my clothes when after the show, I'll have to face the ultimate price of mortality, but I'm trying to take ownership of my feelings, claim them.

"You're fucking hot, Lil," Michael says, his gaze raking me from head to toe, his hands dark with ink, touching the curled red strands of my hair with a sort of sexual reverence that leaves me completely off-balance. I need that right now, to stumble and watch the world shift and change around me. "Seriously. I wanted you from the first second I saw you."

Michael—*Mikey*—steps up close to me, dressed entirely in black but looking anything but mournful. He's a slice of sex, a piece of night sky that makes the glimmer of the stars look so much prettier because of the contrast he provides.

"It should've been me that dragged you onto this bus," he whispers against my ear, putting his hands on the narrow curve of my waist. "It should've been me that held you that first night when you cried."

"No, it shouldn't have," I say, refusing to let a single tear fall until I get to Gloversville. That's my rule for tonight: no crying until I'm home. "Because then you would've been a cheater, and I don't date cheaters."

Mikey sighs.

"I'm *already* a cheater," he says, but he meets my eyes when he says it, owns his mistake. "But I won't be one with you."

I smile as he drops a kiss to my mouth, refusing to part his lips, just breathing against me.

The trick works, making my nibbles pebble, my cunt tighten, my skin flush. It's hard to think about crying when hormones are crashing into my heart like tidal waves.

"Let's go," he says, taking my hand and pulling me through the quiet darkness of the bus, outside and toward a squat white building squashed between two much taller ones. There's a set of steps and a big stone arch that lead into the backstage area where the rest of my boys are waiting.

Paxton is smoking a cigarette—despite the fact that it's illegal in New York State to smoke inside—and tossing glares at Octavia. As soon as he sees me, he curls his arm around my neck and pulls me away from Michael, putting his lips to my ear.

"You are in big bloody trouble," he tells me, but he's had all day to get used to the fact that I invited Octavia to stay. Technically, I had no right to extend that offer to her. I guess I was pulling a Muse there, overreaching a little. But surprisingly, Paxton didn't unleash any unwarranted anger my way. "I swear to god if she oversteps her boundaries by a single inch, I'm canning Octavia's arse and having yours for breakfast."

He lets go of me and continues to puff on his cigarette, his wicked pouty mouth twisting into its usual slash of a smile. As he leans back, resuming his position against the wall, I catch Muse's eyes and try not to grin too stupidly at him.

"What's the plan for tonight?" Cope asks, standing next to Ransom and watching me carefully. They're all doing that right now, staring at me like they're worried. I wonder if it's my lack of emotion that's stressing them out, or their fear of what's to come.

"It's okay, you guys," I say, slipping my hands together behind my head, crossing my ankles. This is the perfect moment for my strength pose. "I've got this. Stop freaking out and play an amazing show to knock the socks off these New Yorkers."

"Don't hide what you're feeling, not right now," Ransom says, stealing Pax's cigarette and taking a few drags on it with hands that are remarkably steady. He's got one of those long, loose tanks on with the giant armholes. I wish he'd wear them everyday; I can see all his muscles when he moves.

And fuck, did he get twice as handsome since making up with Pax?

Ransom smiles at me through the stubble on his face and smokes his stolen cigarette.

"I'm not hiding anything," I promise as I smooth my hands down the front of the ruched dress. It hits me mid-thigh and has a square neckline that shows off my cleavage. It's my own dress, salvaged from one of my boxes. I'd actually bought it to wear to a Halloween party with Kevin once upon a time, but he'd called late that night, after I was all dressed and ready to go, and cancelled on me.

I wonder if that was the night he caught the disease he gave me?

I shiver.

I can't deal with thoughts of Kevin right now.

"I'm *waiting* to process my emotions. I'm saving them for later."

"Lil, this is a week's worth of fresh, raw feelings that you've got in the bank. Once you let that wall down, it might come as a bit of a shock." Muse tilts his head to the side, his mohawk in these vibrant silver spikes on top of his head. "The first week you were with us, you cried a lot. Which is good. That's what you should be doing in a situation like this, but since Atlanta … not much, Cutie."

"I'll be fine," I say, feeling this flutter in my chest that surprisingly enough doesn't have anything to do with the boys, just nerves. Tight, tight bundles of nerves.

"You don't have to be tough," he tells me, meeting my gaze with his copper-emerald-sapphire one. "Just remember that: we're here for you."

"And I'm here for you—to cheer you on. Please just get up on that stage and play."

"I'm the king of holding it all in," Muse says one last time, just before Octavia calls Beauty in Lies up to the stage, "and my advice is: fucking *don't.*"

He leans forward and kisses me on either cheek, on my forehead, and *then* my lips. The other boys do their own variations of the same thing—Paxton never kisses without sliding his tongue between my lips which I don't at all mind—and then they pull away, disappearing through the black curtain.

To my left there's a set of steps to the second floor, leading to a hallway with private opera boxes. Octavia told me during our coffee date that the first one is reserved for staff; that's where I decide to watch the show from.

I show my VIP badge to the security guard at the bottom of the steps and head up, pushing past a small black curtain and finding myself in a curved balcony. It protrudes out over the churning crowd below, a few theater style seats lined up in two small rows.

I skirt around them and head to the railing, curling my

fingers around it and leaning forward, hair swinging with the motion, and manage to catch the first glimpse of Beauty in Lies, briefly frozen, waiting to start the show. As I clap with everyone else, the building shutters, the music pouring from the speakers and seducing the audience. Me, I've already been seduced. The only thing that can make me like these guys any better is time. Otherwise, I'm completely fucking sold.

In serious lust.

Feeling the cliff of logic and reason crumble beneath my feet, falling into the abyss of love, that mysterious force that's wielded for both good and evil, that's triumphant at times, apologetic at others. It's dangerous, too, especially in a situation like this, with five guys balanced on the tip of my heart, using me as a compass to point the whole group in the right direction.

If I want this to work, I have to be strong as hell. Dating—being in *love* with—five people offers five times the affection, five times the romance, five times the sex. But it also requires five times the work. Being a queen, even one with such ardent worshippers, requires sacrifice and balance, a steady hand and the heavy weight of responsibility.

But I want this. So damn much.

As hard as it'll be to visit that town, that house, those memories, I remind myself that I could be doing this alone, stumbling into Gloversville with nobody and nothing, opening the door to an empty living room and having to carry the weight of my father's ashes alone.

I got lucky though; I got backup.

A few roadies slip into the balcony with me, pausing when they see me standing there.

"You're welcome to stay," I tell them, inviting them over

with a smile, wondering what it'd be like to work on the tour, so close to the boys and yet so far away at the same time. That was me with my own life not that long ago, working my ass off for goals and dreams that weren't mine, taking care of a man with an ego big enough to match up to an entire rock band's worth of cockiness. But at the end of it all, what did I have left? Less than these people will have after this tour is over. At least they got to see the shows.

Fuck.

I was a roadie in my own *life,* going through the motions, hanging out, waiting around for something to happen. I'm not saying these guys don't work hard—they do—but then again, so did I. I worked really hard at cooking, cleaning, entertaining. I didn't dig deep and try to listen to my own music.

I won't make that same mistake this time.

First, I say goodbye to dad properly. Then, I embrace the gift I've been given.

I start chasing my dream, even if right now all it looks like is an incorporeal cloud in the distance.

As I watch the boys, it occurs to me that right now, they're my muses, the endless well pouring a creative fire into my blood. Halfway through their first song, I end up sprinting back to the bus to grab my tablet, taking it back to the balcony to sit in one of the theater chairs so I can draw.

I draw them, their music, my own feelings.

The concert winds to a close, but as it does, I realize that I have an idea.

I know what I'm going to do with my art.

I'm going to paint my journey from self-appointed roadie to groupie to … the woman I want to be, someone with serious moxie. I'm going to paint my hurts and my struggles, the boys and theirs. And then I'm going to snag a fucking gallery.

Even if I never make a cent, I want people to at least see my work. If I can do that, well, I'd consider that a success. We all have stories to tell and this, this is mine.

Once my boys play their last notes, I've got a series of concept sketches and an idea. Clearly, I still have a lot of work ahead of me, but I feel like I've got direction now, someplace for that compass to point.

When I meet the guys downstairs, I don't even speak, I just turn the screen over and show them the picture I sketched.

"This is what your music looks like inside my head," I tell them.

The expressions on their faces tell me all I need to know.

I'm on the right track.

New York City isn't the easiest place to park a massive entourage of buses and trailers, especially when the venue the label booked has other acts pulling in at ungodly hours of the morning. So as soon as the show's done, the staff starts packing up and getting ready to make the seven hour drive into Canada.

"There's no show tomorrow night," Copeland says as he takes my hand and pulls me into the minivan to sit beside him, "so there's no rush, okay? We'll just take as much time as you need."

"I'm fine, really," I say, still high from the rush of creation, from making art, from interpreting the things I feel for the guys and their music into something that can be seen and experienced by other people.

But come on, my dad is fucking dead.

I *know* that I'm going to feel something, and I'm sure it'll be awful. For right now though, I'm holding it together.

Cope curls his long fingers through mine, bathing my skin with his heat, challenging my heart to a race, one that it'll never win because with him around, it refuses to pause that galloping beat, sprinting endless loops around the track.

My eyes lift up to meet his, a cool aqua blue in the dark.

His faux hawk is still perfect, even after rocking out hard enough to shake me up a little, light a fire under my ass.

"I want to have a gallery show," I confess to him as we wait for the others to change, gather whatever they might need for the car ride and pile in with us. I'm pretty sure Michael's driving again. I don't think anyone cares enough to challenge him on that one. I still think Paxton is slightly more dominant, but he's also a spoiled shit. I can't imagine him actually wanting to take the wheel. "And I don't want to rent out a place either. I want to earn a spot somewhere, get people talking."

"With the kind of work you started tonight, I don't think it'll be all that difficult," Cope says, our thighs lined up, his jeans pressed up to my naked calf, half a naked thigh. I pick at the edge of the black dress with my other hand.

"The chances of making money at that sort of thing are slim to none, but I think I care more about people seeing my work than I do about raking in a fortune." I pause and suck on my lower lip for a second, playing with the charms on my bracelet. "Do you think that NDA I signed will affect my ability to paint you guys?"

"No," Cope says firmly. "You might not have read it, but Muse has."

"You're kidding me?" I ask, turning to look at Cope. I think I might be gaping. Copeland just grins at me.

"Nope. It's pretty basic actually, very dry. It's mostly there to protect the label and their interests, not us. If you wanted to, you could snap a photo of you naked with all of us and post it on Facebook."

I grin back at him.

"Why would I want to share that? You guys are mine. The social media buzzards can eat carrion for all I care."

Cope laughs and leans his shoulder into mine, resting our heads together.

"When we get back to Seattle, I want you to meet my mom. It'll probably be an awful introduction. She might even scare the shit out of you. Fuck, she might even convince you to get as far away from me as possible."

"No," I tell him as he squeezes my hand, "that won't happen. I'm dating you, not your mother. And you know, you were right that we should be taking care of each other. You can lean on me if you need to. I'm not going to break."

"You mean you'll take me on another bookstore date if I want one?"

"I bet you need a lot of bookstore dates considering how much you read."

"I bet you're right. I'm used to going alone; it'll be nice to have somebody around to stack my purchases on."

"Hah, so I'm your romance novel mule now, am I?" I ask and Cope laughs, the sound as light and weightless as birds' wings. Obviously he's not just the carefree boy next door that he pretends to be, but I think he is inherently gentle, giving, a caretaker.

"We're just about ready," Muse says, surprising me by climbing into the driver's seat. He looks at me and Cope in the rearview mirror, his glasses perched on his nose. "Michael has shitty night vision," he explains without my even having to ask. "And Paxton's usually at least partially buzzed at all times. It just makes sense for me to drive."

"I told you I'd do it," Ran says, slipping into the van and climbing into the back row. He pauses briefly to give me a kiss on the forehead.

"I thought you and Pax might want some snogging time in the backseat," Muse says, timing his delivery perfectly with Paxton's arrival at the van's open door.

"Be careful or I might just come for you next," he says and I almost choke on my own breath when I turn to look at him … and find him wearing jeans and a t-shirt. "What?" he asks, like he's so damn innocent. But I see that mouth curving into an evil smile. "I can't dress down and look lazy and unkempt like the rest of these bastards?"

The tight black Beauty in Lies tee stretches across Pax's muscles, leaving both his arms bare and dripping with tattoos. I hardly ever get to see those since they're always covered up. It's too dim with just the tiny overhead light on in the van to make out details, but the overall effect is *stunning.* Oh, and that ass in denim … I pinch it when he moves past me to sit with Ransom.

For a few minutes there, it just feels like we're going on a road trip.

I almost forget what's waiting at the end of it.

Michael appears with Octavia, speaking briefly with her outside before he turns and shuts the back door for me, climbing into the front seat and buckling his belt.

"As long as we're in Montréal for the show the day after tomorrow, we can do whatever we want."

"Are … your security guards coming with us?" I ask, almost dreading the answer. Having random strangers following us in a mall, at a club, or on a beach is one thing. But at my dad's house? I don't like the idea of it.

"No, there's no need for them with what we're doing," Mikey says as Muse starts the engine and the headlights flare to life. "It's just us, Lil."

He glances over his shoulder to meet my gaze as I breathe out a small sigh of relief.

The van rolls forward, toward the already open gate, and

onto a still busy New York street. For a while there nobody speaks. Me, because I'm checking out the shimmering lights of the city, the towering skyscrapers with a thousand winking eyes. Cope because he's watching me watch the city. Ran and Pax … I glance at them surreptitiously.

There are definitely hands inside of pants back there.

I bite my lip to hold back a girly giggle. I have no idea why watching them together excites me so much; it just does. I have an intense urge to crawl back there and get in on the action, but I don't want to let go of Cope's hand. That, and I also refuse to take my eyes off my pink leather purse, sitting on the seat next to me. Inside of it are my mother's ashes. I feel strangely protective of her tonight, maybe because I know I'm going to make the boys walk to the cemetery with me to spread her ashes.

Jesus.

I breathe out suddenly, my pulse racing.

I still need to call the cemetery and see about getting my dad's name added to the Goode family mausoleum. I wonder briefly why I haven't done it already, but inside, I know. I wasn't ready to take that step, that final act that would seal his name in stone forever. *Roy Goode.*

Deep breath, Lil.

"I found the listing for the house," Cope says quietly a while later. He shows me his phone, but I can't look at any of the pictures. No way. I just need to get there and say goodbye in person. "The listing price is pretty low."

"Gloversville isn't exactly hot ticket real estate," I say, making my voice light. Or I try to anyway. It comes out sounding kind of … husky? "That's not surprising."

"You know," Cope starts, scrolling through the listing details, "it wouldn't be that big of a purchase for the five of us to chip in on—"

Before he can finish that sentence, I lean in and kiss him with everything I've got, a surge of feeling bursting up from my heart like a sea of butterflies.

"Cope," I say against his mouth as I pull back slightly, "that's one of the sweetest, most considerate offers I've ever heard in my life." He smiles against my lips, but I don't think he knows what I'm going to say next. "But that house … I've decided that it's actually a good thing to let it go. I want some other family to move in there and enjoy the kind of life that we used to have in it. After losing everyone that called that place home with me, it just *isn't* home anymore, you know?"

"Ah," he says, his breath warm, inviting me to kiss him again. "Fuck, you're right."

"It's stupid and cliché, but home really *is* where the heart is. Right now, my heart is here with the five of you."

"Goddamn it, Lil," Michael says, looking back at me again. "When you talk like that … It makes me fucking crazy."

"Well, it's true," I say, sweeping back red hair with my right hand. "So if you guys live in Seattle, then that's where I'll make my home. Although I admit I'm a little sad that we won't all be together anymore."

There's a long stretch of silence that follows.

I wonder what they're all thinking about, but by then, I'm starting to recognize the countryside and sweat begins to drip down the sides of my face.

When people think of New York, all they think about is the Big Apple. But honestly, there are vast swaths of countryside, farmland, and forest. That's what we're driving through now, the relatively quiet parts. Even though it's dark, the moon sheds just enough light that I get flashes of déjà vu, of traveling this same stretch with my dad to NYC, to Schenectady to visit my estranged aunt, Bess.

"Did you know my dad actually has a sister?" I say into the quiet of the van. I think my boys are trying to be respectful by staying silent, giving me a chance to think. I'm not sure that I want to get too deep into my thoughts right now. "So I guess I do *technically* have family left. I've met her a handful of times, but not one of those visits was pleasant."

"What's she like?" Cope asks as I hear this shuddering sigh from the backseat that makes my nipples harden, despite the situation. And then Ransom is folding his arms on the back of the seat between me and Cope, watching me carefully.

"She's a veterinarian," I say, realizing that's not exactly the question Cope was asking. "Devoutly religious. I guess my grandparents were, too. I mean, not that my dad *wasn't* religious, but he wasn't a zealot either. Aunt Bess is … too judgmental, aggressive to a fault. My dad cut her off completely after Yasmine died."

"How come, darling?" Ransom asks, his voice sliding around me like a silken ribbon.

"Well," I start, wondering if this might affect either Ran or Pax negatively. "Yasmine identified as bisexual. Between dating asshole metalcore boys," I say with a slight smile, "she sometimes dated asshole metalcore girls, too." A small laugh escapes me as I sweep my fingers through my hair. "My aunt came to the funeral with a *God Hates Fags* sign. I haven't seen her since. Frankly, I don't really care. I thought about contacting her to let her know that …" I stop and swallow hard. I guess I just can't casually say *my dad passed.* Nope. It won't come out. "Anyway, fuck her."

"Fuck her," Paxton agrees from behind me. "I don't have much tolerance for bigots. You'll see, when you meet my parents. There's more than one reason we don't get along."

"Paxton's parents are the fucking devil," Michael says from the front, scaring the crap out of me. I'm already nervous about meeting them; that doesn't help. "No wonder we all ended up here, starting a new family. Looks like we either lost the good ones or ended up with the shittiest blood relations known to man."

I notice that Muse isn't weighing in on the conversation and decide to change the subject. He might just be too focused on driving to join in, but my guess is that he really doesn't want to talk about his family. The only things he's told me about his past are that he was emancipated at fifteen, that he worked in a magic shop, and that he shares his middle name with his uncle.

"I have my house key from before I moved to Arizona. The locks haven't been changed in years, so getting inside isn't a problem." I poke at my purse with the toe of my black heel. These ones have a silver skull and crossbones buckle across the front. "I don't know what my stepmom left in the house, but if there's a lot of stuff we can cart it over to my dad's storage unit."

"Did she have access to that, your stepmom?" Muse asks, finally rejoining the conversation.

See, I think I was right.

"Nope. Just me and dad. I have the key for that, too, if we need it."

I take another deep breath and lean my head back against the seat, still clutching Cope's hand. Ransom turns his face toward me and presses several loving kisses to my temple.

The stubble on his face tickles my skin, making me smile.

His fingers start to massage my scalp and I close my eyes for a second, just to take a moment to collect myself, prepare my heart for the sight of the familiar turned distant, the homely turned foreign, the living turned dead.

But I guess I drift off to sleep because when I open them, we're pulling into my parents' driveway.

My lashes part, eyes opening, head lifting, my gaze taking in the quiet suburban street with a detached sort of acknowledgement. *Yes,* my heart says, *we once lived here, but we don't know this place anymore.* That thought's fine and dandy, a good shield against the pain, but as soon as I open the minivan's sliding door I know it to be a lie.

Setting my high heel on the pavement, I see two pairs of children's handprints with dates scrawled in messy lines below them. Above them, the words *Lil & Yas.*

Fucking fuck.

I grab my purse and carefully pull my phone out, snapping a photo before I can think better of it. I might not want to look at this right now, but later …

"I can be your photographer," Cope says, sweeping hair back from my face, "so you can just relax and look around."

"Okay," I say. I think my eyes are already watering. Yep. When I reach my fingers up, I find warm saltwater on my cheeks. "Thank you, Cope."

I lift my gaze from the driveway and pan down the row of houses on either side of the street. There are a few differences here and there—a new mailbox, a fresh coat of paint, a stump where there used to be a tree—but otherwise, I may as well have stepped into a time warp.

Walking around the front of the van, I see the *For Sale* sign swaying gently in the nighttime breeze, stuck right in the center of my dad's fastidiously kept lawn. It's been a while since he was strong enough to care for it properly, but it still looks fantastic. I figure he probably hired someone to take over when he no longer could.

"Let me get my key," I say as my boys cluster around me, giving me the small burst of strength needed to move up the walkway, as familiar to me as my own hand, and pull the ring of keys from my purse. I unlock the front door and push it open before I can change my mind.

It occurs to me how many times I stood here after dates with Kevin, lingering on the porch so I didn't have to leave his side. Half the time, Dad was in the living room peeking at us through the curtains, trying to make sure we didn't take our goodbye kissing too far.

"Welcome home," I whisper, because there's nobody else left to say it.

Grief is a weird emotion, isn't it? So disconcerting. It's like there's this part of your life missing, this part that you *ache* for. After a while, it gets easier to pretend it was never there, but that doesn't make the want go away. And it's those little moments every now and again, those reminders of a time past that tear the scab off, make the pain feel fresh.

I think that's what happens to me when I walk into the gaping emptiness of my childhood home. Living in Phoenix, there were no reminders of Mom, of Yasmine. Being on tour with Beauty and Lies, there were no reminders of Dad.

Here, there are signs and symbols everywhere, happy ghosts smiling and laughing, hugging, *living.* I see the dent in the wall as soon as I take a few steps into the room, that place where Yas and I accidentally crashed our new bikes—after we were told a dozen times not to ride them in the house. Yes, that spot has been patched and painted over, but there's a dip that I can feel when I run my palm across it.

"Picture, please," I tell Cope, trying to keep my voice steady, full aware that tears are just streaming down my cheeks. I don't let the guys see, keeping my face turned away from them, my melancholy quiet. If one of them hugs me right now … I might just break down.

I move past the foyer, across scuffed hardwood floors and into the living room.

There, the hole above the fireplace where one of Mom's paintings hung my entire life. Even after Dad married Susan, he kept the colorful canvas there, and every now and again I'd catch him looking up at it with a slight glaze in his eyes, a gentle smile.

That painting is now sitting on the floor, leaning against the bricks of the fireplace. There's a pile of random meaningless shit next to it, gouged from my childhood bedroom. Susan stacked my old headboard, my nightstand, and bedside lamps in here, too.

I hardly register any of it.

There, on the fireplace mantle is a small urn, similar to the one in my purse.

That … *vase* is all that's left of the man that put bandages on my wounds, held me when I cried over boys, kissed my forehead before I fell asleep at night.

Fuck.

I need to get out of here.

"I can't breathe," I say, turning and pushing through my boys until I'm out in the yard again, breathing in cool damp air.

I make it about ten steps outside the door before I fall to my knees. I'm not trying to be dramatic; it just happens. I mean, Jesus, my dad's been dead all of fourteen days. Fourteen. That's not even long enough to heal a shallow scratch.

"Oh, sweet thing," Ransom says, kneeling down next to me. The violet scent follows him to the pavement as he sweeps his arms around me and holds me tight. I lean into him because I know he understands. I'm not being whiny; I'm not trying to make a scene. I'm just fucking grieving, fighting to heal. Everyone has their own process and this is mine. This … is *mine.*

Copeland squats down on the other side of me, his face completely free of judgment, his look sympathetic and sweet. I know he wants to take care of me, but I'm not going to let him. There are four other boys that can do that right now and he deserves a break from Cara, from his grandma, from his mom. But then … he reaches out his arms to hug me, too, and I can't resist.

I melt into the pair of them, sobbing until the initial shock of the moment passes and I'm left with a runny nose and burning eyes.

"Do you want us to load up the stuff in the living room?" Muse asks, leaning over me, pushing hair back from my forehead. His glasses almost fall off his face, but he rescues them at the last minute with a hand covered in black bat tattoos.

"Yes, please," I whisper hoarsely. "And anything else you find. I want it all. Everything."

"Got it," Derek says, standing back up and heading inside to do what he does best—make sure the practicalities are out of the way so everyone else can revel in their emotions. That poor fucking man.

I sniffle and run my arm across my face, staring at the thick trunk of the tree that decorates the front corner of the yard. I think it's a called a champion oak or something. It *looks* like a champion, stretching its massive arms to the starry night sky.

"You just tell us when you're ready to go back in, wonderful," Ransom says, his soft voice the perfect pitch and cadence for the moment.

I sit there for a while, glancing to my left to see Michael, Paxton, and Muse loading up the back of the van. It's going to be a tight fit to get us all in there with my stuff. A visit to the storage unit is definitely in order.

"I'm ready," I whisper after the van door is closed, my stuff loaded.

"Hey, love," Pax says, pausing in front of me, much more subdued than usual. I appreciate that. "We got everything but the, uh …" He stares down at me for a few seconds, gorgeous, but almost like a stranger in his jeans and t-shirt. I can't decide if I miss the suits or not. "We left the ashes inside," he continues, using some of that skill from the stage to make his words melodious and easy to listen to.

"Thank you," I say, letting Cope and Ran help me to my feet.

I brush off my knees and turn to find Michael and Muse waiting on the porch for me.

Heading back to the front door, I slip an arm around each of their waists and lead them back inside the dark living room. It's an older house, so most of the rooms don't actually have any lights of their own. My mom used to joke about it and say she was just glad for the excuse to buy a lot of lamps.

It doesn't matter to me. In fact, it's probably better that I only see the familiar rooms in a bath of moonlight.

"Let me give you guys the tour," I say, taking Dad off the mantle and adding him to the plastic bag that holds Mom. She's already spilled inside and if he spills, too, then at least they'll be together again. That's how I'm going to sprinkle their ashes, mixed together, next to the Goode family mausoleum where Yasmine is buried. Well, technically it's just her name inside the actual structure, her body buried in the small plot behind it. "Obviously, we have the living room here," I say, totally detached as I take the guys through to my dad's office, then back through the living room and into the kitchen.

Cope takes pictures of everything, the flash on my phone highlighting dark nooks and crannies as we make our way up the stairs to the bedrooms.

"This was my sister's room," I say, opening a door to an empty square box that looks nothing at all like the palace Yasmine had turned it into, draping everything in pink and glitter and crystals. It's because of her that I like the color pink so damn much. I stare into the room for a long time, the guys' bodies keeping me warm despite the empty cold of the house. I think it's in the mid-forties outside, and there's no heater running in here so it's seriously fucking chilly, like ghosts are passing through my body as I close the door and move back down the hallway.

The door to mom's art studio is cracked, and I kick it the rest of the way open with my heel, staring at the floral patterned wallpaper that Susan put up when she moved in.

"Mom's art studio—although it was a hell of a lot cooler before my stepmother got ahold of it."

The guys follow me into the room, even though there's

nothing really there to see. Four walls, a closet with sliding doors, a window. But to me, this room is so much *more* than that. This is where my love for art was born.

I tell the boys that.

"My mom gave birth to my creativity in this room," I say, stepping over to the window and squinting into the darkness like I can see the cemetery if I try hard enough. During the day you can, the green hills dotted with gray gravestones. My mom used to say it was peaceful, that she enjoyed the view. Personally, I'm not a fan of graveyards.

Michael puts an arm around my shoulders and pulls me close, giving me an uncharacteristically gentle kiss that soothes some of the angst bubbling up inside of me.

"That must be where you got your talent, too," he whispers, giving me one more kiss before I pull away and take his hand, leading him into the hallway and staring at the two doors on the opposite end.

My parents' room, the carefully selected lavender walls my mom chose painted over with some of Susan's beige … and my room.

I skip the bathroom, but Cope doesn't, slipping inside and taking a bunch of pictures that I'm sure I'll be grateful for later. I mean, there are memories in there, too. Bath time with Yasmine when we were kids, getting my first period, putting makeup on before school.

I start down the hall and then pause to take off my heels. I can't take the sound of them clicking across the floors, the sound too similar to the cadence of mom's shoes as she swept down the hall to peek in my bedroom, dressed in her evening best, to tell me that she was about to head out on a date with dad.

"I've got 'em, love," Paxton says, curling his fingers

through the straps and taking the pair of heels from my too tight grip. I lean my forehead into his chest and he goes still for a second. But then with a deep breath, he relaxes and lays his hand on the back of my head. "And I've got you, too, if you need me."

"I might," I say, my voice echoing in the empty house as I stand up and look into Pax's grey eyes. They're surprisingly empathetic right now, reflecting some of the emotion that I know he's still holding back. This thing with Ransom is a good first step, but he still has a ways to go. Somehow, seeing his pain reflected back makes me feel a little better, less alone.

God.

I'm not alone *at all,* am I?

I turn back to look at my boys, at Michael and Muse and Ransom and Copeland.

"Thanks for doing this with me," I say before I forget to do it.

"No thanks required," Pax says, putting his hand on my shoulder. I reach up to squeeze his tattooed fingers, and then move silent as a ghost across the floor, pushing the door to my parents' room open. It doesn't look anything like I remember—new crown molding, new baseboards, different paint colors.

"My mom and dad's room," I say with zero inflection, moving away before the hideous new décor choices fade away and memories start to peek through ugly beige paint and pressboard moldings. "My room."

I grab the last handle and twist it, sweeping inside and feeling my breath rush out in a gasp.

My bedroom … it looks exactly the same. The walls are painted a soft yellow, and in one corner, near the window, there's the mural my mother painted. Taking inspiration from the tree in our front yard, she painted intricate little branches dotted with fall reddened leaves. Hidden amongst the foliage is a tiny nest with little eggs in it, a pair of hummingbirds watching over it from a nearby branch. One of them is brown and speckled, the other brilliant shimmery green with a red chest.

There's a mattress and box spring sitting in the middle of the room. I can tell by the familiar floral pattern that this is literally the same mattress I slept on for most of my life.

"I lost my virginity on this," I say as I point at it and smile through a new rush of tears. These, too, at least are silent. I step into the room, running my hand over the ceramic light switch cover that my mother painted and glazed. It has tiny flowers in pink and yellow all over it.

"Do you need a screwdriver?" Muse asks as I hand him my purse.

"There's a multitool in there, attached to my keys. It should have one," I say, smiling back at him. He returns the expression and then slips his hand into the bag, grabbing my key ring and starting in on the light switch.

Cope keeps photographing everything, his bottom lip tucked slightly under his teeth, his eyes flicking back to me every now and again like he's checking up on me.

Mikey, Pax, Ran, and I pause in a row in front of the window.

From here, we can see the minivan in the driveway, the gentle unassuming row of suburban houses, each with a single porch light and vibrantly green lawn. There are flowers everywhere, the first hints of spring coloring the neighborhood.

"It's so weird, being here," I say, voice echoing again.

"Surreal."

"I thought the same thing," Ransom says, voice tight, "when I visited my mom's place to pack up her stuff. In the end, I gathered the things that meant the most to me and then left, leaving the front door open behind me. I have no idea what happened to the rest of it."

I cuddle up to him and he pulls me close.

We stand there until Muse and Cope are finished, joining us in front of the glass, all six of our reflections visible against the squeaky clean surface. I like that, seeing them standing beside me like that.

My boys. My rockstars. My lovers.

"Is it okay if I lie down for a little bit?" I ask.

"Of course it is," Cope says, responding for the entire band.

I turn around and crawl onto the mattress, curling up on my side and breathing in the familiar scent of rosewater perfume. I practically soaked my bed with it back in the day. Closing my eyes, I just lay there and take in the fact that this is a forever sort of goodbye, a farewell to a different life. And then I just make myself realize how damn lucky I am that I ended up on that fucking bus with those fucking guys.

Bodies crowd in around mine, warm ones, bodies that smell like pomegranates, like laundry soap, maybe even a little bit like sex, sweat from the show. Hard, muscular arms curl around me, tuck me close, breaking the violent cycle of my grieving thoughts and lulling me to sleep.

I wake up before anybody else, blinking at the gentle grey-blue morning light, stretching my arms above my head and then rolling onto my back to stare up at the ceiling. There are arms and legs all over me, but I don't mind. Despite the fact that six people just fell asleep on a queen size mattress on the floor of an empty room, I'm comfortable. Shit, I slept like a baby.

I sit up suddenly and realize that my damn glasses are missing, patting around with my hands until I find a bit of plastic underneath the thick sleeve of Ransom's hoodie. I clean the lenses off as best I can with the soft inner fabric of my sleeveless hoodie, and then slip them back on my face.

The sun is *just* barely peeking its face up over the roofs of the houses on the opposite side of the street, teasing the little room with early morning color. Even though this is a sad moment for Lilith, even though it kills me to see her in so much pain, I feel a sense of peace wash over me. This is how things needed to happen, the only way for her to make a clean break from her grief and start the slow process of healing, a process I never managed to actually stumble into.

I glance over at the mural on the wall next to the window, the painting so delicately and finely detailed that it pops off the wall like a photograph. Lilith's mother was really goddamn talented. I mean, to make a plain tree so intriguing that it draws the eye, that's skill.

I'm staring at it, listening to the sound of the others breathing around me when I see them.

The hummingbirds.

My mouth sets in a thin line and my heart starts to pound.

Hummingbirds outside my bedroom window …

A mattress.

The sound of breathing.

Holy shit. Shit. Shit, shit, shit.

Before I realize what I'm doing, I'm standing up and sprinting from that room as fast as my legs can carry me, stumbling at the top of the stairs, coming precariously close to toppling over them. I fall down the first few, find my feet, and then pound down the rest, skidding across the wood floors and out the front door.

Just like Lilith, I make it about halfway across the yard and then stop, bending over at the waist, breathing so hard that I get dizzy. I put my head between my knees and squeeze my eyes shut tight.

Hideous memories assault me as I stand in Lil's front yard, my body quivering uncontrollably, just like Ransom's.

Hummingbirds, flitting back and forth in front of the glass, pausing to drink from the fake red flowers adorning the feeder. Watching them. Wishing I could hear the cute sounds they make at each other. But the sound of the mattress is too loud, the heavy breathing ...

I stumble over to the base of the tree and throw up, shoving my arm across my mouth and desperately struggling to control my breathing before I pass out.

No. No. No. I don't want any of that. I don't want to

remember that. What little boy wants to remember that? I can't. I won't.

I shove my shirt up, press my fingers tight to the fresh tattoo on my hip and rub it until it burns, until the physical pain reminds me that I'm here, that I'm safe, that I met a girl and started to fall in love with her, that I get to play a concert in Canada tomorrow, and then one in Ireland. In England. Scotland. France.

I am not that little boy anymore.

I lower myself to my knees and throw up again.

"Derek."

It's Lilith's voice, that soothing feminine throaty sound. Her hand touches my back, and I jump, startling her.

"Oh my god, are you okay?" she asks, panic lacing her voice when she sees all the puke on her lawn. Fuck. I did not want her to see me like this. "What happened? Are you not feeling well?"

"I …" I start to speak, but the words get caught in my throat, my breath too panicky, too rapid to speak.

Lilith kneels down next to me and wraps her arms around me, pulling my head to her breasts, pressing my face to the soft, sweet smelling warmth of her skin. I close my eyes and wrap my own arms around her slender waist, squeezing her tight, listening to the sound of her heart fluttering and beating in fear for me.

"It's okay, Muse," she says, stroking her fingertips across the shaved darkness of my hair on either side of my mussed up mohawk. "It's okay. I've got you."

"I'm sorry," I whisper, my voice fucked-up, throat aching from the acidity of my puke. I definitely don't feel like a glamorous rock star right now. I just … hell, I don't know what I feel like. And this is why I block everything out, why

I refuse to acknowledge my own pain. It's so much easier to let myself be empathetic, let everyone else's emotions sweep over me, take control of my heart. If I do that, I don't have to feel this gut-wrenching, god-awful nightmare wash over me. "I'm sorry, Lilith. You're going through a lot right now; you don't need this shit."

"Muse," she says, her voice scolding. "Don't. You always put yourself in the background. And while I think it's cute and admirable as hell, it's not necessary one hundred percent of the time. I thought you just warned me about holding back and hiding my emotions."

"You're right," I whisper, leaning back, sitting up so I can look her in the face. "I did. Because I didn't want you to end up like me, with this festering wound inside of you."

I look down at my knees. I have to tell her, I know that. Everybody else has spilled their guts to this girl, bared their souls, invited her to bury the bodies of their demons.

"I've been running from this my entire life. Usually I can push it down, pack it away. But lately … fuck." I run a hand over my face and glance away, toward the open front door. A gentle breeze teases the green grass underneath us, making it ripple like the surface of a pond. "I guess I can't run from it forever."

"You don't have to tell me if—"

"Yes, I do," I say, lifting my face to stare into hers. She's so beautiful, so fucking beautiful. It's no surprise to me that she's managed to hook us all. I wish I could kiss her right now, but … you know. "Lilith," I start, forcing my hands to sit still in my lap. I make myself look at her, right at her, straight into eyes already shimmering with unshed tears. I swallow hard, try out a dozen different ways to say it. "More than once … when I was a kid …" I stutter, breathing hard again, my eyes wide and my mouth dry. "Lilith, I was raped."

The day is warm, sunny, cheerful. But I can't enjoy it, not even as I take a walk through my old neighborhood with my boys, Muse's hand clutched tight inside of mine. I can't let go of it, not even with sweat slicking our palms, my nails digging into his skin. He doesn't try to pull away either, squeezing my fist back, the only physical sign of the confession he gave me this morning.

Lilith, I was raped.

Little Muse, little Derek … my little Derek. He didn't give me any other details, but I heard the hints. More than once. A kid.

I almost threw up, too. Fucking hell.

Emancipated at fifteen … considering suicide.

I just can't. I can't. I fucking can't.

I sweep the palm of my right hand over my hair, charm bracelet jingling with the motion.

And now I've got to go release my parents' ashes to the wind.

"You were brave this morning," I whisper, so only Muse can hear me. I think the other guys already know about his past because they didn't say anything when they found us holding each other on the front lawn like that. And they didn't look surprised either.

"Maybe," Muse says, looking at the sidewalk through the thick lenses of his glasses. He looks the same as he always does, tattooed, pierced, sexy as hell. When he looks up at me, he even smiles. It's that same goddamn look. *I get what I want. Look at me, I'm cheeky. I'm playful.* Fuck him. Why does he do that? But I know why. A past like his, it can't be erased. It literally changes the shape of who you are, forces you to adapt in ways you never thought you could. You *have* to, if you want to go on living. "I think you're brave, coming back here like this."

I snort.

"Not really," I say and he squeezes my hand even harder.

"Really," he tells me, the look on his face, the sound of his voice brooking no arguments.

We keep walking, the other boys talking amongst themselves, trying to keep the mood up. They stop only when we reach the cemetery gates.

"Right this way, guys," I say, opening the waist-high gate and stepping inside, feeling a little silly in the tight black dress now that I'm here, barefoot in the grass of a graveyard. Then again, what *would* feel right here? Some big baggy frock? What would that change? Nothing. Whatever feelings I'm looking for right now—peace, acceptance, love—those things have to come from within.

I follow a curving dirt path through the cemetery, enjoying the warmth of the naked earth beneath my feet. Not wearing shoes, now *that* was a good choice.

But shit … I can't stop thinking about Derek. He must see something of my worry for him on my face because he lets out a deep sigh.

"Don't worry about me, Lil. I didn't tell you that to upset

you. It happened. I've been free for a long time now. I just …" Muses pauses abruptly, bringing the entire group to a halt. "Wanted to tell the woman I'm falling in love with my truth. So now you know. If I decide I need to talk more about it, I'll tell you. Until then, please don't let it taint what we just found together." He looks up at me as I get stupidly teary again. I can't help it. I fucking *ache* for him. "Lil, you make my lonely traveler not so fucking lonely anymore."

My breathing hitches, my hand tingling where it's wrapped around his.

I let go but only so I can put my arms around his neck and squeeze him tight. Muse hugs me back, so fiercely that my feet rise up off the ground, the softness of my body pressed firmly against the muscular planes of his. More tears slide down my face, hitting the red sleeveless hoodie draped over his shoulders.

"You're so poetic," I whisper against his ear, "are you sure you're only twenty-one?"

He laughs, the sound untainted by his confession, that crack on his face already pulled back together, hiding the rest of his truth. But this kind of pain, I can't and won't force it. Just like I thought before, I have to wait for him to come to me. With Pax, with Michael, Ran, Cope, I can pry and dig and peel apart their layers.

Muse has to give me his.

I decide to give him mine first, as a gesture of good will.

The woman I'm falling in love with …

I press my lips even tighter to his ear, making him shiver.

"Love has no prerequisite," I quote after Ransom. "I love you, Muse."

He sets me carefully back on my feet and looks down at me, one hand cupping my face, his breathing rapid-fire and erratic, but in a good way this time. He seems surprised, but how could I not love someone willing to split themselves in half just to tell me about their past?

I bite my lip and turn away, but Muse grabs my arm and tugs me back, pulling me close and crushing my mouth with his. As usual, he planned for everything, so he had clean clothes, a toothbrush, toothpaste, and mouthwash handy this morning. Figures.

I kiss his mint flavored mouth, letting his tongue sweep mine, his hands curl around my waist.

After a few minutes, Michael clears his throat and we pause, sharing another look before I pull away again and turn around, walking backward so I can stare at all five boys.

"It's just past these trees," I tell them, "the Goode family burial plot."

The closer I get, the better I start to feel. I know it doesn't make any sense, but it's true. Each step helps me to breathe a little easier, helps my shoulders relax, dries the tears on my face.

Birds chirp from the branches of the trees, and the wind rustles and teases wildflowers and freshly mowed grass. Here and there brightly colored bouquets adorn grey headstones, white obelisks, angels watching over the discarded shells of their charges.

I know this isn't a magic cure-all, like, I spread these ashes and everything is just perfect. My dad will still be dead, and it will still be day fifteen without him, and I'll still miss him like fucking crazy.

But it's a good first step.

I know without a doubt that I can at least say goodbye to this place, move on from here, from Arizona, from Susan, from Kevin. Those things, I can definitely leave behind with a sense of peace and not worry about them again.

“Here it is,” I say, pausing our group in front of a small square building with weathered stone sides, a tall rounded door made of some sort of rusting metal, and a series of tiny windows that look in on a central platform. A vase with faux flowers sits permanently in residence on top of it, and on the wall in the back, small stone squares are cordoned off, the names of distant relatives—and Yasmine—chiseled in big block letters.

I stare at the squat stone building for a moment, Ransom's flirty violet scent swirling with a gentle breeze and wrapping around me.

Walking around the building, I find the patch of undisturbed grass where all the bodies are buried. There's a small metal fence connected to the back of the mausoleum that borders the plot. This is where I sit down, taking the bag with both urns in it out of the pink purse.

“Please sit down,” I say, looking up at them, all dressed up and beautiful still, even after the car ride and our rough night on the bare mattress.

“You sure you want us here for this?” Michael asks, looking slightly uncomfortable, like he thinks he's overstepping his boundaries or something. I reach up and grab his hand, tugging on it until he sits his tattooed rockstar ass down on the grass next to me.

Copeland takes my other side, then Paxton, Muse, Ransom, ending the circle with Michael and me.

“Thank you for bringing me here,” I tell them again. I can't say it enough. Kevin would never have gone out of his way to do half the things these boys have done for me. And I'm not just talking about the money they spent on my new clothes or my tablet or the airfare for the world tour portion of this trip. There's that, obviously, but it's so much more than that.

What I'm *really* talking about are the hugs, the honesty, the tears both given and received, the sex, the acceptance, the lack of judgment, the music, the hot cups of tea, the protectiveness, the inclusivity. The love. I feel a lot of love from these guys—a *lot* of it.

"You don't have to keep thanking us for that, love," Paxton says, one knee cocked up, looking like a blonde god in his tight t-shirt and jeans. He taps his fingers against his leg and meets my eyes across the circle.

"Maybe not, but I want to," I say, staring at the spilled urns inside the bag.

I lay it flat on the ground in front of me, near the center of the circle, and then I take the multitool from my purse and use it to carefully crush the urns into shards, shaking the bag and mixing everything up into a gray-white-blue-green amalgamation.

A butterfly lands on my bare shoulder and I pause, glancing over at it, its blue and black wings stilling. A breeze blows and then it takes off again, flapping toward the fluffy white clouds dotting the sky.

That's either another message from fate … or a really weird coincidence.

I suppose I don't much mind either way.

I unzip the bag and stare inside for a long, long time. The more I look at the stuff in the bag, the more convinced I am that this … it's not Mom and Dad, is it? No. They're gone and these ashes are just that, ashes. A few tears plop inside the plastic, sliding down the sides and collecting debris. I let them fall for a second and then pull the sides of the bag as hard as I can, splitting it in half.

Ashes and bits of ceramic fall to the grass.

The wind starts right in on the ash portion of it, picking bits of it up and taking it away the same way it did the butterfly. I watch it go, liquid dripping down my cheeks, and then I turn my gaze back to my boys, licking the salty taste from my lower lip.

"Do you want to say a prayer or something?" Michael asks softly, but I just shake my head.

The sound of the breeze in trees, the chatter of birds, the distant hum of insects. That's prayer enough for me; human words can't compete with nature's song.

Closing my eyes, I reach down and take the hand of the man on either side of me.

Moments pass, sunshine warming my skin.

I let as many tears fall as my heart wants, tilting my head back slightly and embracing the moment. When they finally stop, when I crack my eyes and drop my chin, I see Paxton with two lines of wetness of his face.

With a tentative finger, he reaches up and touches his cheek.

"Holy shit," he whispers, and I smile.

See, I told you he wasn't an asshole.

Emotionally exhausted.

That's me, Lilith Tempest Goode, the girlfriend of Beauty in Lies, lover of five gorgeous men. Adult orphan. Artist. Groupie.

And currently, I'm curled up in the backseat of a rental van with two of my boyfriends. My head rests in Muse's lap, his legs stretched out along the seat, Paxton curled up in what would be an adorable fetal position if he wasn't covered in tattoos and smirking in his sleep.

The drive from Gloversville, New York to Montréal, Québec is about four hours. I sleep through most of it, missing my dad with a fierce ache that gentles and soothes the longer I lay entwined with these two men. At one point, I snap to in a panic, thinking I've left my passport on the bus, but Muse assures me that *all* of our passports are currently tucked in the duffel bag riding between Copeland and Ransom in the center row.

After that, everything's a blur, scenery rushing by outside the window, the gentle murmur of Michael's voice as he drives and talks with Ran and Cope. I drift in and out of actual sleep, coming to only when we're pulling into a parking lot, rain driving against the roof of the van.

"We're in Canada already?" I ask, blinking as I struggle to sit up without elbowing Muse in the stomach or kicking Pax in the face. "I missed it? My first moment outside the United States."

"Sorry, sweet thing," Ransom says, hooking an arm on the back of his seat and glancing over at me. His smile is too soft, even buried in all that stubble, to say he's really apologetic about it. "But you were so cute passed out back there."

I stretch and yawn as Muse adjusts himself to sit next to me, also yawning and stretching.

Paxton just mumbles some curse words and flops his body against the window.

"Please tell me we don't have a show tonight," he murmurs as Michael parks next to Beauty in Lies' tour bus and shuts off the engine.

"Nope. Tomorrow," Cope says as Ransom grabs the sliding door and pulls it open, letting in a rush of cold air that makes me shiver.

Pax continues to curse as he climbs out with me following after him, Muse right behind us.

Since it's raining so hard, we don't hang out in the parking for long, heading onto the bus and shaking water droplets off our skin, a few of the boys shedding their shirts.

"I'm gonna go check in with Octavia," Muse says, grabbing an umbrella from one of the bottom cabinets in the kitchen and heading back outside.

Me, I plod into the Bat Cave, yank my stretchy black dress off and throw it on the floor, climbing into the silken sheets in my bra and panties. It's only about six o'clock, but after seeing my childhood home transformed into an empty skeleton, learning about Muse's past, spreading my parents' ashes, and unloading all of my keepsakes into a storage unit, I'm so tired I'll probably sleep straight through to tomorrow.

"Fuck, baby girl," Ransom says, climbing in next to me in boxers and a hoodie. Automatically, he curls his body around mine like we were made to fit together like this. "I know nothing actually happened to me today, but damn it if I'm not falling asleep standing up."

I wrap my arms around his and burrow close, enjoying this little private moment together.

"Seeing me go through that stirred up your own emotions. It's completely reasonable," I whisper, feeling like I should keep my voice low to match his.

"Mm," he murmurs against my hair, sending warm shivers of pleasure down my spine. Ransom just makes these fucking noises sometimes that drive me up the wall—in a good way. I wiggle closer to him and feel the thickness of his cock inside his boxers.

"I like having you to myself for a second," I say, smiling slyly at Pax when he pauses in the doorway to the Bat Cave, completely nude. "Now that Paxton is trying to steal you away, I'm jealous."

"Oh, please," he drawls, waving a hand holding a cigarette, perfuming the air with the scent of tobacco. Obviously I'm not a fan of cigarettes, but seeing him stand there covered in tattoos, speaking in an English accent, and smoking one all at the same time … that turns me on. "You can bloody have him."

"So you say until the two of you are jacking each other off in the backseat of a van."

Ransom chuckles and Pax smirks, ashing his cigarette into the trash can at the end of the bed, the one that was once upon a time filled with four condoms from four different dudes. I blush a little as Paxton abandons his smoke in the metal *rubbish bin* as he calls it, and joins us on the bed.

"You liked that, did you?" Pax asks, leaning back against the pillows and lacing his fingers behind his neck. He's so completely unashamed of his erection, proud of it more like. But those tears … he definitely had no idea how to deal with those.

"Maybe," I say, although the answer is actually *definitely.*

I close my eyes for a moment, feeling this brief respite from my grief. I did what I had to do, went home, said goodbye. And yet, my journey didn't end there. It's a good feeling, knowing I still have something left to do, somewhere to go … some*one* to hold.

"Octavia's going to have a roadie return the van for us," I hear Muse saying from the living room, already back from his errand. I count slowly under my breath, seeing how long it takes the other guys to join us. Once a few of us get in here, it's like there's this magnetic pull on everyone else.

Or maybe they can just sense that my fatigue drifted away as soon as I felt Ransom's cock pressing up against my ass …

"All taken care of," Muse says, slipping into the room and raising his pierced brow at Pax's blatant nudity. "Honestly, what she did to Lilith was fucked beyond fucked, but Octavia is damn good at what she does. All we have to do is show up at the concert tomorrow and then plop our asses in another van for a ride to the airport. Done, done, done."

He shrugs out of his clothes, all the way down to his skivvies, and joins us.

"Yeah, well, I've got my eye on her," Paxton says, determined not to let it go. It's actually kind of cute in a way, how protective he is of me. But he says Michael knows how to hold a grudge? I think Pax is the king of it. "Maybe I should bring her to meet my parents, too? If they like her, she's done. Sacked. Out the door. Those selfish cads have awful taste in friends, business partners, lovers."

"Sons," Michael adds when he enters the room, damp from a quickie shower. "They clearly fucked you up royally, so I don't see why you'd expect much else from them."

He climbs onto the bad and stretches out on his tummy, flashing his new tattoo to the room and putting his violet gaze on level with mine.

I reach a hand out and tease the razored strands of his black hair. Ransom has dark hair, too, but his is distinctly chocolate flavored. Michael's is as dark as a starless sky.

"Sorry," Cope says, slipping into the room a few moments later. "I had a ton of fucking voicemails from both my mom and her doctor."

"Is everything okay?" I ask and he sighs, kicking off his shoes in the door and adding to our collective clothing mess. I wonder what it's going to be like staying in hotels with these guys? Do we each get our own rooms? Would I even *want* my own room? No, I don't think so. Getting my own place together in Seattle, some kind of permanent base of operations sounds like a good idea. But on the road, I just want all my men to myself.

"Everything's fine. I usually get at least two calls a day from my mother. Maybe one a week from her doctor. It's just the same old, same old." Cope smiles at me, like he's already over it. But not like Muse, not like he's pushed his feelings down in order to deal with them. I think he really is just used to taking care of his mom; he's done it his whole life.

Once Copeland gets under the covers, I feel it.

Feminine satisfaction, female triumph.

Mine.

Fuck.

It really does feel good to say that.

All of these guys, they belong to me.

Without saying a word, I reach under the covers and push my panties down, encouraging Ransom by wiggling against him. At the same time, I reach out and cup the side of Michael's face, drawing him in for a kiss.

And just like that, I shift the mood the way I want it.

I want sex.

It's an emotional sounding board for me now, and not just because I'm trying to fuck the bad feelings away or anything like that. It's an easy form of connection, this silken glide of bodies on bodies, hands, mouths, cocks, *cunt.* Just one of those. And anyway, the act with these guys is so much more than *just* sex. When we're all in one room like this, there's this transcendent feeling of togetherness, family, romance.

I've never felt anything like it.

Ransom slides into me from behind me, spooning me while Michael fucks my mouth with wickedly decadent flicks of his tongue. He reaches around my back while we kiss, unhooking my bra, making the act of pulling the straps down my arms erotic with his confident surety, his slowness.

When he wraps his jewel toned hands around my breasts and squeezes them, I cry out, arching into his touch. My pelvis tilts back naturally, welcoming Ransom inside, his cock hitting my G-spot in exactly the right place.

I let him move inside of me until his breathing gets too harsh, too ragged, and then I pull away, sitting up and shimmying out of my panties.

Climbing up on Michael's lap, I take him next, letting the heavy weight of his violet gaze wash over me, reveling in the thick heaviness of his cock. He licks his full lower lip and then relaxes slowly, a wild male giving into my demands. He's not necessarily relinquishing control … just sharing it.

I sigh with pleasure when Muse moves up behind us, kissing the side of my neck and then cupping my ass, kneading my tender flesh with strong fingers. He teases one of those against my ass, slicking lube from his hand against me, warming me up to take his cock. When he enters me from behind, the feeling is almost … transcendent.

The two men share my body seamlessly, the three of us moving as easily as if we were just two.

"You look like a goddess," Cope whispers in my ear, just before he straddles Michael's head and I lean forward to take his cock into my mouth, his long musician's fingers pressing gently into the back of my head.

Yes, group sex takes a *ton* of maneuvering, but once all those pieces are in play, it's so worth it.

It's like planning ahead on a chessboard, staying patient, waiting for that one final moment when you checkmate the king … or in this case, king*s*.

Me, I'm the *queen;* I can move as many spaces as I want.

The guys can't be shy though either. I mean, right now, straight-as-fuck Michael (probably the guy in the group with the lowest chance of ever touching or looking at another man) has Copeland's body pretty intimately acquainted with the area just a few inches above his face.

The way his hands knead my hips though, I figure he's too far gone with pleasure to care. I can feel my body wrapping him tight, liquid and wet, my sex tightening on Michael's cock like a vise.

Ran and Pax move over to me, kneeling on my right and left like knights. One is dark-haired, dark-eyed. The other blonde with a pale grey-blue gaze. Together they make a beautiful contrast.

I slide my mouth off of Cope's shaft and lean into Ransom, sucking and licking and caressing his cock instead, letting him borrow my sharp tongue, my hungry lips. And then I do the same for Paxton. I switch between the three men, loving the amount of control I have over them right now. The looks on their faces … they'd do anything for me.

Well, I think they'd do anything for me anyway.

I know I'd do the same for them.

I stop short of letting any of them come, pulling away from Muse and Michael like I did to Ransom. The groans of frustration they make are basic, primal, curving my lips up with amusement.

The air in the room feels languid, hot, charged.

Compared to last week, something is definitely different in here. I can't figure out if it's me or one of them, or some sort of combination.

Cope's the first to take my hips, pull them up and mount me from behind as I stretch on all fours like a cat, biting my lip, closing my eyes against the curved length of his shaft. He really does know how to use his body to bring a woman pleasure. It's obvious in every move he makes that he's thinking about more than just himself. Even naked, he still smells like denim and soap, fresh and clean and inviting.

Between movements, the boys touch themselves, hands wrapped around their shafts, showing me how they like to be pleasured, giving me tips without even knowing that they're doing it. I watch them as Cope rides me, leaning into the thrust of his pelvis, listening to the sweet sound of our bodies joining.

Paxton, aggressive as ever, gets on his knees in front of me, fisting some of my hair in his hand and sliding his dick between my lips. He pumps his hips in time with Cope's, trapping me between their bodies, electrifying me, making the nerve endings in every part of my body tingle like they've been galvanized. Lightning and thunder, that's what the two of them feel like, sound like, right now.

I'm pretty sure Pax plans on breaking my unspoken rule for the night and coming without permission when Ransom grabs him by his hair and kisses him in a way that I swear I can feel, pleasure rippling through Pax's body and into mine.

Ran shoves him off of me and I pull away from Cope with a sly smile, rolling onto my back again. I survey the men around me, feeling wily, like a fox. No, a *vixen.* See, I'm all about metaphors tonight. It's the only way I can describe the indescribable, explain this sudden violent surge of need inside of me.

If I think about it, I imagine that this is my body celebrating, a farewell party to the metaphorical roadie that she used to be, just someone to carry around the boss' equipment. Now, *she* is the musician.

"You're having a grand old time, aren't you, Miss Lilith Tempest Goode?" Pax growls as I yank Muse on top of me and help him find my ass again, breathing a sigh of pleasurable relief as he slides into me and kisses me with his glasses slipping down his nose.

I find that so fucking hot.

"I have five men all to myself," I say, my voice breathless but husky, almost unrecognizable. My nails dig into Derek's back as his lips trail across my jaw, up to my ear. "Why wouldn't I be?"

"I'm all yours," Muse confirms, making me shiver, my ankles wrapping tight behind his back, holding him against me, encouraging him to move faster, harder, deeper. Sweat drips down his body, scalds me when it hits my skin. With him pressed up against me like this, all I can smell is that smoky scent of his, like a hot cup of tea on a cold morning.

I close my eyes as Muse groans against my throat, coming and quivering in my arms, triggering an orgasm for me, too.

My spirit and my heart felt like they got some closure today, leaving my body unplugged and unfettered. I think that's why my orgasm with Muse hits me so hard. There are no barriers right now, no landmines of grief inside of me. Even Muse's confession doesn't stop the pleasure from obliterating me in violent waves. I'm just glad he told me the truth, that he trusts me enough to talk to me, that he cares enough about what I think.

Muse rolls off and I leave him on his back, panting.

Satisfied.

One down …

I steal Ransom away from Pax with a single kiss to the cheek, drawing his attention away from their make out session and over to me.

He lays back and pulls me on top, so I can straddle him. My goal here is to get Pax and Michael together, just so I can see what it'd be like to have the two alpha males at the same time. So I grab Cope before either of them can approach me, encouraging him to take me from behind.

Our bodies locked together, I ride the ardent wave with my skin tingling, sweat pouring down my body. Strands of my long red hair get stuck to my forehead, the sides of my face, trail over Ransom's skin as I lean down to kiss him.

They're both so worked up that neither of them takes long, Ransom going first, Copeland next, both of them crying out, worshipping me with their hands, their voices, their cocks.

"You know you have serious fucking stamina," Muse says, lying on his side and watching me as Cope sits back and I climb off of Ransom. "Like, superhuman stamina."

"I *am* superhuman," I say with a smirk worthy of Paxton. "I'm a woman; we all are."

"You fucking paired me with him on *purpose,*" Michael growls, the sound sending shivers down my spine. "You know that I think he's a worthless piece of shit."

"Don't be intimidated, Mikey," Pax says, his sly smile sharp enough to cut. "And you might just learn something."

I straddle Pax the way I did Ransom, Michael behind me.

But instead of taking me from behind, he slides his slick cock into my swollen sex alongside Paxton's, making me shiver and go still, my body melting, surrendering. I can't breathe as he starts to move, his hands locked on my hips, almost hard enough to bruise.

Pax doesn't look surprised at all, pulling my face down to his, kissing me and refusing to let Michael do all the work, arching his hips up off the bed and pleasuring me with every micro movement he makes.

The two of them work me until I can't take it anymore, climaxing so hard that I can feel my body bearing down on them, squeezing them together until it's impossible for them to resist coming with me.

When that rainbow of color arches against the backs of my tightly closed eyelids, I know I'm not the only one that sees it.

Apparently Paxton speaks fluent French which just makes him that much more attractive to me as I lean against the wall at the edge of the stage and listen to him address the crowd with words that I can't understand but that I fucking *feel.*

"Are you ready for Dublin?" Octavia asks, leaning in close to me so she can be heard over the deafening roar of the crowd and the first few notes plucked from Michael's guitar.

"More than ready," I tell her, this jittery feeling inside of me that has nothing to do with how sore I am right now. And god, I'm *really* freaking sore, but I wanted them all last night, so I made it happen. I figure there's probably not a lot of room on a private plane for sex anyway. Instead of hanging out on the bus by ourselves between destinations, we'll be crammed together in an aircraft with Octavia, her assistant, a pair of bodyguards, and the flight crew.

I'm curious to see how *that* goes.

"Have you ever been out of the country?" I ask as we move a ways away to talk. I don't need to see my boys to feel them, to hear their music reverberate inside the very depths of my soul. It pounds through the floor, finds its way into my blood, my bones.

"A couple of times," she says, her white sneaker tapping along with the rhythm of the song. The way she moves, I can tell she's a serious fan of her band's music, that she's not their manager just because it pays well or because she had a crush on Pax; she really does like their sound. "But always for business. I'm not sure that I've ever actually been allowed to have fun in another country."

I laugh and lean forward, putting a hand on her arm.

"You should come out with us sometime. I hear Tokyo's a blast."

Octavia flushes a little, flashing me a little more of that uncertain side of herself, the one she tries to keep hidden with a professional facade. Maybe it'll actually be fun, getting to know her? I could use a girlfriend. I seriously don't have a single one. Most of my high school friends dispersed after graduation—me right along with them them. And the women I befriended in Phoenix basically abandoned me when I broke up with Kevin, choosing to stay *his* friend instead of mine. I wonder what lies he must've told them about me?

"I'd like that," she says finally, and we smile at each other, pausing as one song ends and another starts up almost right away, the clatter of the drums making my heart pump faster, my body tighten up—as if I need more sex at this moment in time.

But I guess my boys can't help it if everything they play is either laced in sex … or heartache.

There doesn't seem to be much in between.

I grab a bottle of water from one of the refreshment tables and sneak back to the curtain to watch, waiting for that blissful moment when the guys say goodbye to the crowd and come back to me. No matter how many times it happens, I get that wild flutter of excitement in my belly, the flicker of butterfly wings beating in time with my heart.

Tonight, it's extra exciting because I know what we're doing and where we're headed.

The world.

And then home.

It doesn't matter if I've never been to Seattle. If my boys are there, it'll feel like home. I know that because each and every city we've visited since I started getting to know them, it's felt like home.

When the last note of the night is played, and the crowd bids Beauty in Lies farewell with a raucous chorus of cheering, I bite my lip and wait on my tiptoes for them to shed their instruments and head across the brightly lit stage into the shadows.

I lift my arms out and Muse grabs me around the waist, spinning me and dropping me back to my feet for a kiss as vibrant and silken as the petals on a red, red rose.

"I'm scared of planes," he whispers in my ear and I chuckle. "Will you hold my hand when we take off?"

"I will," I promise as he lets go of me and I greet the other guys, tucking my hands in their sweaty ones, letting Cope and Ran lead me down the steps and out the back door. There's already a van waiting for us, like an airport shuttle but blacker, sleeker, definitely a lot more swag.

"I can't believe we don't even get a break to shower," Michael says, mopping at his forehead with a bandana and leaning back into the leather seat. Outside, it's finally stopped raining, the night quiet and still, at complete odds with the excited beating of my heart.

"There's a shower on the plane," Cope says and Michael

lifts his head, giving his friend a skeptical look.

"You're shitting me."

"The label chartered us a *Lineage 1000E,*" he says and Michael shrugs.

"That doesn't mean a damn thing to me. I take it it's fancy?"

"Oh, it's *fancy,*" Cope says, his smile almost wicked. It's a different look for him, that's for sure.

Paxton says nothing, his gaze focused out the window, his expression telling me he's clearly lost in thought. My only guess is that it has something to do with his parents. His phone's been ringing off the hook today, and his mood's been decidedly sour.

"Do you think there'll be room to draw on it?" I ask, my mind drifting to the cramped quarters of economy seating. You'd think with how wealthy Kevin's father is that he'd have sprung for first class when he flew me down to Phoenix to visit the first time. But no, he bought the cheapest seats available, ones that didn't even allow a *carry-on.* I had to upgrade at the counter with my own money just to take my suitcase.

"Room to draw, dance, do a fucking cartwheel," Pax says, suddenly rejoining the conversation to look back at us. "There's even a room with a queen size bed in it."

"Bullshit," I say, flushing from head to toe.

"There is. Trust me, I've been on a Lineage before. It's like a flying hotel suite. My foppish parents won't fly in anything less posh."

Paxton parks his head on his hand and looks at the rest of us with raised blonde brows.

"Well, you bloody asked," he says with a slight shrug, but there's something about the set of his shoulders that says there's a lot he's not saying. I decide to let it go for now, too excited by the idea of the trip to worry about it at the moment.

When we get to the airstrip, the plane takes us straight over to the open door of the jet. No security checkpoints, no TSA, no lines. I wonder about customs, but I doubt the guys know anything about that either, so I don't bother to ask.

"Jesus Christ," Muse breathes as we climb out of the van and stand on the still damp pavement, looking up the steps at the interior of the plane. "This is way beyond our pay grade, Paxton."

"Yeah, well," he says, breezing past us and up the steps like he owns the place.

"This is not from the label," Muse says, looking over at Cope. "Who told you it was?"

"Paxton," Cope says, playing with the sweatband on his right wrist. The two of them exchange a glance as Ransom and Michael pause next to us.

"Yeah," Muse says with a harsh laugh, rubbing at his temples with two bat covered fingers. "Well, that's a bunch of bullshit."

"So whose is it then?" Ran asks, looking confused as he stands there with his hands tucked in the front pocket of his hoodie, the wind teasing the hood off his head and ruffling his dark hair.

"Um, the Blackwells?" Muse says, raising both of his dark brows at us. "Either they own it or they rented it or what the fuck ever, but I will bet you every cent I have in the bank that this plane right here is from Paxton's family."

"After Harper died, they cut him off financially," Ransom says, voice low and tinged with worry. "Why would they be doing this now?"

Nobody has an answer for that.

"Fuck this," Michael says, tucking his bandana in his pocket. "I'm not looking a gift horse in the mouth. Let's just get on and enjoy the flight. When it comes to Pax's crazy family, I don't get involved. He can deal with that shit on his own."

Michael moves past us, up the steps, and inside.

Muse takes a deep breath and then reaches down for my hand, curling our fingers together.

"You ready, Cutie?" he asks and I nod, my heart still pounding, unsure about the slight turn of events. I have no idea why Pax's family would upgrade our plane ride, but I'm guessing we'll find out eventually.

Based on his mood, I imagine that it's probably nothing good.

"I'm ready," I say, walking up the steep set of stairs with Derek by my side, Ran and Cope behind us.

As soon as we hit the top step, I'm sure of it.

I really am Cinderella, and this … this is my carriage. Not the one the fairy godmother gave me though, the one that turns back into a pumpkin. This is the real deal, the prince's carriage, the one that'll take me back to the castle so I can live happily ever after.

I take a deep breath and step inside, a million pounds lighter after saying goodbye to my family, to Gloversville. But I know that like anything else, this feeling is temporary. Emotions aren't stagnant waters to be treaded indefinitely. There are droughts, floods, tsunamis, hurricanes, whirlpools. And that's just one person's worth of baggage.

But five?

Five princes in a fine carriage, one princess.

No matter how many slippers they slide on my feet, no

matter how many balls we visit, I still have to be able to pick up a sword and fight for myself. I have to make a life that's *mine,* that's not dependent on anyone else. It's still okay to wear the beautiful dress and enjoy the fairytale, but there has to be something else beyond the colorful pages of that book, something real.

This jet … it doesn't look real to me with its plush seats, flatscreen TVs, polished wood accents.

Those are just fucking baubles.

The only thing that looks real to me right now is the expression on Paxton Blackwell's face as he pours amber liquid into a glass tumbler and lifts it to his lips for a drink.

I let go of Muse's hand for a moment and make my way over to him.

My arms slide around his waist; my cheek rests against his back.

The rapid thundering of his heart, the sharp intake of his breath, that's what's real. He might be a prince, but he's also still just a man. I close my eyes and hold him tight, wondering yet again if meeting these boys, if stumbling onto their bus, if standing here holding Pax is all coincidence … or if it's fate. If a butterfly really can flap its wings and stir up a storm.

"I love you, Pax," I say because no matter how much money his family has, no matter what they've done or will do to him, they can't buy that or take it away. They can't buy me.

He goes so still that for a second I wonder if I've made a terrible mistake. But then his hand drops and covers mine where they're clenched together around the front of his waist, pressed up tight against his crisp suit jacket and the starched white of his shirt. The thing is, even in all those fancy clothes, he still smells faintly of sweat from the show.

"Miss Lily, I …" he starts, but I reach up and cover his lips with my hand. I don't need to hear him say it back. It doesn't matter. What I said is true, whether it was coincidence … or whether it was fate. If he wants to say it to me, he can say it later, when we're no longer in a carriage with footmen and white horses.

I might be Cinderella right now, but inside, I'll always be the girl sleeping in front of the hearth, her clothes darkened with soot, her hands chapped and blistered from the harsh realities of life and death. The girl without a father or a mother or a sister. But the girl who, although she'd never rejoice at the loss of her loved ones, is starting to be okay with who she's becoming.

Grief and love … the only true immortals in this world.

But I can tell you with all due certainty that the latter … most definitely cancels out the former.

Especially if you have love five times over.

Moxie

Rock-Hard Beautiful, Book 3

COMING SOON!

Beautiful Survivors

five runaway teens, one epic love story

COMING SOON!

Pack Ebon Red

the Seven Mates of Zara Wolf.

COMING SOON!

Sign up for an exclusive first look at the hottest new releases, contests, and exclusives from bestselling author C.M. Stunich and get **three free** eBooks as a thank you!

Sign up here at

WWW.CMSTUNICH.COM

Discover your next five star read

in C.M. Stunich's (aka Violet Blaze's) collection and discover more kick-ass heroines, smoking hot heroes, and stories filled with wit, humor, and heart.

KEEP UP WITH ALL THE FUN ... AND EARN SOME FREE BOOKS!

JOIN THE C.M. STUNICH NEWSLETTER – Get three free books just for signing up http://eepurl.com/DEsEf

TWEET ME ON TWITTER, BABE – Come sing the social media song with me https://twitter.com/CMStunich

SNAPCHAT WITH ME – Get exclusive behind the scenes looks at covers, blurbs, book signings and more http://www.snapchat.com/add/cmstunich

LISTEN TO MY BOOK PLAYLISTS – Share your fave music with me and I'll give you my playlists (I'm super active on here!) https://open.spotify.com/user/CMStunich

FRIEND ME ON FACEBOOK – Okay, I'm actually at the 5,000 friend limit, but if you click the "follow" button on my profile page, you'll see way more of my killer posts https://facebook.com/cmstunich

CHECK OUT THE NEW SITE – (under construction) but it looks kick-a$$ so far, right? You can order signed books here! http://www.cmstunich.com

READ VIOLET BLAZE – Read the books from my hot as hellfire pen name, Violet Blaze http://www.violetblazebooks.com

SUBSCRIBE TO MY RSS FEED – Press that little orange button in the corner and copy that RSS feed so you can get all the latest updates http://www.cmstunich.com/blog

AMAZON, BABY – If you click the follow button here, you'll get an email each time I put out a new book. Pretty sweet, huh? http://amazon.com/author/cmstunich http://amazon.com/author/violetblaze

PINTEREST – Lots of hot half-naked men. Oh, and half-naked men. Plus, tattooed guys holding babies (who are half-naked) http://pinterest.com/cmstunich

INSTAGRAM – Cute cat pictures. And half-naked guys. Yep, that again. http://instagram.com/cmstunich

GRAB A SMOKIN' HOT READ – Check out my books, grab one or two or five. Fall in love over and over again. Satisfaction guaranteed, baby. ;)

AMAZONhttp://amazon.com/author/cmstunich
B&Nhttp://tinyurl.com/cmbarnes
iTUNEShttp://tinyurl.com/cmitunesbooks
GOOGLE PLAYhttp://tinyurl.com/cmgoogle
KOBOhttp://tinyurl.com/cmkobobooks
VIOLET BLAZEhttp://amazon.com/author/violetblaze

P.S. I heart the f*ck out of you! Thanks for reading! I love your faces.

<3 C.M. Stunich aka Violet Blaze

ABOUT THE AUTHOR

C.M. Stunich is a self-admitted bibliophile with a love for exotic teas and a whole host of characters who live full time inside the strange, swirling vortex of her thoughts. Some folks might call this crazy, but Caitlin Morgan doesn't mind – especially considering she has to write biographies in the third person. Oh, and half the host of characters in her head are searing hot bad boys with dirty mouths and skillful hands (among other things). If being crazy means hanging out with them everyday, C.M. has decided to have herself committed.

She hates tapioca pudding, loves to binge on cheesy horror movies, and is a slave to many cats. When she's not vacuuming fur off of her couch, C.M. can be found with her nose buried in a book or her eyes glued to a computer screen. She's the author of over thirty novels – romance, new adult, fantasy, and young adult included. Please, come and join her inside her crazy. There's a heck of a lot to do there.

Oh, and Caitlin loves to chat (incessantly), so feel free to e-mail her, send her a Facebook message, or put up smoke signals. She's already looking forward to it.